Threesome

Laurence Watts

&

Kevin Burnard

Copyright © 2020 Laurence Watts & Kevin Burnard.

All rights reserved.

Front cover photograph by Brian Groff.

ISBN: 1734460742
ISBN-13: 978-1734460742

CAUTION

All rights in the three plays published herein are strictly reserved and application for performance etc., should be made by professionals and amateurs to MB Books, LLC.

No performance may be given unless a license has been obtained.

CONTENTS

Introduction	1
Hollywood	3
Murder At Magpie Hall	109
The Gay Divorce	253
About the Authors	395

INTRODUCTION

Threesome is a collection of three plays: three comedies, to be precise.

Hollywood is set in 2020's Los Angeles around Oscar-weekend; *Murder At Magpie Hall* is set in one of England's stately homes in the early 20th century; while *The Gay Divorce* is set in modern-day San Francisco, focusing on the death throes of a once-happy marriage.

Kevin and I wrote these plays over two years, beginning in early 2019.

We hope you enjoy reading them as much as we enjoyed writing them.

Laurence Watts
December 2020

HOLLYWOOD

A Play in Two Acts

By

Laurence Watts and Kevin Burnard

Cast of Characters

Tiffany Beckworth	-An American film star in her 30s
Robbie Shard	-An American film star in his 30s
Sir Anthony Russell/ Trudy Fishburn	-A British actor in his 50s/ -An American actress in her 40s, portrayed in drag
Dame Margaret McCarthy/ Reporter	-A British actress in her 50s/ -A cable news reporter (voice only)

Scene:
A luxury apartment in Hollywood, Los Angeles.

Time:
2020s.

STAGE PLAN

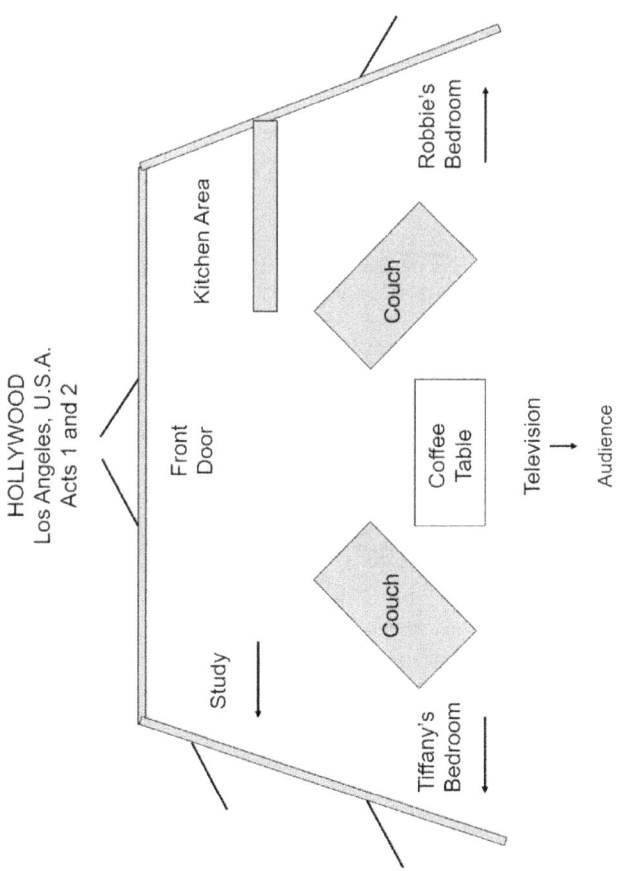

ACT I

Scene 1

SETTING: The front room of an apartment in Beverly Hills, Los Angeles.

There are three doors on the sides of the room. At the center is a grand double door, down C, leading outside. There are two mirrored doors, leading to opposite bedrooms: Tiffany's bedroom, up L and Robbie's bedroom/the guest room, up R, respectively. Near Tiffany's room is another door, down L, leading to the drawing room/study. To the right, opposite it, is an open kitchen. In the center of the room are two couches and a coffee table, facing front. On the coffee table is a fruit basket, a bottle of bourbon and four glasses.

AT RISE: TIFFANY BECKWORTH lounges on the left couch, cell phone to her ear, bourbon on the table.

TIFFANY

So, once I've won, what do we do? What's the game plan? When do we meet with the studios? I'm thinking my own superhero movie. Women can do that now, right? With a cape. I'd look good in a cape. And tights. Although, I'd have a body double for the close-ups, right? I wonder where they'd get one that looks like me? Ooh, or maybe something sad like, something set in World War II? I could be a spy. Or a lover. Or a Nazi. Or a Nazi spy who's also a great lover. That could be my superpower! I could be the world's greatest lover... but also a Nazi. You know, to show my range. What did Meryl do after she won? The first time. Theater? Who does theater? How would we do retakes? And how would they airbrush my boobs? No, that doesn't sound right. I know how much we spent on them, but they still droop when it's wet. And theaters are always damp. And the people that go and see plays are all so boring.

(TIFFANY chugs her bourbon.)

Have you been in touch with Ellen? When was the last time we did her? I mean, I'm funny! We could do Oprah, but she doesn't get the ratings these days, does she? But whatever we do, we're not going to fuck it up like Halle Berry, right? I want money, but I need something that's critically acclaimed as well.

(ROBBIE SHARD enters through the front doors. He puts down his keys and stares at her.)

THREESOME

One minute.

ROBBIE
What the fuck are you wearing?

TIFFANY
(into phone)

The bitch just came home.

(ROBBIE has a seat next to Tiffany. He squeezes her in a half-ironic, half-sincere hug)

TIFFANY
Husband.

ROBBIE
My darling wife. Wait, you didn't go out like that, did you?

TIFFANY
They're lounge pants. And for your information, I've been home all day plotting my victory with my agent.

ROBBIE
I think you mean plotting *our* victory.

TIFFANY
You really think you've got a shot? Honey, only one of us won an MTV Movie Award.

ROBBIE
It was for best on-screen kiss!

TIFFANY
And I nailed it.

ROBBIE
Rumor has it you nailed him as well.

TIFFANY
Don't judge me by your own low standards.

ROBBIE
They're actually pretty high... Today's was a personal trainer.

TIFFANY
Ooh. Do tell…

ROBBIE
My lips are sealed.

TIFFANY
Actually, we need to talk about that.

ROBBIE
(defensively)

I don't think there's anything to discuss.

TIFFANY
As long as the clickbait agrees with you.

ROBBIE
Oh, mind your own bullshit!

TIFFANY
I just need to know… are you bringing him to the awards tomorrow?

ROBBIE
Who?

TIFFANY
Daniel.

ROBBIE
Do I detect a hint of jealousy?

TIFFANY
None. We both deserve better than you.

ROBBIE
You're not his type, sweetie. Weren't you talking to someone when I came in?

TIFFANY

Just my agent. He's still on the line, say hi.

ROBBIE

You left him on hold?

TIFFANY

He's paid to wait for me.

ROBBIE
(his watch beeps with a scheduling alert)

Well, it's time…

TIFFANY

Not again!

(ROBBIE approaches TIFFANY, brandishing his phone threateningly. They break into fake smiles as he holds it up to record a video.)

ROBBIE

Hey guys!

TIFFANY

Hi! Thanks for following us! We are so excited for the Academy Awards tomorrow!

ROBBIE

I hope you win.

TIFFANY

No, I hope you do.

(TIFFANY and ROBBIE have the most sickening kiss in human history.)

Sending love to you all!

ROBBIE

More updates soon!

(ROBBIE puts down the phone.)

TIFFANY

You're so fake.

ROBBIE

As fake as my beautiful wife's tits.

(He tastes his lips and points to the half-empty bourbon bottle.)

It's a little bit early isn't it? Even for you.

TIFFANY

Awards season is stressful! Was that for Instagram?

ROBBIE

Who knows where they put it. I have people to worry about that kind of thing. Seriously though, have you been drinking all day?

TIFFANY

Just to take the edge off of things. I'm so nervous. Aren't you?

ROBBIE

I have a different coping mechanism.

(ROBBIE sits on the right sofa and reaches for the bourbon to pour himself a glass.)

TIFFANY

Tell me about the personal trainer then. Was it hot?

(ROBBIE extends three fingers horizontally across his glass up to the liquor line.)

ROBBIE

Three fingers.

TIFFANY

Too much information! You're disgusting.

ROBBIE

(ROBBIE takes a long sip.)

I'm not in the mood to fight. We're supposed to be supportive, right?

(TIFFANY rolls her eyes as ROBBIE reaches for her, but extends a hand for him to kiss)

THREESOME

Let's practice the acceptance speeches, that'll calm you down.

TIFFANY
OK.

ROBBIE
(reassuringly)

Deep breaths. You're a winner. Everyone loves you and you're very, very pretty.

TIFFANY
I love it when you're being sincere.

ROBBIE
I'll get mine.

(ROBBIE gets up and walks toward his bedroom door, stage right.)

Your agent's still on the line, by the way.

(ROBBIE exits.)

TIFFANY
Oh, yeah.

(TIFFANY picks her phone back up.)

Robbie just came home. He's feeling very emotional, so I said I'll listen to his acceptance speech. I know! Well, I try and be supportive. No, I was surprised he was nominated as well. Still, whatever happens, it's good for me. OK. Talk later.

(TIFFANY hangs up the phone and puts it down. ROBBIE returns from his room.)

ROBBIE
Who wrote yours?

TIFFANY
My publicist.

ROBBIE

Have you read it yet?

TIFFANY

No.

ROBBIE

Liar! I could hear you in your room, last night, muttering thanks to the Academy in your sleep.

(TIFFANY pulls out her script from where it was hidden under the couch)

TIFFANY

Who wrote yours?

ROBBIE

One of the writers from the show.

TIFFANY

Any good?

ROBBIE

We won a Daytime Emmy, remember?

TIFFANY

The speech, darling.

ROBBIE

Of course, it is.

TIFFANY

Shall I be the judge?

ROBBIE

Ladies first.

TIFFANY

Fine.

(reading her speech, suddenly emotional)

Oh my God, I can't believe this is happening!

THREESOME

ROBBIE
They scripted that?

TIFFANY
(stoic)

Of course.

(back on the verge of tears)

First of all, I just want to pay tribute to all the other actresses who were nominated in this category. You are all so talented, it's an honor for me just to be mentioned in the same breath as you. I love you all so, so much.

ROBBIE
Ugh.

TIFFANY
In my heart you are all winners.

ROBBIE
(sipping his drink)

Code for "fuck off, losers."

TIFFANY
Right, but apparently, I can't actually say that...

(back to emotional speech mode)

I would like to thank Peter for his amazing direction, Jim for developing such a rich array of characters in what was an impeccable script. Martine, Jackson, Paul, Davey, Mary-Anne, Windham...

ROBBIE
Who's Mary-Anne?

TIFFANY
No idea.

ROBBIE
Well then, who's Windham?

TIFFANY
I don't know that one either. I'm an actress - I just say the line.

(turns the page)

When I was a child…

ROBBIE
Please…

TIFFANY
…I remember crying at the end of *Steel Magnolias*. And my mother wrapped an arm around me and tried to comfort me by explaining that all the women onscreen were just acting.

ROBBIE
She should have smothered you.

TIFFANY
And in that moment, I knew that what I wanted more than anything else in this world was to be was an actress, so that I could touch other people the way that Sally, Julia, and Dolly touched me.

ROBBIE
First names, eh?

TIFFANY
I'll have won, so I can do that.

(back to speech)

So, the message I have for every little girl out there, watching tonight…

ROBBIE
You'll have put half of them to sleep to sleep by now.

TIFFANY
(crying now)

Is… Keep dreaming. Because dreams really do come true. Thank you.

ROBBIE
(slow clapping)

And to think, I thought you couldn't act. You deserve an award for that speech alone. Waterproof mascara, I hope?

TIFFANY
Do I look like an amateur?

(serious again)

OK, I've shown you mine. You show me yours.

ROBBIE
(glances down to his pages and then at the first row of the audience)

Oh my, from here I can see right down Angelina's dress.

TIFFANY
You're actually going to say that?

ROBBIE
(aside to TIFFANY)

They think it will make me sound straight.

(continuing)

…Anyway, I only have eyes for my darling wife.

(digressing)

Which reminds me, you didn't thank me in your speech!

TIFFANY
What the hell did you do to help me win?

ROBBIE
I've loved and supported you for the last three years!

TIFFANY
Please. I out-earned you two-to-one last year. And what little work you get is because you're married to me. I make you look successful.

ROBBIE

And I make you look tolerable. Everyone likes me. The studio has statistics to prove it. No one liked you until we got married.

TIFFANY

That is bullshit.

ROBBIE

Your likeability ratings were 43% in men under 30, 26% in men between 30 and 40, and 15% among single parent vegan mothers. All up at least 20 points now, thanks to me!

TIFFANY

Men over 70 adored me!

ROBBIE

Anyway, if you're not going to mention me in your speech, I'm not going to mention you in mine.

TIFFANY

Fine, I'll slot you in. You can go in between Mary-Anne and Windham.

ROBBIE

(pause)

Bitch. Where was I?

(back to speech)

I would like to thank all the members of the Academy for this incredible honor... Except Jim... who didn't cast me in the Avatar sequel.

(digressing)

It's a joke, but I'm pretty bitter about that.

(continuing)

Of course, no one wins one of these awards on their own, but I'm not going to recite a long list of names of people you don't know...

TIFFANY

Really?

THREESOME

ROBBIE
(aside)

My writer friend says it's boring.

(back to speech)

So instead, I'm going to tell you a joke.

TIFFANY
Oh, no.

ROBBIE
I remember the day I finally connected with my father. Up until that point, I was a brattish, selfish, lonely boy. One day, I was alone with my dad at our beach house in Fort Lauderdale. He looked out of the window at an angry sky and said, "Looks like rain today." "Tell me something I don't know," I shot back at him. And he paused for a moment as if in thought, before replying: "Your mother doesn't have a gag reflex."

(pause)

I think he was joking, but from that day on I always wanted to be an actor, and I dreamt of a day like this when I could thank you all for making it come true.

(TIFFANY is speechless, and maybe laughing a bit in spite of herself. Her phone beeps with a text alert, and she ignores it.)

TIFFANY
You cannot say that!

ROBBIE
I'm an artist. I break boundaries.

TIFFANY
You thought Van Gogh was a moving company.

ROBBIE
I think it would be a great name. It's better than "Two Men Will Move You."

(TIFFANY's phone beeps again with a text alert. She ignores it once more.)

17

                    TIFFANY
Which must be a nightly experience for you...

                    ROBBIE
At least one of us is getting some. How's the dryness, honey?

(TIFFANY's phone beeps for a third time.)

Are you going to answer that?

                    TIFFANY
If it's important, they'll call.

(ROBBIE's phone beeps with a text message, which he reads)

What is it? One of those Amber Alerts?

                    ROBBIE
(suddenly very serious)

Turn on the TV.

                    TIFFANY
Why? Where's the fire?

(TIFFANY picks up the remote and turns on the TV - offstage, looking past audience.)

                    ROBBIE
You may regret saying that. Apparently, it's at The Beverly Hilton.

(ROBBIE takes the remote from TIFFANY and turns up the volume.)

                    REPORTER
(voice only)

I'm standing on Wilshire Boulevard, in Beverly Hills, at the scene of what can only be described as an inferno at The Beverly Hilton. This hotel has a troubled history, being where Whitney Houston was found drowned in a bathtub after an alleged drug overdose. It's a favorite among Hollywood's elite because of its plush fixtures and convenient location. In fact, we've already seen a number of A-listers evacuated and assembled in the parking lot. The hotel is teeming with stars in town for tomorrow's Academy Awards. No word yet on what caused the fire, the number of, if any, fatalities or the plan to put the fire out. Firefighters are arriving as I speak to try and tackle the blaze, but by the look of things... they have their work cut out for them.

ROBBIE

I recognize that firefighter. Third from the right. From what I remember, he has a huge—

TIFFANY

(checking her texts)

Shit! Robbie, check your phone.

ROBBIE

There's nothing a bunch of hysterical costars can tell me that the news cannot.

TIFFANY

Just do it.

(ROBBIE rolls his eyes but checks his phone.)

ROBBIE

No!

TIFFANY

Well, I guess we're supposed to play Airbnb for Tony Russell and Maggie McCarthy.

ROBBIE

Those British assholes.

TIFFANY

There have to be other places they can stay. I'm sure they can manage—

(TIFFANY's phone rings.)

TIFFANY

(happily, into phone)

Roger! No, we were just going to—

(listens)

Oh, I know, it looks awful. My heart sank when I heard the news.

(listens more)

Oh, Roger, darling, of course we'd love to have Sir Anthony Russell and Dame Margaret McCarthy stay with us! It would be such an honor. But wouldn't they be more comfortable at the Hilton? Or the Sheraton?

(pause)

What about the W? The Four Seasons, then?

(pause)

Fuck it, what about a Best Western, Quality Inn or Motel 6?

(listens more)

They're all full? Seriously? What is this, Bethlehem at Christmas? No, I know it's the Oscars, Roger, but there's got to be somewhere else they can stay?

(listens again)

No, we sent the staff away for the weekend. We signed that deal with *Hello!* and they didn't want any candid shots getting out before they go to print. So, it's just us.

(listening)

I know I did a film with him, I'm blonde not stupid. That doesn't mean we're friends! And I've never met her.

(listening again)

Say that again. It would make a great chapter in my autobiography? Or a good story for Ellen? Yes, I'm listening. Well, I suppose so. Love it. OK, Yes. Of course, we will.

ROBBIE

No.

TIFFANY

(scowling)

Yes!

(beaming into phone)

Thanks, Roger. Love you. Kisses! Bye!

(TIFFANY puts down the phone.)

ROBBIE

You didn't.

TIFFANY

It's great PR. Think about it. This is like when Michael Jackson, Marlon Brando, and Elizabeth Taylor had to do that road trip from New York to LA, after 9/11.

ROBBIE

How much did they get? They were all dead by the time they got around to making a film about it.

TIFFANY

(ignoring him)

We'll be heroes.

ROBBIE

Ugh. My room or yours?

TIFFANY

Yours, obviously.

ROBBIE

You've worked with him, right?

TIFFANY

Yes.

ROBBIE

Does he know about us? Or more specifically, me?

TIFFANY
No.

ROBBIE
So, I'm going to have to lie about who I am in my own home?

TIFFANY
We're actors, Robbie; we'll act. Just think of it as a live performance.

ROBBIE
Performing live is exhausting. This is why I never do theater.

(BLACKOUT)

(END OF SCENE)

ACT I

Scene 2

SETTING: Same as Scene 1.

AT RISE: An empty room, with the lights out.

(The doorbell rings. Nothing happens. After a moment, it rings again.)

TIFFANY
(offstage)

Claudio!

ROBBIE
(offstage)

We sent the staff away, remember?

TIFFANY
(offstage)

Oh, right. You get it!

ROBBIE
(offstage)

No, you get it!

TIFFANY
(offstage)

They need your room!

ROBBIE
(offstage)

Fine!

(ROBBIE enters from his bedroom, stage right.)

What kind of house guests arrive at two in the morning?

(TIFFANY enters from her bedroom, stage left)

TIFFANY

Entitled British snobs, that's who!

(ROBBIE opens the front door and SIR ANTHONY RUSSELL and DAME MARGARET MCCARTHY enter the apartment, they each have a tiny bag.)

Tony! So good to see you!

(TIFFANY and ANTHONY embrace. ANTHONY places a hand on TIFFANY'S backside. ROBBIE and MARGARET also hug.)

ANTHONY

Tiffany, darling!

(TIFFANY removes his hand from her butt and pulls away)

TIFFANY

(through gritted teeth)

Friendly as ever, I see!

ROBBIE

(feeling Margaret's cardigan)

Ooh, what's this? I love the fabric!

MARGARET

It's all I managed to salvage from the hotel, apart from some essentials. It's lemur. Or llama. Something beginning with 'L'. They skin them as babies for extra softness. Like veal.

(ROBBIE, visibly disturbed, pulls out of the hug.)

MARGARET

It's a joke. Oh, your face!

TIFFANY

THREESOME

(to ANTHONY)

Have you met my darling husband?

(MARGARET hugs TIFFANY, and ROBBIE hugs ANTHONY. ROBBIE places his hand on ANTHONY's butt.)

ANTHONY
(removing ROBBIE's hand)

So, this is the lucky man!

ROBBIE
Some would say unlucky.

ANTHONY
But you wouldn't, would you?

(ROBBIE stops hugging ANTHONY, and TIFFANY pulls away from MARGARET.)

I wouldn't. She could be the Ophelia to my Hamlet any day.

(MARGARET puts an arm around ANTHONY.)

If not for my darling wife, of course. I need no other. It really is awfully decent of you to take us in like this. Two homeless strays.

MARGARET
Apparently, every hotel in Los Angeles is full. Even the hotels in Glendale, apparently. It's hard to imagine.

TIFFANY
(through gritted teeth)

Isn't it?

ANTHONY
Well, this promises to be very cozy. Then, tomorrow we can all go the awards together.

TIFFANY
I suppose. What time are your cars arriving?

MARGARET
Cars? I think we're getting an Uber, dear.

ANTHONY
I was thinking we could do those scooter things you see on the sidewalks.

TIFFANY
But you're both nominated for Oscars!

ANTHONY
One of the joys of working for small independent studios, I'm afraid.

ROBBIE
(to MARGARET)

You're gunning for best actress, right?

MARGARET
For playing Queen Victoria. Can you believe it? Honestly, I spend an entire career doing Shakespeare and Chaucer, and they finally recognize me for a dreary little role in a film about a Prime Minister whom no one remembers.

TIFFANY
How amazing would it be if you both won best acting awards on the same night?

ANTHONY
It would be miraculous, principally because I'm up for Best Song.

ROBBIE
Best Song?

ANTHONY
Yes, with Bono. Would you like a private performance?

TIFFANY	ROBBIE
Oh, don't trouble yourself.	Please don't.

ANTHONY
Good, because we were drunk when we wrote it. I can't even remember how it goes. But the studio insisted on a collaboration, so there you have it.

THREESOME

MARGARET
And you two are up for gongs as well, I hear?

TIFFANY
For what?

MARGARET
Oscars, dear.

ROBBIE
Yes, Tiffany's up for Best Supporting Actress for playing Mandy in *Memoirs of a Hapless Hooker*. And I got the nod for playing Clive in a modern retelling of *Maurice*, directed by Baz Luhrmann.

MARGARET
Interesting soundtrack, I'd imagine.

ANTHONY
You know, my father knew Forster. Complete fruit, obviously, but apparently funny as hell. He'd be very proud of you.

ROBBIE
That means a lot to me. But not, like, in a weird way. I like funny people, that's all.

MARGARET
You men are lucky. As women, the only roles we get offered are queens and whores. My Victoria was both, naturally.

TIFFANY
I want to play a superhero.

MARGARET
Oh, not that pop garbage, my dear. You're not Joaquin Phoenix. I'm talking about actual roles. Something you can get your teeth into.

ANTHONY
Have either of you heard any more about the fire?

ROBBIE
There's been a few more bodies pulled from the hotel, unfortunately.

MARGARET

Anyone in my category? Just out of curiosity.

ROBBIE
If you've lost all your clothes, what will you be wearing tomorrow?

ANTHONY
Oh, I'm sure we can pick up something in the morning.

TIFFANY
In the morning? I've been planning my outfit for a year. Ever since I saw what Trudy Fishburn wore last time. I'm on my fifth designer, my fourth jeweler and my third make-up artist!

MARGARET
Aren't you up against her? Didn't she play...

TIFFANY
Betsy Ross.

MARGARET
That was it. *The Battle of Baltimore*, now that was a good film.

ANTHONY
Wonderful production values. Great costumes.

TIFFANY
Yes... yes, but a bit slow and serious, don't you think?

ANTHONY
Did you know they actually filmed parts of the movie at Fort McHenry? With real bombs.

TIFFANY
(with relish)

How apt considering how it did at the box office.

ROBBIE
(aside to TIFFANY)

How long have you been waiting to make that joke?

TIFFANY

(aside to ROBBIE)

Months.

ANTHONY
It's not all about the gross, my dear.

TIFFANY
What a strange thing to say.

MARGARET
Not that Trudy stands a chance against you, my dear. I'm sure you'll win. I bet you made an awesome hooker.

ANTHONY
She did.

MARGARET
You watched it without me?

ANTHONY
Oh, you silly thing.

(ANTHONY pulls MARGARET into a passionate embrace and kisses her.)

You were busy with those reshoots, remember?

MARGARET
Oh yes!

(to TIFFANY and ROBBIE)

I'm sorry, we're keeping you both up. Where will we be sleeping?

TIFFANY
In the guest room. Robbie can show you.

ROBBIE
(reluctantly obeying)

It's just over there…

ANTHONY
Wonderful. Margaret, I'm sure you'll be wanting to get some beauty sleep.

MARGARET
Always the romantic. Will you be joining me?

ANTHONY
Actually, I'd like to catch up with our hosts. Would either of you two like to join me for a drink?

(MARGARET kisses ANTHONY and goes into the guest room.)

Tiffany? Still a bourbon girl, I see.

TIFFANY
The only drink I'd need at this hour is coffee. No, I'm going back to sleep. I'll see you all in the morning.

(TIFFANY walks toward her bedroom, left)

ANTHONY
(pouring two glasses of bourbon)

Well then, Robbie, why don't you and I have a nightcap? I'm sure Margaret will be able to unpack on her own.

MARGARET
(offscreen)

Oh, I say!

(TIFFANY stops at her bedroom door to glare at ROBBIE)

ROBBIE
(to TIFFANY)

I put everything away!

(TIFFANY exits, shaking her head. ROBBIE and ANTHONY drink in silence for a moment)

ANTHONY

So, what's she really like?

ROBBIE
Huh?

ANTHONY
Oh, you know. What's it like being married to Tiffany Beckworth?

ROBBIE
She can be intense.

ANTHONY
Really?

ROBBIE
And very loud and demanding.

ANTHONY
An 'on-top' kind of girl, then?

ROBBIE
I wouldn't really—

ANTHONY
Whatever it is, I bet she wears you out.

ROBBIE
(unsure)

Yes?

ANTHONY
How does she like to take it then?

ROBBIE
Oh, uh, she likes—

ANTHONY
Yes?

(A panicked ROBBIE takes a big gulp of his drink and then eyes the liquor line)

ROBBIE
Three fingers.

ANTHONY
Three? Wow.

ROBBIE
Do you and Margaret ever…?

ANTHONY
Not since 2007.

ROBBIE
Oh. Was it a bad year?

ANTHONY
Only for our sex life. I would imagine everything's shriveled up by now.

ROBBIE
You mean to tell me you haven't had sex since 2007?

ANTHONY
Goodness, no! I shagged one of the stewardesses on the flight from London. A man has needs, if you know what I mean?

ROBBIE
Oh, I do.

ANTHONY
But I'm sure Tiffany fulfils every one of yours.

ROBBIE
She sure is a lay.

ANTHONY
How long have you two been together?

ROBBIE
Three years.

ANTHONY
Ah, the honeymoon period. Happy days!

ROBBIE
Very happy. Absolutely.

ANTHONY
Plus, with your profiles, I'm sure it would be hard to keep any infidelity under wraps.

ROBBIE
(slipping)

Oh, I never show my face.

ANTHONY
I'm sorry?

ROBBIE
On my profiles. Nothing. Changing subject for a moment, you've won an Oscar before, right?

ANTHONY
(smiling)

Yes. I'm one for one.

ROBBIE
For Othello, right? I read your Wikipedia entry earlier.

ANTHONY
It was indeed. I got approached to reprise the role for film after a critically acclaimed season up in Stratford.

ROBBIE
What was it like?

ANTHONY
Stratford?

ROBBIE
No, winning an Oscar! Was it everything you imagined?

ANTHONY
It's always an honor to be held in high regard by your peers, but the art itself is the reward, not the trophy.

ROBBIE

But what did it do for your career?

ANTHONY

Well, my agent was very happy. I suppose I've made more money as a result, but I can't say I'm any happier than I was before. I can sleep with any woman I want, but that was true before I won, of course. I bagged Dame Margaret McCarthy, after all!

ROBBIE

So, are you and Margaret officially... open?

ANTHONY

Good God, no. But what she doesn't know won't hurt her.

ROBBIE

I see

ANTHONY

She's never been terribly interested in "all that". But I am. So, I take care of it without her. Some women just aren't switched on that way. Unlike Tiffany, by the sounds of things...

ROBBIE

Right.

ANTHONY

You two should come to London. We could be very accommodating.

ROBBIE

Have you ever considered moving to LA?

ANTHONY

We've talked about it. But we have so many theater friends in London. We'd miss them. Plus, we're not really the Hollywood types. Everyone over here is so...

ROBBIE

Pretty?

ANTHONY

It has its appeal, don't get me wrong. But over here entertainment is an industry. In Britain it's more of an art.

ROBBIE

Tiffany and I were nominated for very artistic films.

ANTHONY

Of course, you were. Disregard my remark. Now, while Margaret and I are here, please just carry-on as normal. Go about your business as if we weren't even here.

ROBBIE

What do you mean?

ANTHONY

I'm just saying, you and Tiffany don't need to tone it down on our account. Even if she is… loud.

ROBBIE

OK.

ANTHONY

Go on, don't let me hold you up.

ROBBIE

Okay. Goodnight?

ANTHONY

(a little creepily)

Goodnight and… good luck.

(ROBBIE, confused, goes to his room, right. He stops, remembers, and crosses back to Tiffany's room, left. ROBBIE exits.)

(ANTHONY remains. He sits on the couch, watching Tiffany's door. Expectantly, he sips his drink.)

(BLACKOUT)

(END OF SCENE)

ACT I

Scene 3

SETTING: Same as Scene 1.

AT RISE: An empty room, daylight streaming through the windows.

(ROBBIE enters through the main doors in workout gear. He's talking on his phone.)

ROBBIE

Hi handsome. Long time, no talk. Of course, I remember. How are things? You're working where now? Oh, I thought you were a waiter. Well congratulations! No, I never knew you studied accountancy. You know *what?*

(whispering, in case anyone hears)

You know every one of this year's Academy Award winners? You're shitting me!

(back to normal volume)

DID I—??? Wait, wait, wait, let me think about this. I mean, of course I want to know... if I've won. But if I didn't, not so much. How do you know already? Well, yes, I guess someone does have to count the votes. I just never imagined it would be someone I'd—

Yeah, we should do it again sometime. Well, I mean, who wouldn't want to fuck an Oscar winner?

(ROBBIE collapses on couch)

What do you mean I didn't win? No, I know what those individual words mean, I just... Well, who did? That can't be true. He was awful. He came nowhere at the Golden Globes, and he's up for a Razzie for the only other movie he released last year! No, you've gotta have it wrong. Well, maybe you should recount them! No, I know you're an auditor... now. And auditors never make mistakes? Do they ever make deliberate mistakes? I mean, who else knows? Look, I'd be prepared to be really nice to you if you were to... I don't care if you have a boyfriend now. I'll fuck him too, if you like! Bring your brother, I don't care! Look, this is my career we're talking about. Shit. Today is going to suck. The only way this could be worse is if either one of those annoying Brits or my darling wife— Oh, my god, did Tiffany win?

(ROBBIE gasps)

Trudy Fishburn? Oh, my god! Tiffany's never going to get over this. And she just fired another therapist, so this is all on me. Did either of the Brits win? Anthony Russell and Margaret McCarthy; they're staying with us. They didn't? Ugh, this place is going to be as much fun as a morgue. Well, a morgue that reeks heavily of liquor. No, I suppose I'm glad I know. Forewarned is forearmed and all that. I can stop rehearsing my speech for starters. No, I appreciate it. OK. It's fine. I'll call you. Bye.

(MARGARET enters in an evening dress)

MARGARET
Well, don't you look like someone just took a shit in your cornflakes? Speaking of which, do you have any cornflakes?

ROBBIE
What?

MARGARET
A big shit. Positively explosive. Is something the matter?

ROBBIE
(reluctantly)

Have you ever been told a secret you really, really shouldn't know?

MARGARET
Is this about Kevin Spacey? Because everyone knows now, don't they?

ROBBIE
What? No. This is different. They question is, do I zip it or spill it?

MARGARET
Well, Kevin Spacey didn't zip it. Had he kept it zipped, he might not have had half the problems he did.

ROBBIE
Like, hypothetically… if you could, would you want to know in advance

whether or not you are going to win tonight?

MARGARET
I'm sure I don't know. Perhaps. Either way, I might not bother going. Why? Do you know?

ROBBIE
(the worst performance of his career)

No, of course not.

MARGARET
Because that would be against the rules. Wouldn't it?

ROBBIE
Exactly.

MARGARET
Heavens, child, you're meant to be an actor and you're as transparent as glass. I'll repeat myself: do you know?

ROBBIE
Maybe.

MARGARET
How do you know?

ROBBIE
I didn't say I knew. But if I did it might be because a "friend" of mine told me. One who counted the votes.

MARGARET
Would this be what is known as a "friend with benefits"?

ROBBIE
Possibly.

MARGARET
And do you trust him?

ROBBIE
Oh my god, who said it was a him?

MARGARET
Darling, if you think Kevin Spacey was indiscreet you should try Googling your own name sometime. Does Tiffany know?

ROBBIE
I only just found out myself.

MARGARET
I mean about the other men!

ROBBIE
Oh, that! Yes, of course she does. She's free to sleep with whoever she wants to as well. She just chooses not to.

MARGARET
Well, I'm sure you're making enough whoopee for the both of you.

ROBBIE
Regardless, she is fully apprised of the situation.

MARGARET
Good. There's nothing worse than clandestine infidelity. That ended my last marriage.

ROBBIE
Oh, I, um…

(he gapes like a fish.)

I didn't know you were married before.

MARGARET
Yes. I'm not quite Elizabeth Taylor, but I've made my fair share of mistakes. That's the trouble with dating actors. You never know who they really are. They're all professional liars.

ROBBIE
It's a rough industry.

MARGARET
It's dreadful. So, did I win?

ROBBIE

Do you want me to lie?

MARGARET
Always. You're an actor.

ROBBIE
Then… Congratulations!

MARGARET
Shit.

ROBBIE
That was my sentiment.

MARGARET
You too? And to think I almost burnt to death to be a runner-up. Well, at least I didn't waste a new dress on the trip.

ROBBIE
Darling, when they're not new, we just call them vintage.

MARGARET
What about Tony?

ROBBIE
Congratulations again.

MARGARET
Congratulations yes or congratulations no? I'm lost now. This is what my first husband did.

ROBBIE
Tony didn't win either.

MARGARET
Bollocks. Well, fuck this, then. We might as well catch an early flight and go home.

(MARGARET knocks on the guest bedroom door to wake ANTHONY)

Darling, get dressed, we're leaving.

ROBBIE

No, you can't leave!

MARGARET
Don't be stupid, of course we can. It's either that or a night of self-flagellation and congratulating a bunch of sycophants who don't deserve it. And Mr. Biggles needs his walkies.

ROBBIE
Screw your dog – I'm assuming Mr. Biggles is a dog and not the name of some poor man you have locked up in your basement...

MARGARET
You assume correctly

If you leave town, they'll know the winners' names leaked! Think of my friend's reputation! Think of my reputation!

MARGARET
Darling, as I mentioned before, your reputation is all over the Internet.

ROBBIE
My friend would lose his job!

MARGARET
He's probably broken the law! Or at least the trust of his employers and the Academy.

ROBBIE
Fine.

(checks his phone)

But you'll miss out on the goodie bag. They've got, uh, limited edition designer tees, a free cruise to Reykjavik, personalized stained-glass portraits, cannabis-infused lip balm...

MARGARET
I don't need any of that. I can't be bribed by things.

ROBBIE
(sensing victory)

...And a limited-edition Louis Vuitton leash, collar and daytime dog romper for the four-legged member of your family.

(ANTHONY enters, half-dressed, the rest of his suit folded over his arm.)

ANTHONY
Did someone say we're leaving? I didn't oversleep, did I?

MARGARET
(to ROBBIE, aflutter)

Oh, Mr. Biggles would look divine!

(to ANTHONY)

Change of plan, darling, we're staying.

(ANTHONY puts on the rest of his suit.)

ANTHONY
Why would we be leaving, anyway?

MARGARET
You didn't win, darling. Neither did I. Nor did Robbie.

ANTHONY
Well, it'd make sense. None of us deserved to win.

(to MARGARET)

Well, except you darling, you were fabulous.

(continuing)

But Bono has certainly seen better days. How do you know?

MARGARET
Robbie bum-fucked one of the men who tallies the votes.

ANTHONY
Oh, good show. I knew you were a team player. Does Tiffany know you're bisexual?

ROBBIE

THREESOME

I'm not bisexual. Everything I told you last night was a lie.

MARGARET
(slow clapping)

Well done, Robbie. At least your performance convinced one of us.

ANTHONY
So, Tiffany's not getting any at the moment?

ROBBIE
Gross! Don't know, don't want to.

MARGARET
Wait, you haven't mentioned whether Tiffany won or not?

ROBBIE
Well, Tiffany…

(TIFFANY enters, jubilant)

TIFFANY
Today's the day! I'm so excited! can't wait to find out who else won.

ROBBIE
Good morning, darling.

TIFFANY
Good morning, lover. You were amazing last night.

(TIFFANY embraces ROBBIE and gives him a deep, tongued kiss.)

What are you wearing? It's so manly. I just got a text, by the way, the stylists are waiting for us.

ROBBIE
Waiting? Where?

TIFFANY
They had the back-door combination. They've been set up in the drawing room for two hours. Hair and makeup are there as well. We're going to have to share, your stylist got caught in the fire.

ROBBIE
(actually concerned)

Is Fernando okay?

TIFFANY

Third degree burns. I mean, I would have thought he could soldier through, but some people just aren't committed to their craft.

(to ANTHONY and MARGARET)

Are you two hungry? There are cornflakes in the cupboard.

MARGARET

The cornflakes are off this morning, my dear.

ROBBIE

No, Tiffany thinks the cornflakes are fine!

(TIFFANY cheerfully fetches them from the kitchen cupboard)

TIFFANY

Of course, they are. It's a brand-new box.

ANTHONY

I hate cornflakes.

MARGARET

And I'm lactose intolerant.

TIFFANY

Well, I don't buy groceries, so that's what we have. Robbie, go take a shower, for God's sake. I need you at your dashing best today.

(TIFFANY kisses ROBBIE again)

Studmuffin.

ROBBIE

Cupcake. Maggie, Tony... let's continue this conversation in a minute.

(ROBBIE exits to the drawing room)

THREESOME

TIFFANY

What conversation?

MARGARET

About cornflakes.

ANTHONY

(sarcastically)

Did you know, cornflakes were invented by Lord Cornflake in 1681 to feed his peasants during a time of economic crisis?

(TIFFANY prepares herself a bowl of cornflakes)

TIFFANY

Really? I thought they were made by some dude in the States to prevent masturbation. He thought they'd be bland enough to stifle male impulses or something. I'm sure your version is more accurate.

(TIFFANY sits on the couch with her cereal. ANTHONY and MARGARET move to the kitchen to find food.)

MARGARET

(quietly to ANTHONY)

Did she win or didn't she?

ANTHONY

You were the one talking to Robbie. I have no idea.

MARGARET

Well, this is awkward. Does she know that we didn't win?

TIFFANY

Margaret, are you excited? I think you've got a great shot today; you were great!

ANTHONY

(to MARGARET)

Apparently not.

MARGARET
(to TIFFANY)

I'm all butterflies and tingles, my dear.

TIFFANY
Oh my God. Me too! I can't wait. Afterwards, we're planning on going to the Governor's Ball, Elton John's, then Vanity Fair, and lastly Madonna's. We didn't get invited to Jay-Z's and Beyonce's because we're not "urban" enough, whatever that means.

ANTHONY
I thought urban was code for…

TIFFANY
Well, they'll regret it. They've not seen me do the Worm. You know, I think people are just envious. They see Robbie and me, two young, beautiful, successful people, and they react. It's sad, but it's understandable. They want what we have: the American Dream.

(ROBBIE enters holding a plate of donuts)

ROBBIE
The stylists had donuts, so I stole some. Tiff, they need you in there.

ANTHONY
Finally, someone in this town with carbs.

MARGARET
Darling, cornflakes are carbs.

ANTHONY
They're corn. Doesn't that make them a vegetable?

TIFFANY
(she hasn't moved)

It doesn't look like they're finished with you.

ROBBIE
My hair's still wet. They said they need you now.

TIFFANY

Fine. Save me a cream-filled.

ANTHONY
We will, if Robbie doesn't get there first.

TIFFANY
What?

ROBBIE
Cornflake joke. Don't worry about it, go get ready!

(TIFFANY exits to drawing room)

What do I do? Do I tell her or not?

MARGARET
Well, did she win?

ROBBIE
Of course, she didn't win.

ANTHONY
What an awful thing to say

MARGARET
Hypocrite, that's what you said.

ROBBIE
He's right, though. She can't act to save her life. If I tell her she hasn't won, she'll be devastated, and she won't be able to hide it.

MARGARET
Why devastated? It's only an award.

ROBBIE
Be realistic; she's never going to be nominated again. They wrote that role specifically with her in mind. But it's worse than that…

ANTHONY
How is it worse?

ROBBIE
Because the winner in Tiffany's category is…

(TIFFANY enters, looking at her phone)

TIFFANY
Robbie, you doofus. They weren't ready for me, it's still you.

ROBBIE
I swear they said they were.

MARGARET
Did you hear that?

TIFFANY
What?

MARGARET
Tiffany, they just called for you.

ANTHONY
I didn't hear anything.

MARGARET AND ROBBIE
Yes, you did.

ANTHONY
Oh, yes, I did. Run along.

TIFFANY
I'm on cloud nine right now. There could be trumpets playing in here and I swear I wouldn't hear them. Oh, and you left me a cream-filled. Thanks!

(TIFFANY puts her phone down to grab a donut off the plate.)

Today is going to be so perfect!

(TIFFANY exits to the drawing room, without her phone.)

MARGARET
She can't hear us, right?

ROBBIE
All clear.

THREESOME

ANTHONY
Go on then. How can this day get any worse?

ROBBIE
Because this year's Academy Award for Best Supporting Actress is going to… Trudy Fishburn.

MARGARET
Oh, well, she deserves it. Loved her performance.

ROBBIE
You didn't love her, she's a bitch, and as long as you're in this house, you'll remember that!

MARGARET
Got it. She's a slut.

ANTHONY
A talentless slut. With no ass.

MARGARET
Tony!

ROBBIE
Perfect. Tiffany will love you.

MARGARET
But she's still going to be devastated and we're still going to have to deal with that. We're just delaying the inevitable.

ROBBIE
No, we're preparing for it. But the important thing is Tiffany can't know about it until it happens.

(TIFFANY enters, furious and upset.)

TIFFANY
Oh my God, this is horrible! Everything's ruined! Today is the worst… day… ever.

(MARGARET, ROBBIE, and ANTHONY stare silently back.)

ROBBIE

Honey?

TIFFANY
Someone has stolen my phone!

(ANTHONY points at it on the coffee table and coughs.)

MARGARET
Isn't that you phone, my dear? On the coffee table?

TIFFANY
Oh my God, you guys are the best! Today's gonna be perfect.

(TIFFANY exits)

ROBBIE
Perfectly awful.

MARGARET
You need to think of ways you can cushion the blow. Think! What does she like?

ROBBIE
Herself.

MARGARET
Anything else?

ROBBIE
Winning.

ANTHONY
Maybe you could get her flowers?

MARGARET
Flowers are what you get a woman if you want to show no thought at all. They die. Just like your dreams.

ROBBIE
And she'll know if they're not organically farmed. She always knows.

ANTHONY
Why are women always so tricky to buy for?

MARGARET
Why are men so stupid that they think they can buy our happiness? We're simple creatures underneath. Sometimes we just need a dog to pet or someone to listen to us.

ROBBIE
She's allergic.

MARGARET
To being listened to?

ROBBIE
Listening takes so much effort. There has to be an easier way.

ANTHONY
Darling, that emotional support thing really is awfully hard work.

MARGARET
How would you know? Unless you read about it somewhere?

ANTHONY
I played a therapist once, remember?

MARGARET
In a film where you got eaten by zombies! You're both pathetic. And you're not taking this seriously. That poor girl's world is going to come crashing down around her perfectly sculpted ears. How are we going to help her get through this?

ROBBIE
Cock.

MARGARET
Spoken like a true homosexual.

ANTHONY
Drugs?

MARGARET
For her?

ANTHONY

For us.

MARGARET

I haven't smoked weed since Woodstock.

ROBBIE

That was 1969!

MARGARET

How old do you think I am? The film *Woodstock*! I played a hippy. It was my method phase.

ANTHONY

Good job you were never cast as a serial killer.

MARGARET

Actually, that's what ended my method phase.

ROBBIE

OK. This is no help at all.

ANTHONY

I'm sorry. We're much better at being witty than we are at helping.

MARGARET

Look, just be there for her and try not to make things any worse than they are. Not a step out of line. No escorts, rough trade, or closeted scientologists. Not tonight. There's only so much she can take.

(TIFFANY enters, looking fabulous and ready for the evening. ROBBIE, MARGARET, and ANTHONY all stand to look at her.)

ROBBIE

Wow!

ANTHONY

Spectacular!

TIFFANY

Thank you. I feel like a princess.

MARGARET

Well, you look like one, my dear.

THREESOME

TIFFANY
Do I look like a winner?

ROBBIE
You look... great.

TIFFANY
Great enough to make Trudy jealous all year?

MARGARET
Trudy who?

ANTHONY
The flat-assed slut.

MARGARET
(pause)

Oh, that one. What a whore.

(ROBBIE gives ANTHONY and MARGARET two thumbs up)

TIFFANY
Right? Robbie, go get dressed. The car will be here soon and you're not even ready.

ROBBIE
Sorry, my love.

(ROBBIE leaves the room. MARGARET motions to TIFFANY to join her on the couch.)

MARGARET
You're really feeling good about tonight, aren't you, dear?

TIFFANY
I feel like my whole life has been leading up to this.

ANTHONY
Do you really mean that?

TIFFANY

I do. And to have you all here, and Robbie, just makes it perfect. How do you feel?

MARGARET
Me? Oh, yes, so excited. Who knows what will happen?

TIFFANY
You could win an Oscar! I read in the paper you're one of the frontrunners.

ANTHONY
Never believe what you read in the papers, my dear.

MARGARET
Just listen to me, Tiffany. Whatever happens tonight, your husband will be there to support you. Remember that.

TIFFANY
And that's what makes it extra special. The two of us: Hollywood's new power couple. My agent already has a "morning after" photoshoot planned for tomorrow. The two of us, one or two Oscars, and margaritas by the poolside. I've picked out our swimsuits. We have projects lined up as well. There's talk of me playing Marilyn Monroe in a new biopic, but, you know, I'd be willing to pass that up to be a superhero. And it all starts tonight.

ANTHONY
Do you think Robbie will win as well?

MARGARET
Tony!

ANTHONY
I mean, that would be the dream, right?

TIFFANY
I suppose. I mean, I think he was good in Maurice, but I don't think he was as good as me. But I'd be happy for him if he won. Even if I didn't. But I just know this is my year. They're all talking about me on Twitter. I Googled myself just now and everyone says I'm a shoe-in.

MARGARET
Have you ever Googled your husband?

TIFFANY

I daren't. I'm still haunted by some fanfiction someone wrote about him, years ago.

ANTHONY
Well, look. If you need any advice afterwards, winner to winner, my door is always open.

TIFFANY
That's really sweet of you, Tony. But I feel like this Oscars is about one generation of actors handing the baton to the next.

(ROBBIE enters, dressed sharply)

TIFFANY
Oh my God, you look amazing! My knight in shining armor.

ROBBIE
Well, your knight in an Armani tuxedo.

(TIFFANY pulls out her phone)

TIFFANY
Everyone needs to see how good we look.

MARGARET
I notice no one's commented on how beautiful I look.

ANTHONY
Darling, you always look gorgeous. Goes without saying, really.

MARGARET
It goes without saying all too often.

(TIFFANY brandishes the phone threateningly)

TIFFANY
You all look great. Come on, join us!

ANTHONY
What for?

MARGARET
It's that the Instabook thing your agent was rambling about?

ANTHONY
That's very kind of you, but we don't believe in social media.

TIFFANY
It's good publicity! We need to preserve this moment. I mean, four potential Oscar winners, this is history right here!

ROBBIE
Tiffany, we should probably tell you—

(TIFFANY hits record on her phone.)

TIFFANY
Squeeze in! Camera's rolling!

(EVERYBODY forces a smile)

TIFFANY
Hi, lovelies! This is Tiffany Beckworth, reporting in before the Oscars! I'm so excited, oh my God! Robbie and I are here with two other nominees, Dame Margaret McCarthy and Sir Anthony Russell, and we're all so honored to be nominated. Anthony, say hello to everyone.

ANTHONY
So, they can see us now?

TIFFANY
Yeah, I'm filming us on my phone.

ANTHONY
(waving)

Hello, instawebbers.

MARGARET
You'll have to forgive us, we're such luddites.

TIFFANY
Is that where you're from in England? That's so cute. Say hi, Robbie!

ROBBIE
"Hi, Robbie!"

TIFFANY

Isn't he hilarious? Great comedian, great actor. We all are. I hope everyone does amazing. But we're all winners already, just to be here. Especially me. Everyone smile and say "Oscars!!!!"

EVERYONE

Oscars!

(CURTAIN)

(END OF ACT)

ACT II

Scene 1

SETTING: The same front room of the same apartment in Beverly Hills, Los Angeles. The next morning. There is a solitary Oscar sitting on the coffee table.

AT RISE: The room is empty, and strewn with empty bottles, champagne glasses, and confetti.

(MARGARET exits her room, lugging a suitcase.)

MARGARET
(to herself)

Passport. Purse. Phone. Phone charger? Bollocks.

(MARGARET re-enters her room. After a moment, ROBBIE enters through the front door. He falls face-first onto the floor.)

MARGARET
(reentering, holding a charger, to herself)

There you are you little bugger.

(MARGARET sees ROBBIE on the floor.)

Speaking of buggers. Are you alive? Darling? Robbie?

ROBBIE
Ugh.

MARGARET
Can I get you anything?

ROBBIE
Ugh.

MARGARET
Would a glass of water help?

THREESOME

ROBBIE
Ugh.

MARGARET
One grunt for yes, two for no.

ROBBIE
Ugh.

MARGARET
Splendid.

(MARGARET goes to the kitchen to fetch water. She returns to ROBBIE with a glass.)

ROBBIE
(looking up at MARGARET)

Ice?

MARGARET
Oh, for heaven's sake. You Americans and your bloody ice cubes.

(MARGARET walks to the kitchen, adds ice and returns.)

Here you go, petal. No, use your hands. Grip it. Take the glass. Take the fucking gla-

(Exasperated, MARGARET throws the contents of the glass over him)

ROBBIE
As I said to Pablo last night, in me, not on me.

MARGARET
Oh, I'm sorry darling. Heavy night?

ROBBIE
Is it morning?

MARGARET
I'm afraid so. I think we lost you after the Governor's Ball. Pablo, was that the name of the man whose face you were eating?

ROBBIE
Face?

MARGARET
You know, from a distance, you looked like one of those suction cup toys people have on their car rear windows. Darling, you weren't terribly discreet.

ROBBIE
Oh, shit. My agent is going to kill me.

(ROBBIE spots the Oscar.)

Wait. Sweet mother of God! Did I win? Is my agent not going to kill me?

MARGARET
Do you really not remember?

ROBBIE
It's 6:20 a.m. and I can't get off the floor, so… no.

(MARGARET grabs an apple from the fruit basket on the coffee table, sits down on the right sofa, and takes a bite.)

MARGARET
What's the last thing you remember?

ROBBIE
For heaven's sake, woman. Did I win?

MARGARET
I'll get there. Now, what's the last thing you remember?

ROBBIE
Pulling up at the Dolby Theater in the limo.

MARGARET
You don't remember the ceremony?

ROBBIE
It's tequila. I have to stop drinking tequila.

MARGARET

The limo didn't have tequila, dear. It's just a thought, but have you considered your amnesia might have something to do with mixing painkillers with hard liquor?

ROBBIE
I stopped taking painkillers when weed went legal.

MARGARET
Well, someone finished off the last of Tony's Oxycontin and it wasn't me. Shame, I was going to. It's good stuff. Better than he deserves.

ROBBIE
Shit, I thought that was my PrEP!

MARGARET
Evidently.

ROBBIE
But did I win?

MARGARET
Did you deserve to win?

ROBBIE
Of course not, but neither did any of the others.

MARGARET
Well, we can agree on that.

(pause)

No, you didn't win. The Academy Award for Best Actor in a Supporting Role went to... Mark Clifton.

ROBBIE
That little bitch.

MARGARET
It's kind of poetic, don't you think? That you, the closeted sword-swallower playing a gay aristocrat, were beaten by an openly gay actor playing a womanizing academic.

ROBBIE

Maybe gay is "in" then? Maybe my agent won't kill me?

MARGARET
Tiffany might. There were an awful lot of camera flashes every time you put your tongue down Pablo's throat. Even before that other fella joined in.

ROBBIE
Ugh. But, wait. If I didn't win, then whose Oscar is that?

MARGARET
All in good time.

(she takes another bite of the apple)

So, they announced your category first. After you didn't win, it looked like you disappeared off to the restroom with one of the seat-fillers. Which meant you weren't sitting in your seat when they announced your wife's category. So, when the cameras zoomed in on Tiffany, all excited and expectant, there was a big red empty seat right next to her.

ROBBIE
Oh, no.

MARGARET
It gets worse.

ROBBIE
It does?

MARGARET
For you. Because when they announced that she had won, she turned to where you should have been sitting and sort of hugged thin air.

ROBBIE
She won?

MARGARET
Oh, yes.

(taking another bite of the apple)

Turns out that little informant of yours didn't entirely get his facts right.

ROBBIE
Well, that's awesome news. Isn't it? I'm married to an Oscar-winner?

MARGARET
Are you? You might want to discuss that with her when she wakes up, because I think being absent for an Academy Award win is ample grounds for divorce.

(ROBBIE scrambles to his feet.)

ROBBIE
No!

MARGARET
She has every right to.

ROBBIE
She has every right to everything. She lawyered the hell out of the prenups.

MARGARET
Well, that's unfortunate. Maybe your friend Pablo has a bed available.

ROBBIE
I'd have to sleep in a twin.

MARGARET
I'm truly sorry for your hardship.

ROBBIE
You aren't really, are you?

MARGARET
Not a dicky bird, but it's fun to watch you squirm. I'm sure it will all make good fodder for you book.

ROBBIE
For what?

MARGARET
Your memoir. At one point you turned to Tony and I and told us, to our faces, that the only reason you let us stay with you was because it would make a good anecdote for your autobiography.

ROBBIE

Oh, God.

MARGARET

It's fine. We're used to it. And you're a young Caucasian male in Hollywood. You'll be fine. But meanwhile, I... must be going.

ROBBIE

Going where?

MARGARET

Home.

ROBBIE

Where's Anthony?

(MARGARET moves to leave.)

MARGARET

Sleeping.

ROBBIE

Does he have a later flight than you?

MARGARET

I have no idea, darling. Goodbye.

(ANTHONY enters from the guest bedroom.)

ANTHONY

(to MARGARET)

Where are you going?

MARGARET

(stopping and turning to him)

Home.

ANTHONY

Our home?

MARGARET

We can let the judge decide that.

ANTHONY
What on earth are you talking about?

ROBBIE
Yes, Margaret, what happened?

MARGARET
Tell me one thing, Tony.

ANTHONY
What?

MARGARET
Was she pretty?

ANTHONY
Who?

MARGARET
The actress you fucked at Elton John's.

ANTHONY
(aloof)

I don't know what you're talking about.

MARGARET
I knew this boy was a poof,

(to ROBBIE)
no offense darling,

(continuing)
within thirty seconds of seeing him, and he's still a better actor than you are.

ROBBIE
Thanks, I think.

ANTHONY
Darling, I would never do anything to—

MARGARET

Oh, don't give me that bullshit. You know I hate these awards ceremonies. We're miles away from home. I never wanted to come. We knew I wasn't going to win, and you didn't have a snowflake's chance in hell. It was always going to be a shitty night. So, why would you go and make a pig's ear of an evening so much bloody worse?

ANTHONY

You didn't enjoy the parties?

MARGARET

It would have been nice to catch up with Elton, but these things are like weddings. You only get ten seconds with the bride and groom before you're stuck at a table surrounded by the kind of people you spend the rest of the year avoiding. I spent two hours with a team nominated for best sound mixing, whatever that is. And they lost, as well! It was like being at a wake. And the only thing that could have made it bearable was you. And where were you?

ANTHONY

Well, darling I was… mingling. Like you said, ten seconds with everyone important.

ROBBIE

Am I somebody important?

MARGARET

Oh, darling, don't be silly.

ROBBIE

So, that's a yes?

MARGARET AND ANTHONY

No!

MARGARET

Anthony Maynard Russell, I will ask you one more time and if you care for the longevity of our marriage, you will answer me truthfully. Who was it you spent twenty minutes with in Elton John's toilet?

ROBBIE

Actually *in* the toilet?

ANTHONY
Of course, we weren't literally in the toilet, you imbecile.

MARGARET
Ha! We!

ANTHONY
I misspoke. I was just... constipated.

MARGARET
For twenty minutes? Elton was busting to take a slash and the poor man was locked out of his own john. Ha! Elton's John! I didn't mean to do it, but that's quite good.

ROBBIE
A slash? Is that a drug thing?

MARGARET AND ANTHONY
No!

ANTHONY
My Oxycontin dosage was off. It does strange things to the bowels. Clogs them up something terrible.

ROBBIE
I know nothing about that.

MARGARET
Just how constipated were you that you needed someone else in there to help you?

ANTHONY
She doesn't matter.

MARGARET
Doesn't she? OK then, what are we talking?

ANTHONY
What do you mean?

MARGARET
Spell it out for me. What on the Anthony Russell menu doesn't matter...

for twenty minutes?

ANTHONY

I don't have to answer that.

MARGARET

You do if you want to stay married.

ROBBIE

I'm so glad you're the ones fighting. Should I take notes?

MARGARET

Write this down: "Sir Anthony Russell is a liar and an adulterer." So, what was on the menu, Tony? Are we talking an aperitif?

ANTHONY

What?

MARGARET

Or did you get all the way to pudding?

ANTHONY

Do you really want to know?

ROBBIE

Oh my God, yes.

MARGARET

Spit it out, Tony.

ANTHONY

It was nothing more than… an amuse-bouche.

ROBBIE

You had to douche?

MARGARET AND ANTHONY

Shut up, Robbie.

(ROBBIE goes to the kitchen and looks through cupboards while MARGARET and ANTHONY continue arguing.)

MARGARET

I see. So, what happens now?

ANTHONY
What do you mean?

MARGARET
What happens to us? Are you likely to get this craving again in the future? I'm assuming this isn't the first time this has happened.

ANTHONY
It doesn't have to change anything. I wouldn't mind if you "snacked" here and there.

MARGARET
I've long lost my appetite. Time to collect the bill, I think. Don't you?

ROBBIE
(pulling cornflakes from the cupboard)

Does anyone else want cornflakes?

MARGARET
Not for me, darling, but I think Tony might still be hungry.

ANTHONY
I'm not. And I'm not willing to throw away our marriage over something so small and unimportant.

MARGARET
Interesting choice of words when the offending article happens to be your penis.

ROBBIE
(pouring cereal into bowl)

Alrighty.

ANTHONY
Do you want me to say I'm sorry?

MARGARET
Do you want to?

ANTHONY
Would it help?

MARGARET
Probably not, but saying "sorry" would be a fucking good place to start.

ANTHONY
Darling, of course I'm sorry.

MARGARET
Are you? This isn't a role, Anthony. This is a marriage between two people who are meant to love one another. And part of loving someone is having respect for that person.

ANTHONY
Of course, I respect you. I want to stay married to you. We work.

MARGARET
Well, that's the thing about marriages, Tony, they take two people. I can't respect you anymore. You see, it's not really about the infidelity. I get it. You're a man. All men, it seems to me, are dogs. Robbie, would you agree with me?

ROBBIE
Doggystyle is pretty popular.

MARGARET
I'll assume that proves my point. Which reminds me, I'm keeping Mr. Biggles.

ANTHONY
I never liked him anyway.

MARGARET
But where and when does it end, Tony? We're actors and we want the world's attention, I get that. But you've won your Oscar. You've been to the premieres and been on television. But it's not enough is it? You're still not satisfied. And I think I've finally realized you never will be. It's not a craft to you, or even a career. It's just about you. And I've had enough.

ANTHONY
Of course, it's not about me. What kind of an out-of-control egomaniac do you take me for?

THREESOME

(TIFFANY slams open her door, a massive smile on her face.)

TIFFANY
(practically singing)

Good morning, peasants! Make way, please, newly crowned Hollywood royalty coming through!

ROBBIE
(smiling)

Good morning, gorgeous.

TIFFANY
Oh, that's strange, I thought they'd usually collected the trash by now.

ROBBIE
It's not Thursday.

TIFFANY
It's a metaphor, dipshit. Here's another one: we're finished.

MARGARET
That's not a metaphor, love.

TIFFANY
Oh, Margaret, you're leaving?

ANTHONY
It's nothing. Margaret's just got her knickers in a twist.

MARGARET
And Tony prefers women that don't wear knickers.

TIFFANY
Put it on the backburner, Robbie and I are about to have a truly epic fight, and I like to have a supportive audience when I kick someone's ass.

ROBBIE
Metaphorically?

TIFFANY

Oh, no. It's never too soon to start stunt training for superhero stuff.

                                    ROBBIE

I prefer my ass un-kicked.

                                    TIFFANY

I think we all know only too well how you like your ass.

                                    ROBBIE

Tiff…

                                    TIFFANY

(interrupting)

You had one job last night! One!

                                    ROBBIE

To win? Well, that wasn't going to happen.

                                    TIFFANY

Two jobs, then! And you fucked up both of them! Now, don't get me wrong. I don't mind being married to a loser, and I don't mind being with a manslut addicted to backroom hookups, or whatever it is you get up to, but I cannot have a partner who misses the biggest moment of my life.

                                    ROBBIE

I didn't think you'd win!

                                    TIFFANY

Well, thanks for the vote of confidence. "Where's your husband, Tiffany?" That was the headline in the New York Post this morning. And you know what? Had I lost, I'd have damn well needed you there, too. But I didn't lose because I'm amazing.

                                    ROBBIE

(sincerely)

You are so amazing.

                                    TIFFANY

So, I made up my own headline.

                                    ROBBIE

THREESOME

What do you mean?

TIFFANY
"Fuckfest at Tiffany's!" What do you think about that one? That will be the headline they'll write when I tell them about the gangbangs you've regularly had here, in our marital home, while I'm on location.

ROBBIE
Don't exaggerate, it happened once. And it was just three of us.

TIFFANY
That's one more than most of us ever have at a time!

ROBBIE
Is it?

MARGARET
Anthony? Any advance on three?

ANTHONY
I had an active youth.

MARGARET
So, did I, actually. Point to Robbie.

ROBBIE
See, Tiff? It's normal.

TIFFANY
It is not!

ROBBIE
This is Hollywood. This city breathes scandal. We've all been through worse. Everything's going to be fine.

(ROBBIE's phone rings. He answers.)

ROBBIE
(into phone)

Hello?

(to the group)

It's my agent.

(back into phone)

Oh. That's... not fine. Really? No, we're good, we're good. Well, fix it! What do you mean, we can't...? Well, send them through and I'll call you back.

(he hangs up)

TIFFANY
So, not fine?

ROBBIE
They have pictures.

TIFFANY
How many and how bad?

MARGARET
I did tell you, Robbie. Terribly indiscrete. I almost took a few myself on my iPhone. Have you seen what TMZ pays these days?

TIFFANY
I need to see this.

ROBBIE
My agent's texting them over.

TIFFANY
Well, let's see.

ROBBIE
No!

(Robbie grabs his phone and runs to the guest bedroom door.)

TIFFANY
Get it, Tony!

(ANTHONY corners ROBBIE. TIFFANY and MARGARET cut him off from behind.)

THREESOME

TIFFANY
Give us the phone, Robbie!

ROBBIE
Never!

(TIFFANY kicks ROBBIE in the shins. He screams and drops the phone.)

You bitch.

(MARGARET scoops up the phone.)

TIFFANY
What are they? What's he doing?

MARGARET
They're still loading. Oh, the first one's here. It's of Robbie, in a kitchen? With someone who looks Puerto Rican.

(ANTHONY squeezes in behind MARGARET for a look.)

ANTHONY
I didn't know it was possible for a man's body to do that.

MARGARET
Yes, you did.

ANTHONY
Not with men!

(ANTHONY grabs the phone from MARGARET. He swipes to the next picture.)

Oh, that's a spectacular one.

MARGARET
(to ANTHONY)

You should have been born gay. You'd have been a lot happier.

ROBBIE
Give me my phone!

ANTHONY
Tiffany, catch!

(ANTHONY tosses the phone to TIFFANY. She catches it.)

TIFFANY
Oh, this is like charades. It's a man. It's Robbie! With another man. This one's African American. In a parking garage?

MARGARET
(looking over TIFFANY's shoulder)

Is that the same gentleman, Robbie? Just how indiscreet were you? Oh, it's that thing that was in the bedroom!

(pointing towards Robbie's bedroom)

That's what it was for. I thought it was to clean around the u-bend.

TIFFANY
You took that to the Oscars?

ROBBIE
Just give it to me, this isn't funny!

TIFFANY
It's hilarious. Tony, catch!

(TIFFANY tosses the phone to ANTHONY. He catches it.)

ANTHONY
The next one is of a... it's still the black guy. Can I say black? Anyway, this time you're in a car. Only, you can only see the back of Robbie's head because... Well, Robbie's busy.

MARGARET
Dogs, like I said.

ANTHONY
Yeah, well, fetch!

(ANTHONY throws the phone to MARGARET.)

MARGARET

Me again? This one's coming through slowly. It's blurry. Oh, it's getting clearer. This ones of a man. Oh, it's not Robbie. It's… Anthony…

ANTHONY

What?

MARGARET

… in a bathroom…

ROBBIE

(to ANTHONY)

We didn't! Did we?

MARGARET

(sitting down on one of the couches)

… with a woman.

ROBBIE

Oh, that's disappointing.

ANTHONY

(suddenly serious)

Margaret, give me the phone. Those fucking paparazzi with their zoom lenses!

ROBBIE

(confused)

With which woman?

(TIFFANY gets up to leave.)

MARGARET

Don't go, Tiffany. It's just getting interesting.

TIFFANY

I've got a thing. An interview…

MARGARET

Tiffany, would you like to tell Robbie who was with Anthony in Elton John's bathroom? On *your* knees?

ROBBIE

You didn't?

TIFFANY

Robbie, I…

ROBBIE

He's twice your age. Maybe three times!

TIFFANY

You hypocrite! You always said we were open!

ROBBIE

Yes, but you're a woman—

TIFFANY

What kind of chauvinistic bullshit is that anyway? You can do whoever the hell you like and you're still America's darling, but the moment Margaret or I step out of line, we get the scarlet fucking letter.

ROBBIE

What are you talking about? I have been in the closet my entire life! Neither one of us do whatever or whoever we want. We have to play by the rules…

TIFFANY

You just got your ass handed to you by an openly gay man, the only thing holding you back in life is that you're a fucking coward.

ROBBIE

I get that you felt abandoned and lonely, but you went with him? I thought you had better taste than that!

ANTHONY

What's wrong with me?

MARGARET

Shut up, Tony. For once, this isn't about you.

THREESOME

TIFFANY
(to ROBBIE)

I was drunk. On success... and champagne, mostly. I remember going to the bathroom and all of a sudden, he was there.

MARGARET
That's how we met. How unoriginal.

(to ANTHONY)

Twenty years later and you're still cruising bathrooms for attention.

ROBBIE
(to TIFFANY)

But... is this the first time you've...?

TIFFANY
Oh, please. I'm not you. You weren't there, Robbie! You were off fucking half of West Hollywood. Who was I supposed to share my win with? This is all your doing.

ANTHONY
You seemed to enjoy it.

TIFFANY
I'd just won an Oscar, Tony, I'd have enjoyed erotic root canal at that moment.

ANTHONY
Is that a thing?

ROBBIE
(to ANTHONY)

You should be ashamed of yourself.

MARGARET
He's right, there.

ANTHONY
(to ROBBIE)

You are in no position to judge anyone.

MARGARET

But I am. Jesus, Anthony. I knew you were a bastard, but fucking one of our hosts? That's just tacky.

(to TIFFANY)

And Tiffany… How dare you?! But also, I'm sorry you now know what I've had to work with for the best part of two decades.

TIFFANY

I'm sorry, Margaret. It just happened.

MARGARET

History is one long list of shit that 'just happened'. But you should learn to show some judgement. And an appreciation for open windows. You're a Hollywood icon now.

TIFFANY

I'm still sorry.

MARGARET

There's no need to be. If these pictures get published, I'm the only one in this room whose reputation comes out of this intact. That's punishment enough. Well, not for you, Anthony, you deserve a good flaying, but it's enough for the two of you.

(to TIFFANY)

And at least you have your Oscar, which is one more than I have. It doesn't look like it will bring you much luck, but maybe you'll at least get one of those stupid superhero gigs.

(TIFFANY's phone rings)

Maybe that's one now.

TIFFANY

(looking at her phone)

It's my agent.

(she looks to Heaven)

A multi-million, multi-film deal, please. With my own personal chef, nutritionist, and personal trainer so I can bench press Robbie's body weight. And I want use of the studio's private jet. And I want little girls across America to play with tiny plastic figurines of my likeness. And I want to be on cereal boxes and Happy Meals. Oh, and my own Lego figurine.

MARGARET

(sincerely, despite it all)

And I hope you get it all.

(aside to ROBBIE)

You do realize she's insane?

ROBBIE

It's her most endearing quality.

(TIFFANY answers the call)

TIFFANY

Hi Roger. What amazing, lucrative job have you got lined up for me? And don't scrimp on the details, I want you to enunciate every zero in my paycheck.

(pause)

Sure, I can sit down. It's that big, then?

ROBBIE

I'm so proud you're my wife.

TIFFANY

(to ROBBIE, quietly)

Soon to be ex-wife.

(continuing)

Sorry Roger, could you repeat that? My roommate was talking over you. Do

I remember *La La Land*? The one with Emma Stone and that cute guy who's in everything?

ROBBIE

Ryan Gosling? He's hot.

MARGARET

A bit, I suppose.

TIFFANY

Why didn't you put me up for that, by the way? He'd make anyone look great. I can dance just as well as Emma Stone. And they could have just filmed me from the waist up. I was reading this thing about CG body doubles... I'm sorry, you were talking. Please continue.

(listening)

The Oscars, right? And Warren Beatty and Faye Dunnaway announced *La La Land* had won best picture, but there was a mistake with the envelopes and then they announced that *Moonlight* had actually won. I remember. Robbie thought the whole things was hilarious.

(deadly-serious pause)

What kind of mistake?

MARGARET

(sympathetically)

Oh, love.

TIFFANY

(starting to whimper a little)

Who should have won, then?

(pause)

Roger, they can't do that. Everyone saw me win. It's on Wikipedia now, it's fact.

(beat)

No, I had my publicist update it last night.

(crying)

Well, why didn't they take it away from me during the ceremony? Why didn't somebody catch this? This is ridiculous. I won!

(pause, punctuated by sobbing breaths)

A statement? No, I can't present it to her. I don't care what the fucking optics are, Roger, I can't do that.

(pause)

Because it would break my heart, that's why! There has to be an alternative.

(pause)

When?

(TIFFANY composes herself)

Yeah, I'll be here.

(TIFFANY limply drops her phone.)

ROBBIE
What happened?

ANTHONY
Do you need a hug?

TIFFANY
(to ANTHONY)

You can stay the fuck away from me, you pervert! In fact, you need to leave, right now.

ANTHONY
I just want to help.

MARGARET
Leaving would help.

ANTHONY

Fine. Are you coming?

MARGARET

I don't think so. I'll make sure your things find their way back to England.

ANTHONY

Is this really goodbye?

MARGARET

I think so. Start moving your things out when you get back to London. I'll stay on in LA for a week or two.

ANTHONY

Will I see you in Cannes?

MARGARET

Poor phrasing, darling. People will think it's a fetish.

ANTHONY

(seriously)

To promote our film.

MARGARET

Yes, if you don't come down with some infectious disease between now and then, but I'm praying you do.

ANTHONY

(appealing to their host)

Tiffany…

TIFFANY

Just get the fuck out.

(ANTHONY exits. A few awkward moments pass)

ROBBIE

What did Roger say?

MARGARET

THREESOME

(to ROBBIE)

Maybe men aren't dogs. The way they retain information, they're more like goldfish.

ROBBIE
What is going on?

MARGARET
Isn't it obvious? Tiffany, do you feel up to telling him, or should I do it?

TIFFANY
I don't know.

MARGARET
I'll do it, then.

TIFFANY
No, I need to. Robbie, can you sit down with me for a moment?

ROBBIE
Okay?

(ROBBIE sits next to TIFFANY on the couch.)

TIFFANY
My Oscar… it… it isn't real.

ROBBIE
I know I wasn't there, but I've seen reruns of them presenting it to you…

TIFFANY
There was a mistake, Robbie. Remember *La La Land*?

ROBBIE
(shaking his head)

Didn't get the part, didn't watch it.

TIFFANY
Not the movie, the award. It was announced as Best Picture, but the Oscar actually went to the one about the gay black guy.

85

ROBBIE

Moonlight! Gay theme. Loved it. The mix up, that's right! So, you're saying...

TIFFANY

When they announced I'd won the Academy Award for Best Supporting Actress, for my break-out work in *Memoirs of a Hapless Hooker*... They made a mistake. I didn't win.

ROBBIE

Then who won?

TIFFANY

(gulping)

She did.

ROBBIE

(aghast)

No!

TIFFANY

Yes.

ROBBIE

Not her?

TIFFANY

Yes.

ROBBIE

(unsure)

Are we a hundred percent sure we're talking about the same 'her'?

MARGARET

Trudy Fishburn, dear.

ROBBIE

But she's a total bitch!

TIFFANY

Robbie, I love you for saying that, but she's on her way over, so please quit shitting on her until after she leaves. And then I'll join you... gladly.

MARGARET
She's coming here? Now?

TIFFANY
Yes.

ROBBIE
Really?

TIFFANY
Yes! They asked me if I wanted to take part in a public handover of the statuette, but I refused. I can't do it. I'd club her with it.

ROBBIE
Tell them you don't want to take part in any handover!

TIFFANY
How would that even work?

ROBBIE
I don't know. Hold it hostage? Sell it on eBay? I'll break it in two and then no one can have it!

TIFFANY AND MARGARET
No.

MARGARET
When is she arriving?

TIFFANY
She's on her way.

MARGARET
So, it could be at any moment?

ROBBIE
I mean, it's kind of exciting.

MARGARET
Robbie!

ROBBIE
Sorry.

MARGARET
Couldn't you just be powdering your nose when she arrives? Then we could say you're predisposed and give her the wretched thing?

(The doorbell rings)

ROBBIE
Oh, my god, it's her! It's the megabitch!

TIFFANY
Quiet!

MARGARET
Are you up to this?

TIFFANY
I think so.

MARGARET
Just think of it as something you have to get through. Like a love scene with Tom Hanks. Just grin and bear it.

TIFFANY
OK. I can do this. I'll get it.

(TIFFANY just stands there. The doorbell rings again.)

ROBBIE
Today, right?

TIFFANY
I'm working on it.

ROBBIE
Are you? Because it looks like you're just standing there.

TIFFANY
Every actor has their process, Robbie. Lay off!

MARGARET

THREESOME

Do you need help, my dear? Here let me give you a little…

(MARGARET pushes TIFFANY by the shoulders. TIFFANY drags her feet as MARGARET moves her to the door.)

It's like her feet are glued or something.

(Doorbell rings again.)

ROBBIE
Come on, Tiff, let's get it over with.

TIFFANY
(shouting)

Coming!

(ROBBIE helps pull TIFFANY to the door. He's a lot better at this than MARGARET. They make it most of the way.)

ROBBIE
You're brave enough to live with me, Tiffany. You've got this.

TIFFANY
You're right.

(ROBBIE and MARGARET release her)

I've got this.

(TIFFANY opens the door, then hides behind it.)

TRUDY
(entering like she owns the place, in a thick southern accent)

What a fabulous day to be alive!

TIFFANY
(sheepishly)

Trudy.

TRUDY

What on earth are you doing back there?

TIFFANY
(coming out from behind the door)

It's a joke. I… wanted to surprise you!

TRUDY
Hilarious.

(TRUDY captures TIFFANY in an awkward hug.)

It's lovely to see you. I just wish it had been in better circumstances. And Margaret, too! Well, this is just like the awards all over again.

MARGARET
Congratulations on your win, Trudy. I'm sorry you didn't get to have your big night.

TRUDY
Oh well, you know what they say: better late than never. It ain't over 'til it's over. Everything comes to she who waits.

MARGARET
(aloof)

What a lovely ensemble of clichés.

TRUDY
Just like your marvelous Victoria. Your scriptwriters were truly robbed.

MARGARET
(prickly)

Whereas your make-up artists were incredible. They almost made you look human.

TRUDY
Let's cut to the chase, shall we? I came here for one thing. Where is he?

ROBBIE
He's on the coffee table.

THREESOME

TRUDY
(walking over)

Well, there's the little fella. Hello, handsome.

(TRUDY walks over to the coffee table.)

May I? I mean, it doesn't look like any of you are actually going to hand him to me.

TIFFANY
(running and grabbing the Oscar)

Actually, can I have a moment?

TRUDY
Whatever makes it easier, sweetheart. This must be so painful for you.

TIFFANY
It's fine! I'm sure you deserve it.

(TIFFANY holds up the award, staring into its eyes.)

This is not goodbye. This is just, 'until we meet again'.

(TIFFANY kisses the statue on the lips, then hands it to a mildly disturbed TRUDY.)

TRUDY
Thanks. I'll be sure to wash it when I get home.

TIFFANY
No, thank you. In my heart we are all winners.

TRUDY
Tell it to your shrink, honey.

MARGARET
OK, I think it's time for you to sling your hook.

TRUDY
No! Not yet, anyway. We need to share this moment with the world.

ROBBIE

On social media?

TRUDY

Four queens of the industry, sorry Robbie, three, united in a moment of history, tragedy, and triumph.

MARGARET

I think I'm going to be sick.

TRUDY

(holding up her phone)

And we're rolling. Hi, guys! I'm here at the house of fellow acting legend Tiffany Beckworth, who's handing over the Best Supporting Actress Oscar to its rightful owner. Me! It's like we've having our own little award ceremony. I just love award ceremonies, don't you?

ROBBIE

Love them.

MARGARET

Thrilled.

TIFFANY

The most relaxing and stress-free time of my life!

TRUDY

I'm so honored to be in the company of such greats, and to be indisputably the best, as this award proves.

TIFFANY

But really, we're all winners.

TRUDY

Especially me. This is Trudy Fishburn, queen of Hollywood, signing off!

(TRUDY puts the phone down)

TIFFANY

Will you be leaving now?

TRUDY

I think I should. My agent wants to discuss some new superhero role he wants me to take.

(TRUDY walks to the door, then stops, turning back to TIFFANY.)

Oh, darling, I just had a brilliant idea.

TIFFANY

What?

TRUDY

Would you like to do it?

TIFFANY

(gasping)

Me? A superhero?

TRUDY

No, honey, that's me. But there's a part going for my sidekick. I think you'd be perfect! Every bit as iconic and powerful as me, only a little bit… less.

TIFFANY

(hollowly)

It sounds like a dream.

TRUDY

Good. I'll have my people call your people. Bye Margaret! And you, Robbie. Nice coverage in The Enquirer by the way. So brave of you to come out like that.

ROBBIE

Fuck off.

TRUDY

(whispering)

So brave.

(TRUDY leaves.)

ROBBIE

(walking over and consoling TIFFANY)

A superhero role! That's amazing. Every cloud has a silver lining.

TIFFANY
(downbeat)

A sidekick, Robbie.

ROBBIE
But with your own costume and powers, right? And with these cinematic universe things, give it… a few years… and they'll spin you off into your own TV show!

TIFFANY
A decade in the shadow of that human bitch-troll?

ROBBIE
It's the best you could have gotten out of this, Tiff. You were never going to win.

TIFFANY
Excuse me?

ROBBIE
I just mean… a friend of mine told me the results ahead of time. It was always going to be Trudy.

TIFFANY
And you kept that a secret?

MARGARET
He told us.

TIFFANY
Incredible. For the first time in his life, Robbie Shard manages to keep a secret, but only from me.

ROBBIE
I thought you wouldn't want to know.

TIFFANY
Were you laughing at me the whole time?

ROBBIE

Look, you wanted to know why I wasn't in the audience when they announced your name? It's because I knew you weren't going to win. And I knew how pissed you'd be, and I didn't want to be there. It's not my fault they screwed up!

TIFFANY

Well, I'm sure as hell pissed now!

ROBBIE

Look, it's not all bad. You got your moment. Half the people are going to remember you winning, not Trudy. I mean, really, who remembers who wins the Oscars? Suck it up, live in Trudy's shadow, get paid, keep working towards your dream. It's what everyone in Hollywood does.

TIFFANY

I can't.

ROBBIE

You so can. You're a total badass.

TIFFANY

I mean, I can't do this anymore.

ROBBIE

Do what?

TIFFANY

You heard Trudy. The Enquirer, Robbie. They know! It's out there now. Everyone knows you're fucking half the world behind my back. Just not the half that has breasts. And not me. I'm second-best to Trudy, and I'm stuck in fake marriage with a wandering slut of a husband. I'm a joke. My whole life is a sham.

(ROBBIE's phone vibrates. He looks down to it.)

ROBBIE

Sorry, I'll turn that off.

TIFFANY

Oh, no. Answer him.

ROBBIE

Who said it's a him?

TIFFANY

I'm not an idiot, Robbie.

ROBBIE

Well, you happen to be right. But we—

TIFFANY

I'm not interested in your excuses. The reason this feels like a sham marriage is because it is a sham. It's a relationship that was put together by our agents for our mutual benefit. And we had a good run. Each of us almost won an Oscar. But I don't see how we can continue. I think I need to be happy, finally. And I think you need to leave. Go have fun with whatever his name is.

ROBBIE

You're overreacting!

TIFFANY

Am I?

ROBBIE

You really want us to break up?

TIFFANY

I think it's what you want. You're just too chickenshit to face up to it. So, yes, what I need is for you to leave. Now. We can have our agents draw up a statement or something. They seem to be good at that.

ROBBIE

Tiff, I don't want—

TIFFANY

(TIFFANY opens the front door.)

Out.

(ROBBIE goes to the door, stopping to take his wife's hand. TIFFANY shakes him off. He walks slowly out, and she slams the door shut behind him. TIFFANY goes back to the sofa and collapses.)

MARGARET
Well, this is an odd turn of events. I woke up this morning, determined to be the first person to leave, and it turns out I'm the last. Is there anything I can do for you before I go?

TIFFANY
Nothing.

MARGARET
(disappointed)

Then I should leave you to wallow in your self-pity.

TIFFANY
Would you quit with the judgement? You just split up with your husband for exactly the same reason that I did.

MARGARET
It's not quite the same, my dear. You were happy to turn a blind eye to Robbie's shenanigans when it suited you. Now, all of a sudden, it doesn't suit you, so you're jumping ship.

TIFFANY
I can do better.

MARGARET
You know, one of these days you're going to have to acknowledge that there's a real person under all that… blonde-ness. Being pretty and bitchy won't last you long in this industry, especially when the prettiness fades. You need someone who will actually stand by you, on whatever terms you both agree.

TIFFANY
The thing you don't get is, Robbie and I, we're not actors. We're not even people. We're stars. We are role models for every little boy and girl out there. We make them happy just by being ourselves, well, not ourselves, but the selves they want us to be. They follow us on social media, they buy the products we use, and they want to read about every detail of our lives. I'm not an actor. I'm just me. And I need people to love me. And now people know its all a lie.

MARGARET
Why did you marry him in the first place?

TIFFANY

Because he's popular. Because for some goddamn reason, people like him more than me. He made me look good for a bit. And because Hello Magazine offered us $1 million for the exclusive photo rights to our wedding.

MARGARET

OK, I'm going to read something to you. I want you to be quiet until I finish.

TIFFANY

Read what?

MARGARET

The Enquirer's online comments section. I was scrolling through them earlier while everyone was talking.

TIFFANY

I never read my own press.

MARGARET

Normally, I would concur, but in this case, I think it's informative:

R0biezgurl69 says "He's so brave. A true hero. I hope he dumps that chick! He'd be better with Tom Hiddleston. Or me!"

Cinemaproguy22 adds: "Is there anyone in Hollywood that doesn't suck dick in one way or another?"

And this one, this one is from lazyeye1996, and he or she says: "Living with that blonde bitch for five years, I'd jump on the first dick I saw, too."

TIFFANY

So, everyone hates me. That's not news. You can leave, too.

MARGARET

I wasn't finished. This one was quite thought-provoking:

"Given the ridiculous standards we hold Hollywood stars to these days, why are we surprised when, once the curtain has been drawn back, what we find is, they are just as flawed and normal as the rest of us."

THREESOME

TIFFANY
Who said that?

MARGARET
Someone called Tiffsboobs420. I think the 420 is a marijuana reference, but the point still stands. Just like broken clocks, even stoners can sometimes be right. My point is this: people are more understanding thee days. I don't think this is as black and white as you make out. And from where I'm sitting, you look more in need of a friend like Robbie than ever before.

TIFFANY
He's not my friend.

MARGARET
He's probably your only true friend. And you managed to go three years without pushing him away, that's got to be a record for you.

TIFFANY
There's no turning this around. Everyone knows he's gay, now. My sex appeal is shot.

MARGARET
Couldn't Robbie come out as bisexual? That seems to be the usual route to take in cases such as these. And everyone finds bisexuals hot. They're so… mysterious. Maybe my next husband should be bisexual. I'll ask my agent for recommendations when I get back to London.

TIFFANY
But I just chucked Robbie out.

MARGARET
He can't have gotten far.

TIFFANY
He'll never forgive me.

MARGARET
Just tell him you're sorry and tell him the truth: he's the person that matters most to you in this world. Well second, after yourself.

TIFFANY
I might use different words.

MARGARET

Use ancient Latin for all I care, just tell him.

TIFFANY

Ugh, he'll be halfway to West Hollywood by now.

MARGARET

Oh, I don't think so.

(MARGARET walks over to the front door)

My guess is he's standing right behind this door.

(MARGARET opens the front door. ROBBIE is standing outside.)

ROBBIE

Is she still pissed at me?

MARGARET

A part of her always will be, but that just proves she actually cares about you.

ROBBIE

I don't think I like that.

MARGARET

Of course you do.

ROBBIE

Maybe.

MARGARET

(grabbing her suitcase)

Right, I'll see the two of you around. Hopefully not at another one of these damned events. You know, I think Maggie Smith has the right idea. She doesn't even show up for these things.

TIFFANY

Goodbye, Margaret.

MARGARET

Until next time. Break a leg.

ROBBIE
Just not one of mine.

(MARGARET exits and shuts the door behind her.)

TIFFANY
Drama queen.

ROBBIE
Spoilt bitch.

TIFFANY
(hugging ROBBIE)

Glad to have you back, kiddo.

ROBBIE
Glad to be back.

(they separate)

So, I was thinking…

TIFFANY
What?

ROBBIE
Let's have a baby.

TIFFANY
Are you kidding? We can't even look after ourselves, let alone another human being.

ROBBIE
We'd have people look after the wretched thing for us, but I was thinking it would bring us closer together. And social media loves babies.

TIFFANY
Margaret thinks you should come out as bisexual.

ROBBIE
That could work, too. Oh my God, we could have a bisexual baby! Has that

been done before? Trans kids are all the rage right now, but I think they're really hard to come by. What do you think?

TIFFANY

I think we need to have a heart-to-heart on the sofa.

(ROBBIE and TIFFANY snuggle up on the sofa. It's almost romantic.)

ROBBIE

Are you alright?

TIFFANY

I just lost my dream to Trudy Fishburn, of course I'm not alright. But in a weird way, I might even be a little less damaged than before. I mean, if I can get through this, I can get through anything.

ROBBIE

You gonna take that sidekick role?

TIFFANY

Trudy's thing?

ROBBIE

Yeah.

TIFFANY

God help me. Yes, I'm going to take it.

ROBBIE

You sure?

TIFFANY

I'll take anything right now. What about you? Got any work lined up?

ROBBIE

Not yet. But I'm sure the CW will want me when I come out as bi.

TIFFANY

You can do better than shitty TV. You were just nominated for an Oscar, for God's sake.

ROBBIE

Tell my agent.

THREESOME

TIFFANY
I will. And you know I'm very good at getting my way.

ROBBIE
Alright. Let me know when you're call him, I'll put my earplugs in.

TIFFANY
Deal.

(TIFFANY and ROBBIE lie quietly next to each other for a moment. It's intimate.)

ROBBIE
I think we should…

TIFFANY
We definitely should…

ROBBIE
Yours or mine?

TIFFANY
Yours.

(ROBBIE reaches down the front of his pants to retrieve his phone. He holds it up in front of them.)

ROBBIE
And we're rolling!

TIFFANY
Hi guys!

ROBBIE
Hi everyone!

TIFFANY
Well, we've had a couple days of triumph and heartache here, and we wanted to give you all a quick update on how things are in the Shard-Beckworth household after a historic awards season!

ROBBIE

You've all probably heard a lot about us over the last few days. Some of it's true, some of it isn't.

TIFFANY

My award for Best Supporting Actress was sadly a mistake. Can you believe it? It actually went to everyone's favorite flag-weaver, Trudy Fishburn. But don't worry, I'll be back!

ROBBIE

And I will always have the memory of my wife receiving an Oscar onstage to treasure.

TIFFANY

And about that…

ROBBIE

You may have noticed I wasn't in the audience when Tiffany received the award. That wasn't an accident, it was a feminist statement.

TIFFANY

My amazing husband wanted to prove that women like me don't need a man standing behind them, or next to them, in order to succeed! He's been very supportive, but wanted the moment to be truly mine. Even if it was meant to be Trudy's moment. He's a real ally of womanhood.

ROBBIE

And especially this woman.

TIFFANY

I wasn't sarcastically hugging thin air! I was hugging myself because, well, I deserve it. All you girls do. So, go ahead and hug yourselves, you rock! And there's one other rumor we need to put to bed, as it were. Robbie, will you?

ROBBIE

I'd like to make one thing clear: outing people is a shameful thing for tabloids to do. It's a struggle for a lot of people and something people should chose to do themselves, in their own time and way.

TIFFANY

But, of course, now you've seen those awful tabloid headlines, we need to say our piece.

ROBBIE

So, I'm bisexual. There I said it. Hi!

TIFFANY
Robbie has never done anything I didn't know about – we're open - and he loves me very, very much. We're a very modern couple in that regard and I encourage everyone out there to explore their own sexuality and not feel they have to fit into any specific box or label. Just be yourself.

ROBBIE
So, that's what we wanted to say. It's been a rough week, but we're standing strong, together, as husband and wife.

TIFFANY
And nothing's going to break that.

ROBBIE
And we'll kick ass at the awards next time.

TIFFANY
Love to you all!

(They both blow a kiss to the camera. ROBBIE puts the phone down.)

Man, our agents are going to hate us for that.

ROBBIE
We're icons. We can choose what kind of stars we want to be.

TIFFANY
Yes, we can.

ROBBIE
And the agents we want to work with.

TIFFANY
Absolutely

ROBBIE
I'm serious about having a baby, by the way. Ooh, you could do the whole baby-bump photoshoot thing with Vanity Fair!

TIFFANY
I think I'd prefer to maintain the structural integrity of my vagina, thank

you very much.

ROBBIE
You could always have a cesarean. Too posh to push to push and all that.

TIFFANY
Since when did you use the word "posh"?

ROBBIE
Since we just had two Brits stay with us in our house. Oh my god! If it's a boy, we could call it Oscar! The blogs would eat that shit up!

TIFFANY
And if it's a girl, we could call it Trudy.

ROBBIE
And we could train her as an assassin to grow up and kill her namesake in cold blood!

TIFFANY
Then we could do a movie together based on the true-life story!

ROBBIE
Ahhhh.

(pause)

We are so fucked up.

TIFFANY
Aren't we? I love us.

ROBBIE
Should I find you another therapist?

TIFFANY
No. The old one will do. Just tell him not to ask any more questions about my dad this time. Or my sister. Or my dog. Or my global humiliation on live TV by being given an Oscar I didn't actually win.

ROBBIE
You know, in a strange way, I think I love you.

                TIFFANY
Yeah? In a strange way, I think I kinda love you too.

(ROBBIE and TIFFANY hug)

                (CURTAIN)

                (END OF ACT)

THREESOME

MURDER AT MAGPIE HALL

A Play in Two Acts

By

Laurence Watts and Kevin Burnard

Cast of Characters

Margaret Woolworth-Spencer	-An upper-class widow and the mistress of Magpie Hall
Hercules Pinot-Noir	-A renowned private detective
Betsy	-Margaret's gluttonous maid
Gertrude Lancaster	-Margaret's wealthier best friend
Reverend Whyte	-The local vicar
Colonel Horseradish	-A salacious military man
Lady Dorothy Swindle	-An older aristocrat
Ivan Othello	-A flamboyant actor
Jones	-A butler

Scene:
A stately home in Witherington, Kent, England.

Time:
Autumn, 1931.

STAGE PLAN

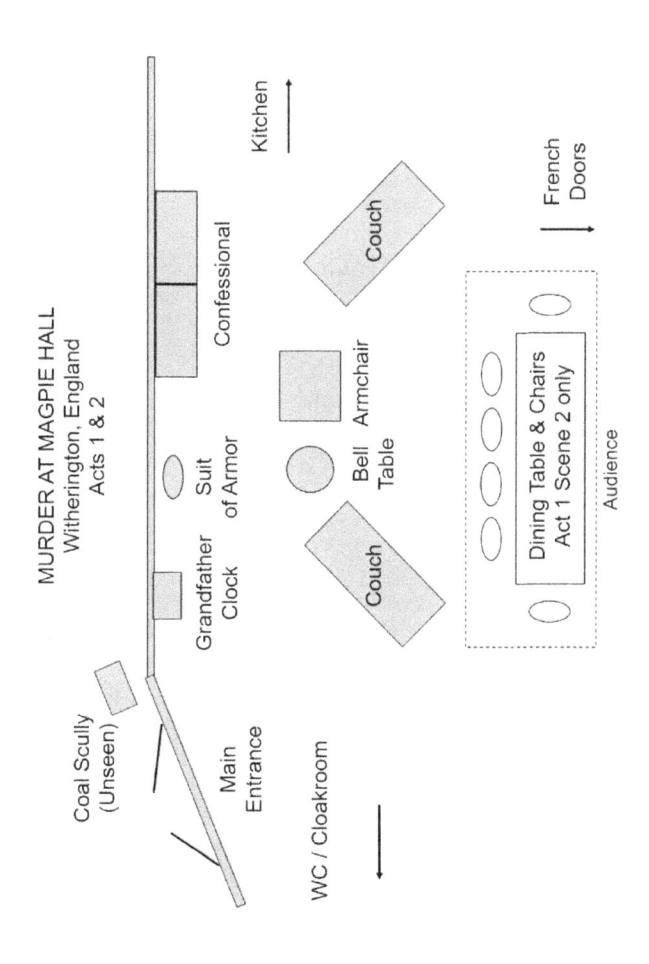

MURDER AT MAGPIE HALL
Witherington, England
Acts 1 & 2

ACT I

Scene 1

SETTING: The sitting room of Magpie Hall. A stately home in Witherington, Kent, England. Early evening.

AT RISE: MAGGIE is sitting in an armchair reading some letters. Her maid BETSY hovers nearby pretending to look busy. MAGGIE finishes reading and gives a bloodcurdling scream.

                        BETSY

Is everything alright, ma'am?

                        MAGGIE

This is murder!

                        BETSY

Murder, ma'am? Shall I send for the police?

                        MAGGIE

No, Betsy, I was speaking metaphorically. I was reacting to these bills.

(pause)

You see, since Mr. Woolworth-Spencer died last month, I have had to oversee the running of Magpie Hall and, I'm afraid to say, the perilous nature of the estate's finances has become painfully clear to me.

                        BETSY

Has it, ma'am?

                        MAGGIE

Yes, it rather has. Having sacked all of the domestic staff except for you and Jones, I just don't see how I can cut back any further? What am I to do?

                        BETSY

I couldn't say ma'am.

                        MAGGIE

Though Henry was a sour, disagreeable stick-in-the-mud, at least he always shielded me from the rigors of managing the estate.

(pause)

I suppose I could sack you. Or Jones. But then who would do all the things that need to be done around here?

(laughs)

It's not like I could do them myself, is it?

BETSY
No, ma'am.

MAGGIE
But why am I bothering you with all this? You are working class, and therefore spend what meagre pay you receive from me on bread and dripping, don't you?

BETSY
Yes, ma'am.

MAGGIE
And alcohol too I suppose… to blind you to your dire social standing? You wouldn't know the first thing about running a country house, would you?

BETSY
Not the first thing, ma'am.

MAGGIE
Let's say no more about it then.

BETSY
Very good ma'am.

MAGGIE
Betsy?

BETSY
Yes, ma'am?

MAGGIE
Please don't think I was checking up on you or anything, but I happened to wander into the pantry this morning and I noticed it was rather bare.

BETSY
(clutching her feather duster to her bosom)

I don't know what you mean ma'am.

MAGGIE
I think you might.

BETSY
(pleading)

A girl's got to eat!

MAGGIE
Yes, but not continuously.

BETSY
(tearfully)

It's my way of dealing with all the uncertainty, ma'am.

MAGGIE
Oh, don't give me that tosh. I'm seriously considering having to sell Magpie Hall! If the rest of us are having to tighten our belts, I don't think it's too much to ask for you to do the same. Literally.

BETSY
Yes, ma'am.

MAGGIE
The good news is that when my late husband died, I found a ham hidden under the pillow on his side of the bed. It's a little old and dusty, but it's not so bad that you can't finish it off.

BETSY
(happily)

Oh, thank you, ma'am.

MAGGIE
Betsy?

THREESOME

BETSY
Yes, ma'am?

MAGGIE
Do you think I should sack Jones?

BETSY
I couldn't say, ma'am.

MAGGIE
Because really, it's either him or you.

BETSY
We've both worked for you our entire lives!

MAGGIE
Of course, you have! Tell me, Betsy…

(beat)

…what does Jones actually do?

BETSY
Do, ma'am?

MAGGIE
I mean, I see you pottering around the house pretending to be busy … dusting things, cleaning things…

(aside)

You've missed a bit by the way, over there behind the lamp…

(back on topic)

But what does Jones actually do?

BETSY
Mr. Jones is the butler, ma'am.

MAGGIE
Yes, I know that, but apart from answering the front door and bringing in the occasional telegram, what does he *do*?

BETSY

I think you should ask him, ma'am.

(The front doorbell rings.)

MAGGIE

I might just do that, Betsy. Unconnected question, who would you say is stronger? You or Jones?

BETSY

Stronger?

MAGGIE

And who would you say eats more?

(BETSY looks confused. JONES appears from stage right and proceeds to stage left to answer the front door. GERTIE enters through the front door.)

JONES

Good evening, madam. You're here to see the lady of the house, I presume.

GERTIE

Well, it would seem rather pointless to come and see Mr. Woolworth-Spencer, now that he's a stiff, wouldn't it?

JONES

Very droll, madam. Wait here, please. I'll announce you.

GERTIE

But I can see Maggie from here.

JONES

One moment, madam.

GERTIE

She can probably hear my voice.

JONES

(insisting)

If you'll just wait.

GERTIE
(calling out)

Maggie!?

(MAGGIE ignores GERTIE for the sake of formality.)

JONES
(announcing)

Miss Gertrude Lancaster!

(MAGGIE stands and welcomes GERTIE)

MAGGIE
Gertie, what a surprise! How lovely to see you.

(MAGGIE and GERTIE kiss one another once on each cheek.)

GERTIE
Maggie, dearest.

MAGGIE
Thank goodness you're here. Now I have someone I can talk to. I was just trying to decide who to sack next – Betsy or Jones. What do you think? Or should I just flip a coin?

GERTIE
(taking MARGARET to the side and lowering her voice)

I rather think that's something that shouldn't be discussed in front of them.

MAGGIE
Ah, good point.

JONES
(trying to save his ass)

Will there be anything else, madam? Anything I can get for either one of you?

MAGGIE
No, that will be all, Jones.

JONES
Very good, ma'am.

(JONES leaves the room.)

MAGGIE
See, I was thinking I'd get rid of Betsy and keep Jones, because if I need to sell the piano, then I could strap it across Jones' back with some rope and he could deliver it to whomever buys it…

GERTIE
(outraged and concerned)

Maggie!??

MAGGIE
What? It'd be perfectly safe. I'd make sure the rope was tight.

GERTIE
I mean, Betsy's still here!

MAGGIE
Oh. So she is.

BETSY
Will that be all, ma'am?

MAGGIE
Yes, Betsy. Thank you.

BETSY
Nothing *I* can get for you?

MAGGIE
No, thank you.

(BETSY exits.)

GERTIE
Maggie, you must be more careful.

MAGGIE
I really don't see what difference it makes.

GERTIE
You mustn't let them know you're thinking of letting them go.

MAGGIE
Why ever not? It keeps them on their toes, doesn't it?

GERTIE
Because things have a habit of going missing when staff know they're heading for the exit!

MAGGIE
You're not suggesting they'd start stealing from me?

GERTIE
Start stealing from you? My dear, they've probably been pilfering this house since the first day they set foot in it! Working class, you see; jealous – all of them. Can't accept their lot in life, unlike us decent upper-class folk.

MAGGIE
That's dreadful.

GERTIE
Leopards and spots, I'm afraid.

(changing subject)

Now tell me, what have you got planned for tonight?

MAGGIE
Tonight? Gertie, whatever do you mean?

GERTIE
Don't be shy, Maggie! I was surprised you didn't mention it yesterday at the church's Fifth Annual Charity Croquet and Shuffleboard Contest, but when the invitation arrived by mail this morning, I assumed it had just slipped your mind.

MAGGIE
I'm afraid you've completely lost me.

GERTIE

Tonight's dinner party, Maggie. The one you invited me to!

MAGGIE

(confused)

A dinner party? Have you gone bonkers? I'm not hosting a dinner party this evening.

GERTIE

Yes, you are, Maggie. Don't lie to me!

MAGGIE

That's a very ugly word, Gertie, and I won't stand for it.

GERTIE

Look here, Margaret. If you've sent me an invitation that you didn't mean to, then just come right out and admit it!

MAGGIE

Gertie, honestly, I'm not hosting a party tonight. I'm really not. I'd planned to have a quiet night in sewing.

GERTIE

Sewing?

MAGGIE

Yes, I thought I'd make something for the lepers in Calcutta.

GERTIE

Really? What were you going to make?

MAGGIE

A noose.

(pause)

But a good one! I think dignity in death is frightfully important, don't you?

GERTIE

(warmly)

Oh, Maggie. You're all heart.

MAGGIE
Aren't I?

(GERTIE hands MAGGIE the invitation she received.)

GERTIE
And such a kind-hearted woman would never exclude her best friend from an evening soiree.

MAGGIE
(examining the invitation)

Good heavens! Well, it certainly looks authentic.

GERTIE
(concerned)

Are you sure you didn't send it and then forget about it? Impending poverty and the prospect of a cruel, yet certain slide down the social ladder can play awful tricks on one's mind.

MAGGIE
I'm adamant, I've never seen this invitation before in my life. And yet, all the details pertain to this house and to a dinner to be held here tonight.

(reading aloud)

'Mrs. Margaret Woolworth-Spencer hereby requests the pleasure of your company for dinner at Magpie Hall, Witherington, on Tuesday the Seventeenth of June. Six for six thirty. Black tie preferred. Carriages at nine.'

(to GERTIE)

I can understand your confusion, but I truly didn't write this.

(a flash of lightning illuminates the room.)

GERTIE
So, there's no dinner then?

MAGGIE

No.

GERTIE

Oh.

MAGGIE

Indeed.

GERTIE

Well, what are you having?

MAGGIE

I've...

(lying)

... already eaten.

GERTIE

Oh. Well, do you think Betsy could knock me up something? I'm frightfully hungry.

MAGGIE

(nervously)

Erm... I'm sure she can rustle up something for you.

(MAGGIE rings the servant bell. BETSY enters.)

BETSY

You rang, ma'am?

MAGGIE

Yes. Miss Lancaster will be staying for dinner. Would you rustle up something for her?

GERTIE

There's no need to go to too much trouble my dear.

BETSY

Very good, ma'am.

GERTIE

Some cold cuts will be fine.

BETSY

Yes, ma'am.

GERTIE

And some roasted vegetables.

BETSY

Yes...

GERTIE

And a cheese course.

BETSY

Will there be anything...?

GERTIE

And some fruit.

BETSY

Yes ma'...

GERTIE

And a glass of red to wash it all down with.

BETSY

(aside to MAGGIE)

The larder's empty! What do you want me to do?

MAGGIE

(aside to BETSY)

Just make her a sandwich. She's not particularly bright. By the time you fetch it she'll probably have forgotten what she asked for.

BETSY

Very good, ma'am.

(BETSY exits stage right. MAGGIE and GERTIE sit down on the couches)

MAGGIE

This fake invitation business is really quite strange, but let's you and I just ignore it and pretend it didn't even happen, shall we?

GERTIE

Let's!

(The front doorbell rings.)

MAGGIE

Well, now who can that be?

GERTIE

Are you expecting someone?

MAGGIE

No.

(JONES enters to answer the front door. REVEREND WHYTE enters through it.)

JONES

Good evening, Reverend.

REVEREND

Good evening, Jones! How is everything?

JONES

Very good, Reverend. Might I take your coat?

REVEREND

How kind! Tell me, Jones, have the last remaining members of your working-class Welsh family died from tuberculosis yet?

JONES

(smiling)

The last one died on Monday, Reverend.

REVEREND

(happily)

That's the ticket! They're in a better place, I assure you.

(beat)

Better than Wales, anyhow.

(The REVEREND tries to walk into the room.)

JONES
(blocking the REVEREND's path)

Mrs. Woolworth-Spencer is in the sitting room.

REVEREND
Yes, I can see that. She's just there.

JONES
(still blocking him)

I'll announce you, Reverend

REVEREND
There's no need, I can see her and Miss Lancaster from here. Hello?!

(He waves at GERTIE, who waves back. MAGGIE ignores him, and JONES stays firm.)

JONES
(announcing)

Reverend Whyte, ma'am.

MAGGIE
(standing and greeting him warmly)

Reverend!

REVEREND
Mrs. Woolworth-Spencer, Miss Lancaster, I do hope I'm not too early?

MAGGIE
Too early for what, Reverend? You're too early for Christmas, that's for sure!

(EVERYONE laughs politely)

REVEREND

I'm here for dinner, of course. I was passing through this end of the village on my way back from afternoon prayer and I thought I'd pop in now, rather than go all the way back to the vicarage and change. I hope my attire is suitable for the occasion.

MAGGIE

Reverend Whyte, am I to believe that you have been invited here to dine this evening?

REVEREND

(searching in his pocket for the invitation)

I have got the right day, haven't I? I'm usually very good with Sundays, but sometimes the rest of the week blurs into one.

MAGGIE

Might I see the invitation?

REVEREND

(handing it over)

I don't understand. What seems to be the problem?

MAGGIE

(sharing it with GERTIE)

Gertie look, it's the same as yours!

GERTIE

Goodness!

(to the REVEREND)

Someone appears to be playing a practical joke, Reverend.

MAGGIE

And not a very amusing one.

REVEREND

Do you mean to say that you didn't send this? Well, what is the world coming to?

MAGGIE
(warmly)

You are *always* welcome in my house, Reverend. Yes, you smell a bit of urine, but that's because you're always surrounded by old people, drawn to the church by the fear of their impending death. That and a possible bladder control problem you might have. But I like you. You've got spunk. But in answer to your question, *no*… the invitation was not sent by me.

REVEREND

Then who sent it?

MAGGIE
(walking over to the bell table)

I'm not sure. But I intend to find out. In the meantime, I have dinner to prepare.

(MAGGIE rings the servant bell.)

BETSY

You rang, ma'am?

MAGGIE

Yes, Betsy. Could you prepare a dinner party for me?

BETSY

Of course, ma'am. When had you in mind?

MAGGIE

Sort of now-ish. Well, in about an hour, to be precise. I'm sure you can rummage something up for us. Perhaps you could use some of that delightful *ham* we have.

BETSY
(adamant, but whispering)

But you said…!

MAGGIE
(quietly but firmly)

I know what I said, but desperate times call for desperate measures!

BETSY
(loudly again)

How many shall I cook for?

MAGGIE
Just the three of us.

GERTIE
But what if more people turn up?

MAGGIE
(exasperated)

Whomever else are we expecting?

(The front doorbell rings again.)

MAGGIE
(annoyed)

Oh, this is beyond the pale!

(JONES walks onto stage to answer the front door. IVAN OTHELLO and LADY DOROTHY SWINDLE enter through it. DOROTHY walks with a cane.)

IVAN
(suavely)

Good evening. I say, would you be a sport and ask one of the lads to take my motor car around the back?

JONES
There are no lads, I'm afraid, sir.

IVAN
Pity. Well, perhaps you'd be a good fellow and do it yourself would you?

(IVAN attempts to hand the keys to JONES, who doesn't take them.)

JONES

I don't think that would be wise, sir. I'm not very good with modern technology.

(to DOROTHY)

May I take your coat, madam?

DOROTHY

Certainly.

JONES

This way.

(announcing them)

Lady Dorothy Swindle and Ivan Othello!

GERTIE

(standing, surprised)

Ivan Othello? The world-famous composer, lyricist, singer, actor and all-round ladies' man?

IVAN

(kissing GERTIE's hand in greeting)

The very same.

GERTIE

Oh, I say! I've gone all aflutter.

IVAN

Don't be alarmed, I usually have that effect on people.

MAGGIE

(blanking IVAN)

Lady Swindle. How lovely to see you again.

IVAN

Usually.

DOROTHY
Margaret. You remember Ivan from my party, of course.

MAGGIE
Of course, I do. Don't worry, Mr. Othello you won't have to sing for your supper tonight.

IVAN
Oh, I'm quite used to it.

MAGGIE
Might I introduce Gertrude Lancaster and Reverend Whyte.

REVEREND	GERTIE
A pleasure to meet you.	Pleased to meet you.

MAGGIE
Tell me, did you come together?

DOROTHY
Why, yes, we did. Mr. Othello was kind enough to give me a lift in his automobile. He's a terrible driver.

IVAN
As I keep telling Her Ladyship, it wasn't my fault; the roads in this area are simply dreadful.

DOROTHY
Still, we got here in one piece. Or, at least, I think we did. I hope we haven't delayed tonight's proceedings.

GERTIE
(about to tell them the whole story)

Well…

MAGGIE
(cutting her off)

Not at all. Dinner will be served shortly.

THREESOME

IVAN
I must say I was surprised to get your invitation, Mrs. Woolworth Spencer. I hadn't realized I'd made such an impression on you at Lady Swindle's party.

MAGGIE
Oh, you made a very strong impression Mr. Othello.

(rolling her eyes)

Very strong.

DOROTHY
I too was surprised by your invitation, Margaret. I hadn't expected you to be entertaining so soon after Henry's death.

MAGGIE
(confused)

Henry?

DOROTHY
Your late husband.

MAGGIE
Oh yes, *him*. Well, I always think you have to grin and bear these things.

DOROTHY
How brave of you. I'd wondered why you appeared so happy at the funeral.

GERTIE
Aren't you going to tell them, Maggie?

IVAN
Tell us what?

MAGGIE
(quickly)

No, I don't think so. Pay no attention, Lady Swindle, my friend is quite insane!

GERTIE

Maggie!

> MAGGIE

Come and look at the gardens instead.

(quietly to GERTIE)

Play along, Gertie. and tell Betsy to prepare dinner for *five*!

(GERTIE nods disappears off stage right.)

> DOROTHY

I shouldn't want to go outside again my dear. The ride down has quite unnerved me.

> MAGGIE

Then, let us look through the French windows.

(DOROTHY, IVAN, and the REVEREND join MAGGIE at the front of the stage, peering out into the garden - the audience.)

> IVAN

It's a lovely house, Mrs. Woolworth-Spencer.

> DOROTHY

Oh, how quaint! You can see the house next door from here.

(pause)

How very modern.

> MAGGIE

(half laughing and gritting her teeth)

Yes. My late husband sold off some of the estate to a couple by the name of Briggs. They own factories in the North, I believe.

> DOROTHY

Oh, how awful. I simply hate new money.

> MAGGIE

So do I. Mainly, of course, because I don't have any…

THREESOME

DOROTHY
Ah.

MAGGIE
And also because the exchange rate between old and new money seems to have been set at one for one.

DOROTHY
And who made *that* decision?

MAGGIE
Quite.

DOROTHY
Tell me, where did the inspiration for tonight's little get-together come from?

MAGGIE
What better way is there to enjoy an evening, than spending it with four of my closest friends?

(pause)

Well, three and Mr. Othello.

(The doorbell rings again.)

DOROTHY
Well, if everyone is here, who can that be?

MAGGIE
(exasperated)

I really have no idea.

(They wait for JONES to appear and open the front door. He is slow. GERTIE reappears on stage)

GERTIE
Shall I just...?

MAGGIE
Not unless you wish never to be invited here again. It's what he's paid to

do! I think.

(through gritted teeth)

However slowly.

(JONES appears from stage right and answers the front door.)

JONES
(announcing)

Colonel Horseradish, ma'am!

MAGGIE
Horsewhips and buggery!

(COLONEL HORSERADISH enters)

COLONEL
Margaret!

MAGGIE
(through gritted teeth)

Colonel! How lovely of you to come.

COLONEL
I was surprised to receive your invitation after our little disagreement last time. For what it's worth, Margaret, I'm truly sorry. I trust my being invited here this evening means all is forgiven.

MAGGIE
Water under the bridge, Colonel. Might I introduce…

(quickly)

…Lady Dorothy Swindle, Reverend Whyte, Ivan Othello and Gertrude Lancaster.

DOROTHY
The Colonel and I have met before.

COLONEL

But of course, Lady Swindle.

DOROTHY
How is your wife?

COLONEL
Still paralyzed from the waist down.

DOROTHY
Well at least she's consistent. There's nothing I hate more than unexpected change.

COLONEL
I couldn't agree more. And having her confined to a wheelchair does make it easier for me to keep tabs on her.

DOROTHY
Quite. "Where is my wife?" "Oh, she's on the ground floor of the house."

COLONEL
Yes, and always in the sitting room since one of the servants accidentally let the air out of her tires whilst trying to tighten the nuts on her wheels.

DOROTHY
It sounds most painful.

COLONEL
She's a good sport, though, bless her.

REVEREND
So, we're up to six now?

MAGGIE
As I was saying, I couldn't think of a nicer way to spend the evening than with five of my closest friends.

REVEREND
Earlier you said four.

MAGGIE
(laughing)

No, I said five, Reverend. All that conversing with God must have affected your hearing! I imagine he has a loud, *booming* voice.

REVEREND
No, you definitely said four.

GERTIE
Well, Maggie probably wasn't counting the Colonel after their little spat, but now he's apologized it's five of her closest friends. Well, four and Mr. Othello.

MAGGIE
Exactly. Less communion wine for you I think, vicar.

(BETSY appears at the edge of stage right, waving at MAGGIE.)

JONES
(noticing)

Ma'am, Betsy wonders if she can have a word with you.

MAGGIE
But of course, do excuse me.

(MAGGIE approaches JONES and BETSY)

BETSY
First of all you said three, then it was five, now it's six people for dinner!

MAGGIE
Well, we'll just have to make do, won't we? I thought you working class people were good at that? Making do.

BETSY
But we don't have enough food!

MAGGIE
It's not my fault. They just keep turning up!

BETSY
It's only a small piece of ham!

MAGGIE
I don't want to hear problems, Betsy, I want to hear solutions. If Jesus

managed to feed five thousand with just some fish and a loaf of bread, I'm sure you can manage a simple meal for six!

BETSY
He was the son of God, ma'am!

MAGGIE
There you go again with the excuses!

(pause)

I've already eaten, and everyone else apart from the Colonel is tiny.

BETSY
I could use some of the leftovers from lunch, I suppose.

MAGGIE
Good idea…

(she has an idea)

I've got it! Pretend its French. Call it "nouveau cuisine". Everyone says they've been to France, but really no one, apart from the Colonel, has been further than Dover.

BETSY
I don't know how to cook nouveau cuisine!

MAGGIE
No one does! Just make it up.

BETSY
I'll give it a go, ma'am.

MAGGIE
That's the spirit.

JONES
Ma'am, since you're only serving a small amount of food, might I suggest a more modest setting for dinner than the dining room?

MAGGIE
That's a cracking idea, Jones. I knew I was right to keep you. But if not in

the dining room, where should we eat?

JONES

I was thinking I could bring one of the smaller tables in here.

MAGGIE

What an excellent idea.

JONES

Thank you, ma'am.

MAGGIE

Will you be able to manage it all on your own?

JONES

No problem, ma'am.

MAGGIE

I knew it! You'd have no problem carrying the piano, would you?

JONES

(confused)

Ma'am?

MAGGIE

It doesn't matter. While I think about it, walk out to the front gate and lock the damned thing will you? I don't want any more uninvited guests turning up.

JONES

Very good, ma'am.

(BLACKOUT)

(END OF SCENE)

ACT I

Scene 2

SETTING: Same as Scene 1.

AT RISE: MAGGIE, GERTIE, DOROTHY, the COLONEL, the REVEREND and IVAN are sitting around a table in the sitting room. They have just finished dinner. BETSY and JONES are on hand.

REVEREND
Well, that was an excellent meal.

MAGGIE
It was rather surprising, wasn't it?

(JONES clears the table)

DOROTHY
And you say it's called *nouveau kitchene*?

MAGGIE
Nouveau cuisine. It's French. You've all been to France, of course?

DOROTHY / GERTIE / COLONEL / IVAN / REVEREND
Oh, yes / Of course / I try to go every year

MAGGIE
Well, after I came back from my last trip, I enrolled Betsy in a course so that she could master it. I do think one has a responsibility to educate one's staff, don't you? It's all I get nowadays.

COLONEL
Well, it explains one thing.

GERTIE
What's that, Colonel?

COLONEL
Why the French are all so thin.

MAGGIE
(changing the subject)

You served in Burma, didn't you Colonel?

COLONEL

And India, Mrs. Woolworth-Spencer.

MAGGIE

Tell me, is it true what they say about Indian men?

COLONEL

(enthusiastically)

As a matter of fact it is! About an inch shorter on average. It's the same all over Asia.

GERTIE

I suppose that means all the doorways are lower?

COLONEL

(confused)

Doorways? Oh, I thought …

MARGARET

More meat, Lady Swindle?

(DOROTHY reluctantly accepts another serving)

IVAN

Is it terribly hot in India, Colonel?

COLONEL

Like the gates of Hell.

REVEREND

One hopes the food is a little better.

COLONEL

I'm not sure it is. Still, you get used to it. I like to think that nowadays I have a cast iron stomach.

DOROTHY

(looking at the scraps on her plate)

What a blessing that must be.

COLONEL
Of course, it's not all beaches and palm trees, you know.

GERTIE
(cheerfully)

Well, no, presumably there are breaks for tea and scones.

COLONEL
It's tough. Men have to *be* tough to survive. You have to have discipline. And you have to install discipline in the locals.

MAGGIE
And how does one do that, Colonel?

COLONEL
Well, the British Army has always found that shooting a few tends to do the trick.

GERTIE
(alarmed)

You shoot them??

COLONEL
Only a few. As an example, you see? For laziness. We shoot soldiers for cowardice, so it is only fair.

DOROTHY
The two words do sound awfully similar.

COLONEL
Exactly. The rest of them are OK. We teach them English.

REVEREND
You teach them cricket as well, don't you?

COLONEL
Damned right we do. Not only is it the greatest sport ever invented, but it's the perfect metaphor for life.

MAGGIE
Dull, long-winded and ultimately pointless?

COLONEL
(ignoring or possibly not hearing her)

Of course, as much as we try and teach it to them, they don't really get it.

DOROTHY
Do you actually let them bat or do you just make them field and bring iced tea and sandwiches in between ends?

COLONEL
Oh, we let them play, Lady Swindle. But mark my words, the day an Indian team beats a British team at cricket will be the day a German wins Wimbledon.

MAGGIE
That's most reassuring.

GERTIE
You must have travelled quite a lot, Mr. Othello, with all your films and musicals?

IVAN
Mainly to America, my dear.

GERTIE
How fascinating.

IVAN
And Morocco.

GERTIE
What are the men like in Morocco?

IVAN
Very… liberating.

DOROTHY
My family has very strong connections with America, Mr. Othello.

IVAN

Really, Lady Swindle?

DOROTHY
Yes, my late husband's family used to run a very profitable business selling package holidays to the Caribbean and American South to the natives in Africa.

MAGGIE
Are you quite sure that's what they did?

DOROTHY
I'm certain of it. Apparently, it was the making of him, because once the natives reached the New World, they liked it so much they didn't want to leave. So, he never suffered the cost of taking them back to Africa.

IVAN
How extraordinary!

DOROTHY
So, he filled the ships with tobacco and brought them back to England, and then did the whole thing over and over again.

GETRUDE
How interesting.

DOROTHY
(changing the subject)

Actually, I'm glad you're here this evening, Reverend, because I've been meaning to ask you about something that's been bothering me.

REVEREND
And what is that, Lady Swindle?

DOROTHY
Well it concerns Teddy.

REVEREND
Teddy? Is he a son of yours?

DOROTHY
Teddy was my West Highland Terrier.

MAGGIE
(quietly to Reverend Whyte)

Disgusting thing it was. It couldn't walk for the last two years of its life. She used to carry it round in a large wicker bag. I often wonder if the Colonel's wife is heading for the same fate.

DOROTHY
My question is this Reverend: when Teddy passed away…

MAGGIE
(again to the Reverend)

He didn't pass away, she left him on a train during a weekend trip to Brighton. She only realised he was missing when the station master sent a telegram to her estate asking her to come and pick up the bag.

DOROTHY
…when Teddy passed away, where did he go?

COLONEL
Well, where did you bury him?

DOROTHY
One of the footmen buried his body in the park under a great oak tree, but I was referring to his soul, Reverend. Dogs do have souls, don't they?

REVEREND
The Bible isn't terribly clear on the matter, Lady Swindle, but I like to believe that he's up in Heaven waiting for you to join him.

GERTIE
(quietly)

Hopefully he won't have to wait *much* longer.

DOROTHY
Well, that's what I thought, but what about the airships?

MAGGIE
(aside)

She's lost it!

REVEREND
What airships, Lady Swindle?

DOROTHY
Well, I used to picture Teddy on a cloud, frolicking with a couple of cherubs, but then the Zeppelins came during the Great War and of course they passed through and over the clouds. And if they could do that, how could Teddy be up there with them?

REVEREND
One has to understand that God created man in his image, Lady Swindle. He could easily have created the clouds we see in the image of Heaven. They need not be Heaven itself.

DOROTHY
Ah, well, that would explain it!

GERTIE
So, where is Heaven then, Reverend if it's not…

(pointing)

…up there?

REVEREND
There's no reason the location of Heaven need obey any of the physical constraints we know here on Earth, Miss Lancaster. Just because we can't point to it doesn't mean it's not there.

MAGGIE
Here's another one for you Reverend. What about all those Indians Colonel Horseradish shot in the Far East?

COLONEL
(defensively)

I only shot a few. There are an *awful* lot of them!

MAGGIE
They don't believe in God. Well, not our god anyway…

REVEREND

Well, that I can be much more candid about.

MAGGIE
Do, go on.

REVEREND
Well I'm fond of expanding on the famous quote by Cecil Rhodes: To be born English is to win first prize in God's lottery for life... To be born Church of England is to win first prize in God's lottery for life-after-death... To be born foreign and an infidel... well, you can always use the lottery ticket to blow your nose on...

ALL
Ha-ha!

GERTIE
(happily)

So, there are no foreigners in Heaven then? That's a relief, as I'd hate having to spend eternity talking to people who couldn't understand what I was saying.

MAGGIE
What about poor people, Reverend? They believe in God and Jesus and whatnot. Well, as much as their tiny brains can understand.

REVEREND
I like to think that there's a special place in Heaven for the poor and disenfranchised.

MAGGIE
I do, too. But I like to think they'd have their section and we'd have ours. Of course, we'd let them into our section every now and then... so they can change the bedsheets and empty the chamber pots.

COLONEL
If you'll excuse me, ladies, Reverend, I always take a stroll after dinner. I find it aids my digestion. Mr. Othello, would you care to join me?

IVAN
I'd love to. I do enjoy the country air when I'm out of London.

COLONEL

THREESOME

Excellent. Bring your cigarettes.

(The COLONEL and IVAN exit through the front door.)

REVEREND
I have to disappear too, I'm afraid, to officiate evening prayer. I shan't be long. I'll cycle there and back soon enough. Just in time for coffee and brandy I shouldn't wonder.

DOROTHY
Would someone mind taking me to the powder room?

GERTIE
I'll take you, Lady Swindle.

DOROTHY
Oh, thank you, my dear.

(to MAGGIE)

It's not that I'm old or incontinent, you know. It's just that I'm aristocratic, and I'm used to having someone else do everything for me.

(GERTIE and DOROTHY leave. BETSY comes back into the room. JONES moves the dining table and chairs offstage.)

BETSY
Did we get away with it, ma'am?

MAGGIE
We certainly did! It really was an excellent meal. Where on earth did you find raisins at such short notice?

BETSY
The rabbit hutch.

MAGGIE
Perhaps the less I know about dinner the better, then.

BETSY
Will you be wanting coffee later?

MAGGIE

That all depends. Do we have any? I don't want to drink a cup full of warm water and dirt or whatever else you have in mind.

BETSY

No, ma'am. We've got plenty of tea, coffee and milk. Shall I use the Royal Doulton or the Wedgewood service?

MAGGIE

It will have to be the Wedgewood. I sold the Royal Doulton last week.

BETSY

Very good, ma'am.

MAGGIE

Oh Betsy, what am I to do for money? At this rate I shall have to marry again.

BETSY

You could always get a job, ma'am.

MAGGIE

(snapping)

This is no time for jokes, Betsy.

BETSY

If you want money, you've got to earn it.

MAGGIE

I just said I'd marry again if I had to!

BETSY

I mean real work!

MAGGIE

Well, clearly you've never been married.

(pause)

Couldn't you get a job and just give the money to me?

BETSY

I already have a job.

MAGGIE
Not if I fire you.

BETSY
(laughing)

I don't think I could earn enough to keep Magpie Hall afloat!

MAGGIE
Well, it was worth a shot.

(sighing again)

Fine, as soon as this evening's over I shall make a list of all the eligible bachelors in Witherington.

BETSY
What about the Colonel, ma'am? He seems very keen on you.

MAGGIE
That's not funny Betsy…

(beat)

Isn't there something menial and blue-collar you could be doing?

BETSY
Well, I was thinking of counting all the clothes pegs to make sure Mr. Jones hasn't stolen any.

MAGGIE
That sounds excellent idea, Betsy! *Can* you count?

BETSY
I think so.

MAGGIE
Good girl! Off you go then.

(GERTIE and DOROTHY reenter)

GERTIE

Come on, Lady Swindle, we're almost there.

DOROTHY
I can see that, Miss Lancaster. I'm lazy, not senile.

MAGGIE
That was quick.

DOROTHY
For lunch, I had a salad of prunes, white beans and chickpeas.

MAGGIE
Well, that sounds lovely.

(aside to Gertie)

How was it for you Gertie?

GERTIE
It was a window into the future, Maggie…

(pause)

…and I did not like what I saw!

MAGGIE
Gravity gets us all in the end, doesn't it? Ah, here come the boys.

(IVAN and the COLONEL reenter.)

IVAN
…and of course, Olivier refused to be outdone and so proceeded to put eleven in his mouth all at once. Noel was furious, but Jill couldn't stop laughing. The London production was reckoned to be superior though.

MAGGIE
Was your walk satisfactory, Gentlemen?

COLONEL
In every regard. Your gamekeeper's frightfully diligent, isn't he? Still working at this hour.

MAGGIE

THREESOME

I don't have a gamekeeper, Colonel. It must have been Jones you saw!

IVAN
I was just sharing some anecdotes of the New York theater scene with the Colonel.

MAGGIE
How fascinating. Do keep them to yourself now that you're back. Nobody likes a show-off.

(The doorbell rings.)

DOROTHY
Is that another guest?

MAGGIE
I sincerely hope not.

GERTIE
Well, who can it be?

MAGGIE
I don't know. Let's wait patiently to find out shall we? I don't think it's going to be anyone we're not expecting.

(They wait.)

GERTIE
(frustrated)

How long are we going to wait for Jones before we simply answer the door ourselves?

MAGGIE
As long as we need to, Gertie. Don't be common!

GERTIE
They might think there's no one in the house and leave.

MAGGIE
Well if they do, whatever they want can't be that important, can it?

(The doorbell goes again. BETSY rushes in to answer it.)

MAGGIE

Betsy? Where's Jones?

BETSY

I couldn't say, ma'am.

(announcing)

Reverend Whyte, ma'am.

MAGGIE

You're back early, Reverend!

REVEREND

Well, the strangest thing happened. I got on my bicycle and rode down the driveway to the lodge, only to find that someone has locked the front gates.

MAGGIE

Oh, of course!

REVEREND

I couldn't get out!

MAGGIE

I'm awfully sorry, Reverend, that was my fault. I told Jones to lock them earlier.

DOROTHY

Whatever made you do that?

MAGGIE

(improvising)

Security. One can never be too careful.

(The doorbell goes again. ALL stand expectantly, but no butler arrives to answer it.)

BETSY

Shall I answer it, ma'am?

MAGGIE

Jones should do it. Go check on him, would you?

BETSY
Yes, ma'am.

(BETSY rushes off stage right.)

MAGGIE
Honestly, you're damned if you keep them and damned if you let them go. In the old days you could just beat them for impudence… or sometimes if you just felt like it… but these days it's all workers' rights, weekends, and work-to-rule.

DOROTHY
I have the same problem with my staff, Mrs. Woolworth Spencer. You're good enough to take them in and then they walk around your house like they own the place.

(The doorbell rings again.)

MAGGIE
(approaching the door, uneasily)

Well, it can't be that difficult can it?

(MAGGIE makes the simple task of opening the front door seem as complicated as defusing a bomb.)

Key, handle. No, that's not it. Maybe it pushes. No.

(it opens)

Ah, there we go!

(There is a fanfare as the door opens. Standing in the doorway is HERCULES PINOT-NOIR, the famous international crime-solving super-sleuth.)

HERCULES
(in a French accent)

It is I, Hercules…

MAGGIE
(interrupting)

Sorry, no hawkers!

(Mrs. Woolworth Spencer slams the door in his face.)

(There is another knock at the front door. MAGGIE opens it again.)

HERCULES

It is I, Hercules....

MAGGIE
(interrupting again)

Now look here, I'd hoped to make myself clear the first time. Whomever you are and whatever you're selling, we don't want any.

(HERCULES barges past her to enter the living room.)

HERCULES

It is I, Hercules Pinot-Noir, the world famous, international, crime-solving super-sleuth.

(pause)

I am here to solve the murder.

MAGGIE

What on earth are you blabbering about? What murder?

HERCULES

The murder that has just happened.

MAGGIE

You must be mistaken.

(BETSY screams from offstage)

HERCULES

I am never mistaken.

(BETSY stumbles on to stage holding a bloody knife.)

THREESOME

MAGGIE
Betsy? What was that noise? What's the matter?

BETSY
It's Jones, ma'am. He's... dead!

(They ALL gasp in shock, except MAGGIE and HERCULES.)

MAGGIE
(disappointed)

Dead?

GERTIE
Well, that solves your conundrum on who to fire.

MAGGIE
(happily)

Oh yes, it does rather, doesn't it? Gosh, there's *always* a silver lining.

IVAN
Well, Mr. Pinot-Noir, we don't need your help because...

(pointing at Betsy)

... the murderer's been caught red-handed.

MAGGIE
What? Oh, my god! Explain yourself, Betsy!

BETSY
I didn't kill him! I just happened to be holding this knife when I found him; I was using it to get the marrow out of some leftover bones.

GERTIE
What on earth would you want with bone marrow?

BETSY
Ah, bone marrow's lovely on a bit of stale bread, Miss Lancaster.

HERCULES

And back to me...

MAGGIE

Yes, back to you. Who are you and how did you know my butler had been murdered?

HERCULES

My reputation precedes me, madam. Surely you will have heard of the Whitlock case?

MAGGIE

No, I'm sorry, I haven't.

(turning to the other guests)

Anyone?

ALL

No / Nope / Never heard of it

HERCULES

What about the Salford Strangler, who choked his victims to death with seaweed?

MAGGIE

I'm afraid not. Any more?

HERCULES

The Portsmouth Poisoner? Who went on a rampage through the South West of England ensnaring his unsuspecting victims with a bag of cyanide-laced Jelly Babies?

GERTIE

Was that the one where the cat got stuck up the tree? And they had to call the fire brigade?

HERCULES

No.

MAGGIE

None of us have heard of you, Mr. Pinot-Noir, but assuming you are who you say you are, why are you here and how did you get on to the estate? I have it on good authority that the front gates are locked!

HERCULES
Two very good questions, madam. You would make a fairly good super-sleuth yourself. The answer to your second question is that I managed to slide in between the bars of your wrought-iron gate. I am used to a European diet and do not have the English pot-belly that many of your countrymen exhibit.

GERTIE
But how did you *just happen* to be in the neighborhood?

HERCULES
It is very simple. Clearly, I am not here by accident. In fact, my being here is very deliberate. I am here, much I guess like all of you… because I was invited.

REVEREND
You invited him, Mrs. Woolworth-Spencer?

DOROTHY
You're awfully late if that's the case. We've already eaten. Though, you didn't miss much.

HERCULES
I am not late. I am exactly on time. My invitation told me to be here at eight o'clock precisely.

(The grandfather clock chimes eight. ALL count the chimes, silently but obviously.)

MAGGIE
Might I see your invitation, Mr. Pinot-Noir?

HERCULES
But of course, madam.

MAGGIE
Gertie! Look! It's exactly the same as all the others, except that the time is different. All the others say six p.m. whereas this one says eight o'clock!

GERTIE
How extraordinary. It's as if whomever sent out the invitations meant for Mr. Pinot-Noir to turn up halfway through the evening.

COLONEL
What do you mean "whomever" sent the invitations? Mrs. Woolworth-Spencer sent out the invitations!

MAGGIE
Ah, well that's where you're wrong, I'm afraid. The truth is we've all been the victims of a rather elaborate joke. Each of your invitations is a forgery. I never intended to host a dinner party this evening and if I had I certainly would have prepared a proper meal.

DOROTHY
So, all that talk about spending time with your closest friends was codswallop.

MAGGIE
In short: yes. Don't get me wrong, I like you Lady Swindle, but you, Colonel…

COLONEL
Then, you haven't forgiven me, Margaret?

MAGGIE
Certainly not. And if I ever catch you rummaging through my closet and trying on my underwear again, I will have you shot! At least have the dignity to buy your own!

GERTIE
Well, really!

DOROTHY
Well, why didn't you tell us?

MAGGIE
Because I didn't want to let whomever's pranking us to win!

(beat)

So, I went along with it.

HERCULES
But by inviting me, our killer has thrown down a challenge: catch me if you can! Well, it is a challenge that I accept. I haven't come across a case I

couldn't solve. So know this, whomever you are, you will be brought to justice before the night is over!!!

DOROTHY
Bravo, Mr. Pinot-Noir!

HERCULES
So, let us begin by examining Jeeves' body.

MAGGIE
Actually, his name was Jones.

HERCULES
Colonel, Mr. Othello, would you please bring the butler's body up for us to inspect.

IVAN
If we must.

(the COLONEL and IVAN exit)

MAGGIE
The good news, Betsy, is that if we both make it through tonight alive, your job is secure.

BETSY
That is not very reassuring, ma'am.

COLONEL
(from offstage)

He's very heavy! We're bringing him up the stairs now.

IVAN
(offstage)

The Colonel's very strong. I'm barely breaking a sweat.

(There is a loud thud, followed by several smaller thuds.)

DOROTHY
What was that?

> IVAN
> (offstage)

Whatever it sounded like, we definitely didn't drop the body.

> COLONEL
> (offstage)

Well, you didn't. You'd have to be helping to have had a part in it.

> IVAN
> (offstage)

But he's all gross and cold!

(IVAN and the COLONEL enter with JONES between them. They each have an arm of his across their shoulders.)

> COLONEL

Why don't we drape him over the sofa?

> IVAN
> (straining)

Good idea!

> HERCULES

There doesn't appear to be a stab wound, so it looks like Betsy is off the hook for now.

> COLONEL

If he didn't die from being stabbed, then how did he die?

(JONES' body flops forward, face down over the back of the sofa. It is clear to everyone that something is sticking out of his back.)

> IVAN

Good God!

> GERTIE

Is it a growth? Did he die of cancer?

> REVEREND

It looks like it's made of feathers.

COLONEL
Is it a blow dart?

DOROTHY
It looks like a bird.

GERTUDE
It *does* look like a bird.

MAGGIE
Well, that's very odd.

DOROTHY
What kind of bird is it?

GERTIE
A dead one.

REVEREND
I'm no ornithologist, but it looks like a pigeon to me.

DOROTHY
A pigeon?

MAGGIE
The question is, how did it impale itself in Jones' back?

IVAN
Maybe it got lost?

GERTIE
Perhaps Jones fell and landed on it?

DOROTHY
Maybe he didn't notice it at first. Like a splinter.

IVAN
Maybe it flew into the kitchen through an open window?

MAGGIE
It would have to have been flying very fast.

DOROTHY
Perhaps it was in a hurry?

MAGGIE
A hurry for what? The number five bus?

DOROTHY
Maybe it was flying south for the winter?

HERCULES
No, this was no accident. Jones was murdered!

GERTIE
Oh, it reminds me of when your poor husband, Henry, was found in a pool of blood having been stabbed twenty times with a knitting needle.

MAGGIE
(changing the subject)

Unrelated, who would like coffee?

HERCULES
An excellent idea. Fetch some while I solve the murder. The most important thing is that no one calls the police.

REVEREND
Whyever not?

HERCULES
For the sake of Mrs. Woolworth-Spencer. Miss Lancaster is correct. Mr. Woolworth-Spencer died in *very* unusual circumstances. People will assume...

MAGGIE
It was an accident!

(pause)

I'd been telling him for weeks not to play on the trampoline so close to my knitting bag. Then he got his feet got caught in the springs, and before you could say "multi-perforation"... he was dead.

THREESOME

GERTIE
No one thinks you killed Henry, Maggie.

MAGGIE
Yes, they do! They call me The Black Widow of Witherington.

DOROTHY
(cheerfully)

Oh, I hadn't heard that one! That's good, I'll make a note of it for later.

IVAN
(to DOROTHY)

I can see it on Broadway. The songs would write themselves.

HERCULES
A police investigation into Jones' demise would set tongues wagging. And then there's Betsy to think about. Before you could say "working-class scapegoat" they'll have her strung up for Jones' murder.

BETSY
I didn't kill him!

MAGGIE
We believe you Betsy, but that doesn't mean a jury of our upper-class peers would agree with us.

DOROTHY
Should we believe her?

MAGGIE
I do. I say we just bury the body in the garden. The Reverend can do a quick ceremony and we'll all say nothing more about it.

IVAN
Is that legal?

MAGGIE
Mr. Othello, the law exists to protect the upper and middle classes, not to persecute us. Betsy will dig the grave first thing in the morning.

HERCULES

Excellent! Now we must figure out who will be murdered next.

GERTIE
(astonished)

Next?

HERCULES
Well, we were summoned here for a reason. All of us are either targets, the detective, or the murderer.

GERTIE
Crickey

MAGGIE
In for a long night, then.

(to Betsy)

Coffee for six please, Betsy. And since you're heading down to the kitchen you might as well take Jones' body with you.

BETSY
Right you are, ma'am.

(BETSY single-handedly drags JONES' body from the stage.)

MAGGIE
Oh, chin up everyone. Honestly, one dead butler and you let the mood turn to misery.

GERTIE
Mr. Othello, you're a dashingly handsome yet strangely single, world-famous singer, composer, lyricist and actor... couldn't you play something on the piano to cheer us all up?

IVAN
(protesting)

One of us could be murdered at any moment, Miss Lancaster!

DOROTHY
Play something good, then; you'll be less of a target.

MAGGIE

Actually, could we not? I think I'm coming down with a headache. Music will just make it worse.

IVAN

That's a relief.

MAGGIE

Ah, here comes the coffee!

(BETSY appears on stage with coffee. HERCULES takes a cup for himself and a cup for IVAN.)

That was quick.

(quietly to BETSY)

You did use boiling water, didn't you?

HERCULES

(handing IVAN a cup)

You needn't fear, I'm here to keep you all safe.

(HERCULES puts a hand on IVAN's arm. Momentarily reassured, IVAN takes a sip of his coffee.)

DOROTHY

What a lovely service, Mrs. Woolworth Spencer.

MAGGIE

Why thank you, Lady Swindle.

DOROTHY

What make is it?

MAGGIE

Royal Doulton.

DOROTHY

How marvelous. I bought a lovely Wedgewood set from Hancocks just the other day with a beautiful blue and yellow floral design.

MAGGIE

A *blue and yellow* floral design?

DOROTHY

Why yes! Not unlike the coloring in the Woolworth-Spencer family crest.

MAGGIE

Do you mind if I ask how much you paid for it, Lady Swindle?

DOROTHY

Something in the region of five guineas, I believe.

MAGGIE

Five guineas!?

GERTIE

Is something the matter Maggie?

MAGGIE

(to Gertie)

He only paid me three guineas for it, the cheapskate!

IVAN

(getting to his feet and putting down the cup)

No, this is madness! We can't just sit here waiting to be picked off one by one! I've never been one for heroics, but I have an adoring public to think about. So, I'm sorry, but I'm leaving.

COLONEL

I'll accompany you.

IVAN

I don't mean to be rude, Colonel, but you might be a murderer.

(to MAGGIE)

Tell Jones to fetch my… oh, never mind. I'll do it myself.

(IVAN leaves through the front door.)

THREESOME

GERTIE

He can't leave! He's just as much a suspect as the rest of us!

MAGGIE

He won't get far. The front gates are locked, and the key is still on Jones' body.

HERCULES

(patting his pocket)

Actually, I have it here. None of you are permitted to leave until this crime is solved.

MAGGIE

Someone might as well go fetch him, then. Colonel, why don't you do it?

COLONEL

Alone?

MAGGIE

Fine, take the Reverend with you.

(The REVEREND and the COLONEL exit through the front door.)

GERTIE

To think, one of us is a murderer. Can you imagine?

(excitedly)

It could even be dashing Ivan Othello!

(sad)

That would be dreadful...

(excitedly again)

… and also rather thrilling. How did you meet Mr. Othello, Lady Swindle? Was it somewhere terribly grand, in London?

DOROTHY

We met at Harrods, my dear.

GERTIE

Oh, that is grand.

DOROTHY

In the parking lot.

MAGGIE

Slightly less grand.

DOROTHY

I'd been up to town to order Christmas hampers – they really do make excellent Christmas presents – and when I came out of the department store, there he was, standing next to my car and talking to my chauffeur.

GERTIE

What were they talking about?

MAGGIE

Well from the way Lady Swindle described Mr. Othello's driving, it certainly wasn't road safety.

DOROTHY

At first, they both seemed quite flustered by my return. Anyway, to cut a long story short we hit if off and Ivan and I have been the closest of friends ever since.

GERTIE

Tongues will wag, Lady Swindle.

DOROTHY

Oh, my dear, I don't entertain the idea that Mr. Othello is interested in me for a second.

GERTIE

You're not over the hill yet, Your Ladyship.

MAGGIE

No, but far enough up to enjoy the view.

GERTIE

Ivan is quite a view.

(HERCULES checks his watch, counting down from ten on his fingers)

DOROTHY
Mr. Othello's more interested in his music and his film grosses than he is in women. I'm sure he'll meet the right girl *one day*.

(the REVEREND enters in a panic.)

REVEREND
Something terrible has happened!

(HERCULES stops counting and perks up)

MAGGIE
What is it? Is it a socialist revolution?

REVEREND
No, it's worse than that!

DOROTHY
What could be worse than that?

REVEREND
It's Mr. Othello! He's dead!

DOROTHY
No!

(the COLONEL enters dragging IVAN's body)

COLONEL
Where do you want him?

MAGGIE
Put him where Jones was, on the sofa!

HERCULES
May I be of assistance?

COLONEL
Please.

(HERCULES assists the COLONEL in laying IVAN's body on the sofa. As they lay him down it is clear he has something protruding through the back of his trousers.)

DOROTHY
Oh, I say!

MAGGIE
Oh, that's most unfriendly!

REVEREND
It looks like the same one that killed Jones!

GERTIE
But it can't be! The pigeon that killed Jones is still stuck in his back!

REVEREND
Perhaps, it was a homing pigeon?

MAGGIE
It's chosen a rather odd place to make its home!

COLONEL
More like a homo-pigeon.

DOROTHY
I've been to some themed parties in my time Mrs. Woolworth-Spencer, but this one takes the biscuit!

GERTIE
It's awful, simply awful!

COLONEL
I knew this sort of thing would happen if we gave women the right to vote!

REVEREND
Perhaps we should all put on protective hats just in case there are any more low-flying pigeons in the area?

DOROTHY
(to the REVEREND)

What a good idea! Do you have any?

GERTIE

(studying IVAN)

Can a man really die from being impaled... in that region?

COLONEL
In Elizabethan times they sometimes killed men by inserting a red-hot poker...

MAGGIE
(cutting him off)

Thank you, Colonel, a simple yes would suffice.

(beat)

It just doesn't make sense. Pigeons aren't ordinarily dangerous.

GERTIE
What about a pigeon with a gun?

MAGGIE
Well, yes, a pigeon with a gun would be dangerous, but both of our pigeons were unarmed.

HERCULES
(irritated)

This is Magpie Hall, is it not?

(beat)

Do you perchance keep *magpies* on the grounds?

MAGGIE
(the penny drops)

Betsy! Check on the magpies and see if there are any missing!

BETSY
Yes, ma'am.

(BETSY exits in a panic via the front door)

GERTIE

Why do you keep magpies on the grounds, Maggie? That's a bit strange, isn't it?

MAGGIE

We always have. It's a tradition.

(pause)

Mr. Pinot-Noir, this is getting darker by the second. Are you absolutely certain this isn't just some big, elaborate misunderstanding?

HERCULES

No, madam. It is most definitely murder!

MAGGIE

How can you be certain?

HERCULES

Because I found *this* pinned to the front door!

(ALL gasp at the piece of paper HERCULES is holding up)

MAGGIE

No, that's a note I left for the postman.

HERCULES

(knowingly)

Yes… but behind it was *this*!

(ALL gasp at the new piece of paper HERCULES is holding up.)

MAGGIE

No. That's last week's note.

HERCULES

(knowingly)

Yes… but pinned underneath it was *this*!

(ALL gasp at a third piece of paper held by HERCULES)

THREESOME

MAGGIE
Oh, I've never seen that before.

HERCULES
It is a letter!

GERTIE
Whom is it addressed to?

HERCULES
To all of you!

REVEREND
But who knew we were all going to be here?

HERCULES
The person who invited you, of course.

MAGGIE
And who was that?

HERCULES
The *murderer!*

DOROTHY
What's his name? Check near the end!

HERCULES
(losing patience)

He's a murderer you stupid woman, he's not going to sign the letter, is he?

(he checks just in case)

It is not signed.

COLONEL
Damn, he's cunning!

HERCULES
Yes, but *he*...

(looking around)

...or possibly *she*... explains in the letter why each of you are here tonight. It is written in the form of a poem.

GERTIE

I love poems. Do go on.

HERCULES

For dramatic effect, I shall read it aloud:

> "Each of you came here tonight expecting to be fed,
> Each of you has things to hide and now you'll end up dead!
> Repent! Repent! The time is nigh! Your sins both great and small.
> Or else you will fall victim to..."

(A long pause. Too long.)

GERTIE

Will fall victim to what?

HERCULES

"...The curse of Magpie Hall!"

(A flash of lightning illuminates the stage and a crash of thunder is heard, as BETSY slams open the door.)

BETSY

(in a frenzy)

The curse is real! It's happening here, tonight!

MAGGIE

What curse? What are you going on about?

BETSY

(more animated than she has ever been)

Folk used to talk about it in the village when I was a little girl. They used to say this place stank of death. And now the death won't stop until the rhyme is through!

REVEREND

What rhyme?

THREESOME

BETSY
I was only talking to Jones about it in the pub the other day. We were taught it as children, you must know it!

MAGGIE
I haven't the foggiest idea what working class children get taught these days, aside from arson and shoplifting...

BETSY
Well, I was never good at those, ma'am. That's why I'm a maid.

HERCULES
Tell us the rhyme, Betsy.

BETSY
The magpie rhyme: one for sorrow, two for joy, three for a girl, four for a boy, five for silver, six for gold, seven for a secret never to be told!

(Another flash of lightning!)

MAGGIE
That old trumpet? That's superstitious old tosh. A rhyme about seeing magpies: seeing one of them on its own is unlucky, seeing two brings you good luck, that sort of nonsense.

DOROTHY
My mother used to recite it on occasion when I was a child.

HERCULES
(excitedly)

Ah, but do you know how the rhyme originated?

MAGGIE
No. Do you?

HERCULES
I do not, but I suspect that Betsy does.

BETSY
(in story-telling mode)

There once lived a man called Ernest Woolworth…

MAGGIE
Ernest Woolworth? My great, great grandfather?

BETSY
The very same, ma'am. Ernest Woolworth was a wealthy industrialist and landowner. He owned a factory up in Lancashire, spinning wool. He was a strict man. Life in his factory was hard and cruel, but as his workers struggled, he became a wealthy man. He built Magpie Hall with the money he made. Then, one day, he was walking through town when he was approached by a gypsy woman…

MAGGIE
Oh, how awful!

REVEREND
Now, now, God wants us to love the unwashed, as well.

HERCULES
Technically, they're called *Romani*.

GERTIE
Isn't that a type of pasta?

BETSY
(impersonating the gypsy woman)

"Please sir, spare a bit of change for an old gypsy woman? The nights are cold and I've not enough to eat."

COLONEL
That really was awfully good.

MAGGIE
Don't encourage her, Colonel!

BETSY
But Ernest Woolworth was a miserly man.

(impersonating Ernest Woolworth)

"Be gone, old Gypsy woman," he shouted, "you'll get nothing from me."

MAGGIE

And quite right too!

BETSY

So, she cursed him!

DOROTHY

What rotten luck.

BETSY

"Ernest Woolworth," the gypsy bellowed, "in seven days, you will be visited by seven black and white birds. Take care to treat them better than you have treated me, for each time one of them leaves, so a member of your family shall die!"

MAGGIE

What utter rot!

BETSY

That's what he said, ma'am, but on the seventh day he came down to breakfast and saw seven black and white birds...

(she points to the French doors)

...sitting on the lawn!

COLONEL

Incredible!

BETSY

He panicked and rode back into town to try and find the gypsy woman, but she had disappeared. He rushed back to Magpie Hall and had the gamesman capture all seven of the birds and clip their wings so they couldn't fly away, thinking that would keep his family safe.

REVEREND

What a good idea!

BETSY

But he was wrong! That night a fox crept on to the estate and killed one of the birds!

GERTIE
(breathlessly)

And then what happened?

BETSY
Ernest woke the next day to find only six birds left. He ran through the house to check his family was safe.

COLONEL
And were they?

BETSY
His youngest son was dead!

MAGGIE
How many sons did he have?

BETSY
Two, and one daughter.

(pause)

The son had been a hemophiliac and had cut himself while polishing his collection of antique bayonets.

(dramatically)

One for sorrow!

(calmly again)

He bled to death.

MAGGIE
Well, then it was a normal, decent upper-class accident. Like my Henry.

BETSY
Mr. Woolworth knew differently, and ordered the remaining six birds to be put in the coop with the chickens.

THREESOME

GERTIE

And then what happened?

BETSY

That night the fox returned. He crept into the wire pen and killed another magpie!

MAGGIE

(disbelieving)

Why didn't he kill a chicken? They're bigger and juicier, after all?

BETSY

He preferred the taste of magpie, ma'am, and the chickens could fly away from him, while the magpies just sat there.

REVEREND

And was there another death?

BETSY

Aye, there was! Ernest's daughter, Susanna, suffered stomach pains that afternoon while riding her horse. The doctor thought she had appendicitis and operated on her using nitrous oxide as an anesthetic.

(pause)

They say she died laughing.

(dramatically)

Two... for joy!

(ALL gasp)

In the days that followed the fox came back, and took another bird each night. Mr. Woolworth's wife and his oldest son died next.

(dramatically)

Three for a girl

(pause)

... four for a boy!

MAGGIE
(pedantically)

Technically his wife was a woman, not a girl…

BETSY
Next, Ernest Woolworth's mother and father, who lived with them on the estate, died one after the other. His mother choked on a silver spoon while taking her medicine, while his father was killed by a falling chandelier… made of gold!

(dramatically)

Five for silver! Six for Gold!

COLONEL
What did Woolworth do after that? There's still one line left in the rhyme!

BETSY
First, he ordered the gamekeeper to track down and shoot the fox, which the gamekeeper duly did.

GERTIE
Why didn't he do that in the first place?

BETSY
Next, he took the last black and white bird and placed it in a cage. Then, he took the caged bird and locked himself with it in his bedroom.

GERTIE
Surely that should have done the trick?

BETSY
Oh, but it didn't! Somehow they gypsy woman knew what Ernest had done and she came to Magpie Hall herself. The house was locked, but being a gypsy she knew how to pick a lock and sneak around the house without being noticed. So, she crept into his bedroom while he was asleep, opened the cage and stole the last bird herself!

GERTIE
What a nasty piece of work she turned out to be! Did she take anything

else?

MAGGIE
I bet she did, the thieving little gypsy wench!

BETSY
No, ma'am, she didn't take nothing else. She only came for the bird. She was an animal lover and she had meant for Mr. Woolworth to take care of the birds, not to clip their wings or keep them in cages. When Ernest woke from his sleep, he looked across the room and saw the cage... empty!

REVEREND
And did he die?

BETSY
The shock killed him. They say he had a heart attack there and then. Since that day it's said that in order for this house to avoid a repeat occurrence, seven magpies must always reside on the grounds! And since Mr. Woolworth's death, this house has always been known as Magpie Hall.

GERTIE
But you have magpies on the grounds right? You said you keep them here. So, we're safe, right?

BETSY
No, Miss Lancaster!

MAGGIE
What do you mean, no?

BETSY
Well, you asked me to go and check, ma'am and... I'm afraid to say... they've all gone!

MAGGIE
Gone?

BETSY
Gone!

MAGGIE
All of them?

GERTIE
That doesn't sound good.

MAGGIE
But it's an old wives' tale. It doesn't even make sense! What about that last line? Seven for a secret never to be told! What was the secret?

BETSY
He never told anyone...

MAGGIE
Well, that seems awfully convenient!

HERCULES
We must confine ourselves to the facts. I presume that no one here actually believes in curses or spells.

MAGGIE
No, Mr. Pinot-Noir, none of us here with the exception of my somewhat excitable maid gives an ounce of credence to that story.

HERCULES
Nevertheless, the story exists, and we have two deaths on our hands. I am forced to conclude that tonight's killer is using magpie rhyme as their blueprint for murder!

DOROTHY
I don't see why that has to be the case.

HERCULES
Madam, the arithmetic would seem to validate my hypothesis.

MAGGIE
What do you mean, the arithmetic?

BETSY
Don't you see, ma'am? There are seven lines to the song, seven magpies missing and seven people here!

MAGGIE
(smugly)

I count nine, including Mr. Pinot-Noir!

THREESOME

BETSY

Seven victims, a murderer and Mr. Pinot-Noir.

MAGGIE

(angrily)

I thought you said you couldn't count!

(beat)

Jones and Mr. Othello make two. Then there's me, Gertie, Lady Swindle, the Colonel, Reverend Whyte and you. Wait, do working class people count?

DOROTHY

If they do, it's not for much.

MAGGIE

Because otherwise there would only be five potential victims, a murderer and Mr. Pinot-Noir. Four if you were to classify Mr. Othello as an artisan!

GERTIE

(hysterically)

I'm calling the police! I don't care about having my name dragged through the mud, so long as I'm alive to see it!

COLONEL

Good idea, Miss Lancaster!

MAGGIE

Tell them to come quickly and to bring a battering ram to break open the main gates!

GERTIE

(picking up the telephone receiver)

I'm … I'm not good with these things, but isn't there meant to be a tone or something? Or an operator?

(MAGGIE walks over and takes the phone from GERTIE.)

MAGGIE
Operator? Hello? The line's dead. Betsy, we did pay the telephone bill, didn't we?

BETSY
Yes, ma'am.

REVEREND
That flash of lightning must have taken out a telegraph pole!

HERCULES
Or someone has cut the line to prevent us from calling out!

REVEREND
Well, one of us should go and fetch help, then.

HERCULES
You are missing the point. *I* was invited here to solve the crime.

GERTIE
Then get on with it!

HERCULES
Fine, I will begin. Prepare to see my highly trained investigative skills in action. Mrs. Woolworth-Spencer, did you murder Jones and Ivan Othello?

MAGGIE
Certainly not.

HERCULES
Miss Lancaster, are you the murderer?

GERTIE
No.

HERCULES
Lady Swindle?

DOROTHY
Of course, not.

HERCULES
Colonel Horseradish, are you the murderer?

THREESOME

COLONEL

Not in this instance.

HERCULES

Reverend Whyte?

REVEREND

With God as my witness, no.

HERCULES

(turning to Betsy)

Which only leaves you, Betsy!

(Lightning flash!)

BETSY

You're just going to take their words for it?

DOROTHY

Members of the upper class do not lie, my dear. We have reputations to uphold.

HERCULES

(to BETSY)

And you were, coincidentally, the person who discovered Jones' body and the only one here with prior knowledge of the curse…

BETSY

Why would I kill either of them? I'd never met Ivan Othello before tonight!

HERCULES

A good point.

(turns to the rest of the room)

What could be her motive?

DOROTHY

Jealousy! It always is.

MAGGIE
(angrily)

She's pregnant with his baby!

GERTIE
But which one? Jones' or Ivan's?

MAGGIE
Both of them, the little harlot.

(beat)

She eats enough for three people.

BETSY
(protesting)

Ma'am!

MAGGIE
Well, you won't get away with it, Betsy. Not this time.

BETSY
I've never committed a crime in my life!

COLONEL
What about dinner?

HERCULES
(to BETSY)

Who else had the opportunity?

BETSY
The Colonel! Or the Reverend! They didn't stay together when looking for Ivan, either one of them could have killed him!

GERTIE
You can't go around accusing a man of the cloth!

HERCULES
I fear we may be making a mistake, anyway.

DOROTHY
What do you mean?

HERCULES
Well, we are all making one, rather large, assumption.

MAGGIE
And what is that?

HERCULES
That there is only *one* murderer.

GERTIE
You mean there's more than one?

HERCULES
There could be. What if Betsy was working with the Reverend? She could have murdered Jones and *he* could have murdered Mr. Othello? In fact, anyone here could have murdered Jones during dinner. How many of you left the table at one point or another to powder your nose or smoke a cigarette?

MAGGIE
This is getting us nowhere then!

HERCULES
Exactly. We should turn instead to motive and the rhyme that Betsy recounted.

MAGGIE
The magpie rhyme?

HERCULES
Yes, specifically the last line. Seven for a secret never to be told!

COLONEL
How does that help us?

HERCULES
Do you remember the note pinned to the front door?

MAGGIE

(remembering the note)

"Please leave any large parcels around the back?"

HERCULES
The one from the murderer!

(pause)

"Repent," he or she said. Repent or you will fall victim to the curse of Magpie Hall. That may be your key to salvation! Perhaps the murderer knows something about each of you and the way to save yourselves is to admit to whatever sins you have committed!

MAGGIE
That's preposterous! We're all upstanding members of the community!

HERCULES
The situation would suggest otherwise, madam.

MAGGIE
What are you suggesting? That the murderer will have a change of heart if we confess and say we're sorry?

HERCULES
That is what the note says.

MAGGIE
But Mr. Othello and Jones didn't have the chance to repent.

HERCULES
That is true, but I am still of the opinion this is our best way forward.

MAGGIE
Well, who would go first?

HERCULES
Perhaps as our hostess, you could go first?

MAGGIE
Me? I've never done anything wrong.

COLONEL

Apart from murdering your husband.

MAGGIE
I didn't murder him! It was an honest-to-God accident. It could have happened to anyone with a penchant for bouncing up and down and a wife who likes knitting.

GERTIE
Well, I believe you, Maggie.

MAGGIE
Thank you, Gertie.

GERTIE
So, maybe there's something *else* you need to share?

MAGGIE
(unsure)

Something else?

GERTIE
Something in your *past*, maybe?

MAGGIE
(dismissively)

I don't know what you're talking about.

GERTIE
Something that perhaps you've only told your *best friend*.

MAGGIE
(with a look and a tone that could kill)

Gertie, you are treading on very thin ice.

GERTIE
Now is not the time to be shy, Maggie. Your life may depend on it.

HERCULES
You know what this secret of Mrs. Woolworth-Spencer's is?

GERTIE

I think I might.

DOROTHY

Well, spit it out, child!

MAGGIE

Gertie, you promised. On your life!

GERTIE

My life appears to be at stake this evening!

MAGGIE

But I'll be ruined!

GERTIE

Oh, you're ruined anyway.

HERCULES

Perhaps you can help her by giving us a clue?

GERTIE

It involves how she met her husband.

(MAGGIE stares intently at GERTIE)

And her profession at the time she met him. You see the truth is she was a...

MAGGIE

(interrupting)

Cancan dancer! At a revue bar in London called the Frisky Flamingo. There! I said it! I hope you're happy!

DOROTHY

You were an exotic dancer? Oh, how humiliating.

COLONEL

Well, that explains the silk underwear.

MAGGIE

(shouting)

Colonel!

GERTIE
See, don't you feel better now?

MAGGIE
(angrily)

No, I don't! Right. I've shared, now each of you had better spill the beans!

REVEREND
You met Mr. Woolworth-Spencer at a revue bar?

MAGGIE
He was one of my regulars. He tipped very generously. We fell in love and he changed my world.

DOROTHY
Oh, this is too delicious!

MAGGIE
I'm glad you're so pleased Lady Swindle, because you're next.

GERTIE
No, I'll go next.

MAGGIE
Gertie?

GERTIE
There's something I've been meaning to get off of my chest for a long time.

MAGGIE
My dearest friend, what is it?

GERTIE
I've wronged someone in this room.

HERCULES
Whom have you wronged Miss Lancaster?

GERTIE

My best friend in the whole wide world…

(MAGGIE gasps)

…Mrs. Woolworth-Spencer.

MAGGIE
Whatever it is, I'm sure it won't affect our friendship.

GERTIE
I had an affair with Henry while you were in London for the season.

MAGGIE
(with venom)

We're *finished*.

DOROTHY
Oh, this just gets better!

GERTIE
It meant nothing, Maggie. I came over to make sure he was OK, since you'd been away for so long. He was lonely, there was moonlight and candlelight, and I don't know how it happened, but he started to kiss me and I started to kiss him back, and then he held me, I held him back, and then I fell backwards on to the bed and…

MAGGIE
You little slut!!!

DOROTHY
Language! There are ladies present!

MAGGIE
Are there?

GERTIE
Maggie, I'm so sorry!

MAGGIE
Sorry? You were intimate with my husband, but you're sorry???

GERTIE

I didn't do it to hurt you.

MAGGIE
No, you did it because you're a brazen hussy, a vixen, and a jezebel!

GERTIE
You said it wouldn't affect our friendship!

MAGGIE
To hell with our friendship!!!!

GERTIE
Oh, Maggie, I'm so sorry!!! If it makes it any better, I didn't enjoy his affection for a moment.

MAGGIE
Well, neither did I; that's hardly the point!

GERTIE
Say you'll forgive me.

MAGGIE
I'm not sure I can, Gertie. Should we both make it through tonight without being hideously impaled by birdlife, I may have to reconsider our friendship.

COLONEL
And to think I expected tonight's soiree to be dull.

HERCULES
Colonel, you are next.

COLONEL
Says who?

HERCULES
Says me.

MAGGIE
Let me save everyone some time: he's a transvestite.

COLONEL
That, madam, is a lie!

MAGGIE

Colonel, how many times have I come home from riding and found you rummaging through my drawers? If you don't get a kick out of wearing them then what was it all for?

COLONEL

Damn it, woman, I love you! I always have. When I received your invitation, so soon after Henry's death, I thought this was my chance. I thought you were ready to forgive me and we could finally be together.

(he gets on one knee and holds up a ring)

Margaret, will you marry me?

MAGGIE

Your *wife* is still alive.

COLONEL

Well, yes, but *barely*. And she won't miss the ring. Please, say yes.

MAGGIE

Never! You're a pervert and a would-be adulterer!

COLONEL

(rising)

The underwear just makes me feel closer to you!

MAGGIE

(pause)

You're wearing it right now, aren't you?

COLONEL

For luck.

MAGGIE

Which pair?

COLONEL

(coyly)

The baby blue ones… with the white fringe.

MAGGIE
(livid)

I bought those in Paris! They were my favorite!

COLONEL
Well, they're my favorite too!

DOROTHY
Oh, heavens!

HERCULES
(pivoting to DOROTHY)

Which brings us to you Lady Swindle. So far, we have unmasked a dancing girl, an adulterer and a pervert. What do you have to share with us?

DOROTHY
Nothing. I am a pillar of society.

MAGGIE
Balderdash, there has to be something! Otherwise you wouldn't be here. Out with it!

GERTIE
Something to do with your family's history as slavers, perhaps?

DOROTHY
I thought I was very clear, my dear, my family were purveyors of package holidays.

MAGGIE
Something to do with your dog, then?

DOROTHY
No, I'm as clean as a whistle.

REVEREND
(cautioning her)

Come now, Lady Swindle…

DOROTHY

What?

REVEREND

Are you sure there's nothing you would like to share?

DOROTHY

What I told you, Reverend, was strictly between you, me and our Lord, Jesus Christ.

REVEREND

And I would never betray your trust, Lady Swindle, but given our current predicament you might want to think a little more about preserving your *mortal* life.

DOROTHY

(sighing)

Do I have to?

REVEREND

You don't have to, but I think it's in your best interest.

GERTIE

Come, Lady Swindle, you're amongst friends.

DOROTHY

Well, Miss Lancaster, I'm afraid you've already stolen my thunder.

GERTIE

Me?

(beat)

You mean?

MAGGIE

Nooo!

DOROTHY

I'm afraid so, Mrs. Woolworth-Spencer. It seems your husband was rather carefree with his affections.

MAGGIE
You had relations with my husband?

DOROTHY
You seem surprised.

MAGGIE
When you were a young girl?

DOROTHY
(smiling and reminiscing)

Oh, no.

MAGGIE
But before I met him, then?

DOROTHY
(quietly)

No, I'm afraid not.

MAGGIE
But you're old enough to have been his mother!

DOROTHY
Indeed I am. And I have to say, I think he quite enjoyed being my naughty little boy.

MAGGIE
I…

(sitting down)

… I feel faint.

DOROTHY
He used to call me Mummy. And sometimes we would pretend he was a stable boy and I was his…

GERTIE
I think we get the picture, Lady Swindle.

DOROTHY

And he liked me to go...

(impersonating a horse)

...Neeeiiiighhhhhh

MAGGIE

(rocking back and forth)

This is not happening. It's a dream and I'm going to wake up any second, still rich.

DOROTHY

Why does every younger generation think they invented sex? Where do they think *they* came from?

GERTIE

From storks, Lady Swindle. And from under rocks.

DOROTHY

Anyway, that's my contribution. That only leaves you, Reverend.

REVEREND

Very well. I'm prepared to lay my soul bare. You're all going to find this very shocking, but the truth is... I don't believe in God.

GERTIE/DOROTHY/COLONEL

Oh./That's it?/We thought it was going to be something serious.

REVEREND

(clarifying)

So, I'm a fraud.

GERTIE /DOROTHY/COLONEL

Well, I suppose so./I guess./Well, yes.

REVEREND

And I therefore tender my resignation as the Reverend of this parish.

DOROTHY

Reverend, if the Church of England fired every vicar who doesn't believe in God, half the congregations would have to close.

COLONEL

It's *nice* if you believe in God, but if you do it's sort of like a bonus, really.

REVEREND

But it means I'm a hypocrite.

MAGGIE

Hypocrisy is such a strong word, Reverend.

(beat)

Look at it from the congregation's point of view. Most of us are only there to look down on *other people*.

(beat)

It's why we typically prefer sermons from the Old Testament to the New. The New Testament is a little too liberal for Christian England.

GERTIE

Which also means there has to be some other secret that you're hiding, Reverend?

REVEREND

There isn't.

MAGGIE

Well, thank goodness for that. At least someone in this room hasn't slept with my late husband.

REVEREND

(guiltily)

Oh.

MAGGIE

What?

REVEREND

Well, it only happened once or twice.

MAGGIE

You had carnal relations with my dead husband?

REVEREND

Not when he was dead.

MAGGIE

(hysterically)

A gay priest? Whoever heard of such a thing?

REVEREND

To be candid, I believe I'm what they term "bisexual", much like your late husband.

MAGGIE

My husband was not bisexual. If anything, he was asexual.

REVEREND

No, he was definitely bisexual. Sometimes we'd pretend I was the stable boy and he…

MAGGIE

(interrupting angrily)

Has the world gone stark raving bonkers?

(to GERTIE)

You're meant to be my best friend…

(to DOROTHY)

You're the chairwoman of the bridge club…

(to the REVEREND)

And you're meant to be a man of God… I'm lost for words.

GERTIE

Well, that's first.

MAGGIE

(shaking her head)

By the time he died, Henry and I hadn't had sex since for *five* years.

(pause)

Well, he couldn't... with the syphilis.

GERTIE

(concerned)

Syphilis?

(GERTIE, DOROTHY and the REVEREND look uncomfortable.)

MAGGIE

Yes, syphilis. Ghastly business. He said he caught it off a toilet-seat in a public lavatory in Brighton. Perhaps you know the one he was referring to, Reverend?

(pause)

The herpes he said he caught from one of his horses.

DOROTHY

(to the COLONEL)

Did she say herpes?

COLONEL

(to DOROTHY)

Sounds like you were the horse.

MAGGIE

But I suppose that was probably a lie. Anyway, with him more or less infertile, we decided to forgo our matrimonial obligations. I suppose it's nice to know he kept himself busy, regardless.

(pause)

It also explains the amount of time he spent in the stables.

(to HERCULES)

Is this what you wanted Mr. Pinot-Noir? Public humiliation?

HERCULES
It has nothing to do with what I want, madam.

MAGGIE
Well, that's easy for you to say. All your secrets remain intact.

HERCULES
And I must correct you, madam. None of you has been publicly humiliated. This has been a very private conversation. Between just us and the murderer.

GERTIE
Wait a second, Betsy hasn't revealed her secret yet!

HERCULES
I was just coming to that.

MAGGIE
Out with it, Betsy. Were you fucking my husband as well?

BETSY
Of course not, ma'am. I mean he tried, don't get me wrong. He chased me around the desk in his study a few times when I brought him coffee, but I always managed to outrun him.

GERTIE
That seems improbable.

BETSY
I can be very quick when I need to be.

GERTIE
So could he.

COLONEL
A country house where the master isn't sleeping with his servants? It's unheard of.

THREESOME

MAGGIE
So, what's it to be Betsy? Adultery, gluttony or petty theft?

BETSY
It's nothing of the sort.

MAGGIE
But there must be something?

BETSY
I'm not claiming to be a saint, ma'am, but compared to all of you I've led a remarkably honest life.

DOROTHY
Working class people are too simple to have secrets. I think we're done. All of this has left me feeling rather moist.

REVEREND
Lady Swindle!

DOROTHY
I mean, I need to use the water closet again

MAGGIE
(sighing)

Gertie, would you do the honors?

GERTIE
Do I have to? I'm still feeling queasy from the last time.

DOROTHY
A little less talcum powder this time, my dear. And a little more contact.

GERTIE
(aside to MAGGIE)

There wasn't any talcum in your bathroom, Maggie, so I just patted her down with a fistful of Epsom salts. They should have dried her out, but apparently not.

(GERTIE takes DOROTHY off stage left)

MAGGIE

(sarcastically)

Are we saved then, Mr. Pinot-Noir?

HERCULES

Madam, my investigation is just beginning.

COLONEL

(to HERCULES)

I'm not sure you're adding any value here.

MAGGIE

My thoughts exactly, Colonel.

(to HERCULES)

Perhaps you should leave?

HERCULES

But madam, if I leave how will you solve the murders?

MAGGIE

We'll handle tonight the same way we British deal with our feelings: we'll bury it deep and never talk about it again. And we'll start with the bodies.

COLONEL

Three feet under should do it.

BETSY

I'll fetch four shovels.

MAGGIE

Three will be sufficient, Betsy, I've done quite enough work hosting, thank you very much. Reverend, you do funerals, right? And Colonel, surely you've buried friends on the battlefield.

COLONEL

Yes, friendly fire, terrible thing. I'm a dab hand at burials.

MAGGIE

Good. In the meantime, I'll get us drinks.

(she rings the bell)

Betsy, drinks for everyone. There, now I'm exhausted.

(GERTIE and DOROTHY re-enter)

DOROTHY
All done!

GERTIE
(aside to MAGGIE)

Quite frankly, I'd rather be murdered than see that again.

HERCULES
Let me help you, Lady Swindle.

(HERCULES helps DOROTHY to a seat on the couch next to IVAN's body and pats her on the leg)

DOROTHY
Oh, you are a gentleman!

MAGGIE
Mr. Pinot-Noir was just leaving.

DOROTHY
Oh, really?

HERCULES
You are making a grave error, Mrs. Woolworth-Spencer.

MAGGIE
I disagree. Everything was just peachy until you turned up.

HERCULES
But If I leave, who will solve the third murder?

REVEREND
The third murder? There have only been two.

DOROTHY

All of a sudden, I feel rather faint.

(DOROTHY falls sideways on the sofa, dead.)

COLONEL
Lady Swindle!

REVEREND
Good heavens!

The REVEREND rushes over to DOROTHY.

MAGGIE
Gertie, what did you do to her?

GERTIE
She was fine a minute ago!

REVEREND
She's dead!

GERTIE
Are you sure? It's so often hard to tell when they're that old.

COLONEL
Are there any signs of a magpie?

REVEREND
Nothing visible.

MAGGIE
What if it's someplace you can't see?

(All eyes turn to GERTIE)

GERTIE
Fine! But this is the *very* last time.

(GERTIE approaches and lifts DOROTHY's dress. A magpie can be seen protruding from between Lady Swindle's legs.)

MAGGIE
(recoiling)

How unladylike!

HERCULES
That takes us to three. Do you still want me to leave? Only I am capable of solving this dastardly scheme. If I leave, any of you may be next!

COLONEL
Sod that.

(The COLONEL draws a revolver.)

MAGGIE
(pointing at the COLONEL)

He's the murderer! He's unmasked himself!

COLONEL
I am not! But one of you is, and I have no intention of being next. Reveal yourself!

GERTIE
Don't be stupid, Colonel. What kind of murderer is going to reveal themselves so you can shoot them?

(The COLONEL points the gun at GERTIE.)

COLONEL
Only a *murderer* would know how a murderer thinks!

(beat)

You were alone with Lady Swindle in the powder room! You were obsessed with Mr. Othello and knew you could never have him. You killed Jones to... I don't know, but I'm sure you had a reason. I don't actually care. None of us are closer to Mrs. Woolworth-Spencer than you; you could have known about the curse and planned this whole evening! Confess, Miss Lancaster, or I'll shoot!

GERTIE
Colonel, this is madness.

COLONEL

This is how we handled things in Burma. I don't need a private investigator or the police to solve this. I'm quite prepared to be both judge and executioner.

GERTIE
For goodness sake, somebody say something!

HERCULES
Monsieur, think very carefully about what you are about to do.

COLONEL
I already have.

MAGGIE
I'm not following your logic, Colonel.

COLONEL
And how many native uprisings have you stopped, Mrs. Woolworth-Spencer?

MAGGIE
Fair point.

HERCULES
In my experience, it's at times like these when the lights usually go out.

GERTIE
That doesn't sound like a good thing.

HERCULES
Let's call it a shot in the dark.

(Blackout. EVERYONE screams. There is a gunshot.)

(CURTAIN)

(END OF ACT)

ACT 2

Scene 1

SETTING: The same sitting room of Magpie Hall.

AT RISE: MAGGIE, GERTIE, the REVEREND, BETSY and HERCULES are standing over the dead body of the COLONEL. There are feathers everywhere.

MAGGIE
Well, that was unexpected. Is he dead?

REVEREND
I'll check.

(The REVEREND kicks the COLONEL's hand, sending the gun skittering across the floor. The COLONEL does not react.)

REVEREND
He's dead.

(HERCULES examines the gun.)

MAGGIE
How are you doing, Gertie? No hard feelings, right?

GERTIE
He could have killed me!

MAGGIE
Well, yes. A lot of things *could* have happened, but we can't let ourselves get upset by what might have been, can we?

REVEREND
It looks like him shot himself.

MAGGIE
Well then, that makes four.

HERCULES
(correcting the REVEREND)

No, monsieur. It would appear that the gun backfired on him

MAGGIE

Well, that was lucky, eh Gertie? If you make it out of here alive you should buy a lottery ticket.

REVEREND

(removing a feather from the corner of his mouth)

Why are there feathers everywhere?

HERCULES

That is why the gun backfired. Someone stuffed a magpie into the barrel of the Colonel's gun.

GERTIE

That's ridiculous. How would one even fit?

REVEREND

So, the gun essentially exploded? Oh, yes! I can see little bits of beak implanted in the Colonel's lifeless face.

BETSY

(alarmed)

Lady Swindle and the Colonel! Three for a girl, four for a boy. The killer planned this, ma'am!

MAGGIE

I see your point, Betsy. What's next in the damned rhyme, then?

BETSY

Silver and gold, ma'am.

MAGGIE

Well, we sold all of ours, didn't we? So, we're safe?

BETSY

Yes, ma'am, but I believe Miss Lancaster purchased some of it.

GERTIE

Shit.

REVEREND
Live in the moment, my dear. It's no good dwelling on horrid things.

GERTIE
Isn't the Bible *full* of horrid things?

REVEREND
Well, *yes*, but we say it's about love. People seem to prefer that.

MAGGIE
What should we do, Mr. Pinot-Noir?

HERCULES
Oh, *now* you want my help?

MAGGIE
I mean, it's free, right? You're not charging us or anything?

HERCULES
(perking up)

The thrill is in the chase, Mrs. Woolworth-Spencer.

REVEREND
We need to do something with the bodies. This place is starting to look like a morgue.

MAGGIE
Do we need the bodies, Mr. Pinot-Noir? I mean, for evidence?

GERTIE
Good point, Maggie. We still don't even know how Lady Swindle passed.

HERCULES
Surely "impaling by magpie" covers that?

GERTIE
Yes, but how? There certainly wasn't anything lodged "down there" when we were powdering her nose.

MAGGIE
And why should we believe you? The Colonel was right, you were alone

with her longest. You had the best opportunity.

GERTIE

Maggie, you know me! You trust me!

MAGGIE

You slept with my husband.

REVEREND

Jesus preached forgiveness, Mrs. Wooldworth-Spencer.

MAGGIE

You slept with him, too. My husband that is, not Jesus.

REVEREND

(ignoring her)

Shall we, Miss Lancaster?

GERTIE

Maggie, where should we put them?

MAGGIE

Fine, but I'm not forgiving any of you.

(beat)

I suggest we put Jones' body outside for the cats and dump Lady Swindle, the Colonel and Mr. Othello in the skully. We've run out of coal, so there's plenty of room. There's a trapdoor by the front door. While we're doing that, Mr. Pinot-Noir, you should hurry up and solve this crime. How difficult can it be? There are only four of us left.

HERCULES

For now.

MAGGIE

I beg your pardon?

HERCULES

I was just agreeing with you.

MAGGIE

THREESOME

Okay everyone, let's get to work.

BETSY
May I eat after, ma'am? Dragging bodies is awfully tiring.

MAGGIE
Anything from the larder, second-to-bottom shelf.

BETSY
But there's barely any…

MARGARET
Take it or leave it, Betsy.

BETSY
Very good, ma'am.

(BETSY drags JONES' body on stage and out the front door. The REVEREND takes DOROTHY while GERTIE goes to IVAN's body and lingers.)

HERCULES
(to MAGGIE)

You see, at first, I thought the murderer was Jones.

MAGGIE
He was the first to be killed.

HERCULES
But was he really dead? In past cases of mine, the first victim was only "playing dead", as you say.

MAGGIE
He was definitely dead.

HERCULES
Exactly. So, I ruled him out as a potential suspect.

(beat)

Then I thought there could be more than one murderer! And I suspected Ivan Othello might be working in conjunction with Lady Swindle. After all, the two of the arrived together. Were they having an illicit affair?

(The REVEREND reenters and takes out the COLONEL's body.)

GERTIE
(starting to drag IVAN)

I hope not. He deserved better than that old crone.

(beat)

Do we have to get rid of him?

MAGGIE
What would you do with him if we didn't?

GERTIE
I know an excellent taxidermist; he does the best stags.

(pause)

I think Ivan would look beautiful mounted on my bedroom wall, don't you?

MAGGIE
In your bedroom, Gertie? No, I don't.

GERTIE
Fine.

(GERTIE takes IVAN's body out the front door. The REVEREND reenters.)

HERCULES
(continuing)

If they were not lovers, were they instead out for revenge? Was Ivan Othello secretly Lady Swindle's illegitimate son from an affair she had with one of the gentlemen here tonight? The Colonel? Or the Reverend?

MAGGIE
But now Lady Swindle and Mr. Othello are dead too.

HERCULES

(knowingly)

And thus, I deduced neither of them was the murderer.

                    MAGGIE
(straining to follow his logic)

OK, next you'll be telling me you thought the Colonel did it?

                    HERCULES
Exactly! He had military training. He had killed before.

                    MAGGIE
Only colonials! It's still a leap to imagine him killing members of the British gentry.

                    HERCULES
And yet he threatened to kill Miss Lancaster, and then the rest of us!

                    MAGGIE
So, that's it then? He was the murderer? And now he's dead because his gun backfired?

                    REVEREND
(cheerfully)

Excellent! We can all go home!

                    HERCULES
But then I deduced he was yet another victim!

                    REVEREND
Balls!

                    MAGGIE
(to HERCULES)

But why? He had a motive too! He was driven to insanity by me turning down his advances!

                    HERCULES
There are too many loose ends, my dear. Who put the magpie in his gun? Who summoned us all here in the first place? Where there are mysteries,

there's more murder!

REVEREND
But what do we do to stop it, man? Isn't that why you're here? To help us solve the murder *before* the rhyme is complete?

HERCULES
I am trying my very best, but this killer is proving most elusive. It is as if he, or she, is always one step ahead of me.

(BETSY reenters through the front door)

BETSY
(to MAGGIE)

Second-to-bottom, you said?

MAGGIE
Yes, Betsy.

BETSY
Thank you, ma'am.

(BETSY exits stage right. GERTIE reenters through the front door.)

MAGGIE
So, all that airing of our dirty laundry did us no good?

HERCULES
Did it made you feel better?

MAGGIE
We're not here for therapy, Mr. Pinot-Noir, we're here to survive!

GERTIE
(interrupting)

I feel like we should say a few words.

MAGGIE
I beg your pardon?

GERTIE

THREESOME

Especially for lovely Ivan... if it's goodbye.

MAGGIE
Is that really necessary?

GERTIE
(slightly hysterically)

Yes!

MAGGIE
Very well, Reverend, would you do the honors?

(The REVEREND, MAGGIE, GERTIE and HERCULES gather in the center of the stage.)

REVEREND
Dearly beloved. We are gathered here today to honor the lives of Lady Dorothy Swindle, Ivan Othello, Colonel Horseradish and Jones... did Jones have a first name?

MAGGIE
I don't think so.

(beat)

He was *Welsh*.

REVEREND
Ah. Let us start with Lady Swindle. Dorothy was an upstanding member of the community...

MAGGIE
(coughing under her breath)

Whore!

REVEREND
... Chairwomen of the Witherington Hospital and Sanctuary for Abandoned Cocker Spaniels, and Patron of the British Royal Society of Incontinent Spinsters. May she rest in peace.

MAGGIE, GERTIE and HERCULES

(repeating)

May she rest in peace.

REVEREND
Next, we say farewell to Colonel Archibald Bernard Horseradish...

MAGGIE
(coughing under her breath)

Pervert!

REVEREND
... former Commander of Her Majesty's 2nd Infantry Division, Viceroy of East India, and founder of the Annual Witherington Tiddlywinks Championship. May he rest in peace.

MAGGIE, GERTIE and HERCULES
(repeating)

May he rest in peace.

HERCULES
(to the rest of the grieving party)

Would you excuse me for a second, I have to go and, as you say, make a deposit.

(HERCULES skips off the stage in the direction of the kitchen, rubbing his hands diabolically as he exits)

REVEREND
Next, we say goodbye to Ivan Othello, composer, lyricist and all-round family entertainer.

MAGGIE
(coughing under her breath)

Homosexual!

REVEREND
Whose work included such ballads as "A Gay Time in Paris"...

THREESOME

GERTIE

Which was beautiful.

REVEREND

"An Even Gayer Time in Berlin"...

GERTIE

So lovely.

REVEREND

And "Hip, Hip, Hooray, It's A Good Day To Be Gay... In San Jose."

GERTIE

That was my favorite!

REVEREND

May he rest in peace.

MAGGIE and GERTIE

(repeating)

May he rest in peace.

REVEREND

And lastly, to Jones.

MAGGIE

(coughing under her breath)

Layabout!

REVEREND

(turning to MAGGIE for an idea of what to say)

Who...

MAGGIE

(shrugging)

... opened doors?

REVEREND

...who opened some of the finest doors in all of Christendom. May he rest in peace.

MAGGIE and GERTIE
(repeating)

May he rest in peace.

REVEREND

Amen.

MAGGIE and GERTIE

Amen.

(HERCULES reenters, dusting his hands)

HERCULES

Amen.

MAGGIE

Well, hopefully that's all the unpleasantness over and done with?

GERTIE

You mean the murders?

MAGGIE
(smiling)

No, having to say nice things about people *just* because they're dead.

(Suddenly BETSY rushes on to stage with a magpie shoved down her throat, its feet and tailfeathers are sticking out her mouth. She is holding a knife and fork in her hands.)

MAGGIE

Betsy!

HERCULES
(pointing)

Another murder! Who could have done this?

(BETSY runs back and forth, arms flailing.)

THREESOME

MAGGIE
For God's sake, someone help her!

GERTIE
She's only staff, Maggie.

MAGGIE
She's not just staff, she's part of the family! Like a dog. Or a footstool you've grown really attached to. Oh, Betsy, what have they done to you?

(BETSY screams through a mouthful of magpie, entirely unintelligible.)

MAGGIE
Someone help her!

REVEREND
How?

MAGGIE
I don't know. If only someone had invented some kind of anti-choking maneuver that could help her!

REVEREND
I'm not aware of any.

GERTIE
Me neither.

(MAGGIE takes a collapsing BETSY in her arms)

MAGGIE
Betsy, fight, you stupid girl. I need you! How am I going to dust the parlor? Or cook food? Or do the washing up, or whatever it is you call it? Oh, Betsy, you never even told me how to unclog the toilets. Fight, Betsy! Fight!

(BETSY gurgles and shakes)

REVEREND
Betsy, one grunt for yes, two for no. Did you see the murderer?

BETSY
GRUNT.

REVEREND

Excellent! Now we're getting somewhere.

GERTIE

Are they in this room?

BETSY

(nodding violently)

GRUNT.

MAGGIE

Betsy...

(beat)

... where do we keep the keys to the larder?

GERTIE

(chastising her)

Maggie, we don't have long!

BETSY

(violently shaking her head)

GRUNT, GRUNT.

MAGGIE

Well, really.

(beat)

You're a very poor maid, disobeying me like that.

BETSY

GRUNT, GRUNT.

(BETSY raises a hand to point at HERCULES)

MAGGIE

Mr. Pinot-Noir has the keys?

(happily)

Oh, thank you, Betsy, that's a huge help!!!

                    BETSY

(violently shaking her head again)

GRUNT, GRUNT.

                    MAGGIE

(to GERTIE and the REVEREND)

Sorry, you were asking about the murderer, weren't you?

                    REVEREND

Betsy, am I the murderer?

                    BETSY

(violently shaking her head again)

GRUNT, GRUNT.

                    REVEREND

Well, that's a relief!

                    GERTIE

It's not me, is it, Betsy? Tell them it's not me!

(BETSY wheezes and collapses, unmoving.)

                    MAGGIE

Betsy?

                    REVEREND

(to GERTIE, shrugging)

Bad luck. Still, at least we know it wasn't me.

                    MAGGIE

Is she… gone?

                    GERTIE

I think so.

MAGGIE

(wailing)

Noooooooooooo.

(regaining her composure)

Was that authentic enough?

GERTIE

Very.

REVEREND

So, what do we do now? Betsy exonerated me. And Mr. Pinot-Noir can't be the murderer, because he's the detective. Which only leaves the two of you.

GERTIE

Whoever heard of a female murderer? We are the fairer sex, Reverend, it's just not in our nature.

HERCULES

You raise a good point, Miss Lancaster. When a woman kills her weapon of choice is usually poison. I'm not sure either of you have the strength to impale someone with a magpie.

MAGGIE

Poison! That's it! Think! The manner in which Lady Swindle died; no one was near her. And Mr. Othello? His coffee could have been tampered with! Perhaps our murderer is a poisoner!

GERTIE

You think I poisoned lovely Ivan?

MAGGIE

You were rather keen on mounting his corpse.

GERTIE

I would have preferred to mount him alive.

MAGGIE

Well, *I'm* simply not capable of murder.

HERCULES
And why is that madam?

MAGGIE
I despise manual work of any kind.

(HERCULES retrieves a purse from behind the couch and rummages through it)

GERTIE
You could have gotten Betsy to do it. Wait a minute! That's what you did. You invited us all here and Betsy was your accomplice! She could have killed Jones! She murdered dinner, that's for sure.

(beat)

And we all know you used to be a can-can dancer. Anyone capable of all that kicking definitely has a violent streak.

MAGGIE
I never wanted any of you here tonight in the first place!

GERTIE
Clearly, that is a lie.

HERCULES
I knew it! Just as I suspected!

(HERCULES retrieves a vial from the bag)

Poison! And not just any poison. The rare venom of the South American Spider-Snake-Pig.

REVEREND
A pig? Whoever heard of a venomous pig?

HERCULES
(knowingly)

Very few people who have lived to tell the tale. What did you think the tusks were for, Reverend?

GERTIE
Well, I've never been to South America.

MAGGIE
You haven't even been to France!

GERTIE
Yes, I have!

MAGGIE
And for the record, I've never been to South America, either.

HERCULES
Nevertheless, would the owner of this purse please stand up?

GERTIE
We're already standing, Mr. Pinot-Noir.

HERCULES
Very well, then would the owner of this bag please step forward.

(There is a moment's pause before both MAGGIE and GETRUDE take a step forward at the same time.)

REVEREND
(astonished)

They both did it?

HERCULES
This is most unexpected. Ladies, please explain yourselves!

GERTIE
It's my bag. Why did you step forward, Maggie?

MAGGIE
What are you talking about, my late husband bought it for me!

GERTIE
Nonsense, he bought it as a gift for me!

REVEREND
Well, whose is it?

HERCULES
We will determine that by examining the contents. Reverend, would you help me please?

(the REVEREND pulls a brush out of the bag and hands it to HERCULES)

A hairbrush.

MAGGIE
That's mine.

REVEREND
So, it was you!

HERCULES
But wait! Please retrieve another item from the bag.

(the REVEREND pulls out a necklace with a locket attached)

Next, we have a locket. Hidden inside of which is…

(he opens it)

… a lipstick stained photo of Ivan Othello.

MAGGIE
That's not mine!

GERTIE
That belongs to me.

(defensively)

He had very defined cheekbones.

MAGGIE
What is your locket doing in my bag?

GERTIE
It's not your bag, you stupid woman. You must have put your hairbrush in my purse by mistake.

(beat)

I shall have to disinfect it.

(the REVEREND retrieves another item and hands it to HERCULES)

HERCULES
Next, we have a compact… containing a lock of someone's hair.

REVEREND
Good God, they're scalping them!

MAGGIE AND GERTIE
That's mine!

HERCULES
Madams, how can this be?

MAGGIE
(emphatically)

That lock of hair was given to me by my late husband on our wedding anniversary, as we watched the sun go down on Waterloo Bridge.

GETRUDE
(just as emphatically)

No, he gave it to me. You were out of town. I was stroking his hair in bed after a particularly strenuous night of passion, and noticed the gray streak, so I offered to cut it off and he gave it to me as a keepsake!

MAGGIE
Slut.

GERTIE
Witch.

REVEREND
He gave you both the same lock of hair?

HERCULES
Mais oui. It is obvious, is it not? Not only did he give you the same lock of

hair, he gave you the same bag, as well. To share.

GERTIE

How could he? We'd notice!

HERCULES

And how often do women misplace their handbags?

MAGGIE

(defensively)

Never.

HERCULES

Then where is your bag now?

MAGGIE AND GERTIE

There!

HERCULES

And if this bag is not yours?

MAGGIE

Um.

GERTIE

It always turns up. Eventually.

HERCULES

Have you ever noticed it containing unfamiliar items? Perhaps you noticed it was slowly getting heavier?

MAGGIE

I always meant to empty it out at some point. Perhaps in a couple of Christmases' time.

GERTIE

Me too.

MAGGIE

And you never know when something might come in handy in an emergency, even if you've never seen it before.

GERTIE

Do you mean to tell me that Mr. Woolworth-Spencer conned us into sharing the same handbag... and we didn't even notice?

REVEREND

I dare say he found the whole thing quite amusing.

MAGGIE

The cad.

GERTIE

Indeed.

REVEREND

So where does that leave us? Whose is the poison? The South American Pygmy Snake thingy?

HERCULES

(emphatically)

South American Spider-Snake-Pig!

GERTIE

It's not mine!

MAGGIE

And it's certainly not mine!

HERCULES

I have an idea. Reverend, I will need your assistance once more. I'm sure the murderer is ready to confess, but perhaps not before me.

REVEREND

Then to whom?

HERCULES

Perhaps she will do so before a greater man.

REVEREND

Me?

HERCULES

I was thinking of God.

REVEREND

Oh, *him*.

HERCULES

Mrs. Woolworth-Spencer, Miss Lancaster, when was the last time either of you entered a confessional?

GERTIE

The upper class don't have sins, Mr. Pinot-Noir.

HERCULES

You've never confessed your adultery to God?

GERTIE

I didn't think he'd be *that* interested. I imagine he's terribly busy.

MAGGIE

Mr. Pinot-Noir, we're English. We either bottle up our feelings or we write them down in a diary that we keep under lock and key.

HERCULES

Confessing is good for the soul.

MAGGIE

So are lemons, but we don't grow those in England, either.

REVEREND

Yet I see, by pure coincidence, you have an antique confessional box in this very room.

MAGGIE

Oh, that was my husband's. No idea what he got up to in it, although there is a hole between the two booths at waist height.

HERCULES

Then this is how we shall proceed. Miss Lancaster, you will go first. You will confess your sins to the Reverend in fear of your eternal soul. Mrs. Woolworth-Spencer will go next. Then I will confer with the Reverend to see what conclusions can be drawn.

MAGGIE

I thought conversations with a priest were meant to be confidential.

HERCULES

Usually, yes. But since the Reverend was exonerated by Betsy, he is likely the next to be murdered.

REVEREND

Yikes.

HERCULES

I think he will be most keen to share what he learns.

REVEREND

We'd better get on with it then.

(GERTIE and the REVEREND enter the antique, wooden confessional box, which is illuminated in such a way that the audience can still see both figures.)

GERTIE

I'm not entirely sure where to begin. Do I just talk about myself? This seems awfully similar to therapy, and I always hated talking about my relationship with papa.

Erm… Aren't I supposed to say, "Forgive me Father, for I have sinned?" Well, I suppose I did. I'm worried I might be a weak woman if I can't resist my best friend's husband like that. Or maybe I'm a strong one, for deciding love matters more than her feelings. I like that more, I think. If love is a sin, then I'm *very* guilty.

But they never love *me*, do they? Mr. Woolworth-Spencer married *her*, then hopped in bed with anyone within fifteen feet who wouldn't fight back. That's not love, is it? And Ivan, lovely Ivan, you know, I really might have murdered *for* him. He was worth it for those cheekbones alone, let alone the rest of him. Or would have been, if he cared at all. No, he's twisted and full of sin, like all the men worth my time. Nobody loves Gertie Lancaster.

I remember pushing Tracy Spooner down the stairs when we were thirteen. She was making eyes at Billy from next door. But he just spent hours at her bedside after that, never appreciating what I did for him by getting her out of the way. I think they got married. I hate them both. It was a beautiful ceremony. Really, they should be dead this evening, not all the other people who died tonight.

I don't think I'm a sinner. Love isn't a sin. Wishing bad things on bad people is only right. I am strong and good, and everyone else is just going to have to deal with that.

You know, talking this out really does make me feel much better. I always had the best of intentions, I can see that now. Thank you, Reverend. I much prefer therapy when my Father doesn't come up.

(GERTIE skips out of the confessional box and rejoins HERCULES.)

GERTIE
(to MAGGIE)

Nailed it.

MAGGIE

Makes a change from you *being nailed*, I suppose.

(MAGGIE enters the confessional box)

MAGGIE

First of all, whatever that harlot said is a lie. Are you listening? OK. Here goes. Forgive me Father, for I have sinned. You see, the thing is…

(she sighs)

…I have a feeling I'm an awful person.

I've lived my life with only one person in mind - myself. I married for money, yet I didn't return my husband's love. Each season, I would go off to London and sleep with countless gentlemen. Sometimes more than one at a time. So, I was unfaithful more times than I can count.

I never treated my staff with the respect they deserved. I loved them like family, but I never treated them as such. Instead I paid them nothing and barely fed them. I don't think I ever once said thank you. And now they're dead.

What else? Once, when I was a can-can dancer at the Frisky Flamingo, I deliberately kicked the girl in the chorus line in front of me. Amanda was her name. She was a trollop. But she didn't deserve to fall, fracture her spine and end up in the poor house eating gruel. Even if I did once see her steal a stick of chewing gum out of Bethany Simpton's overnight bag.

But I'm not a murderer. I don't know who is or why this evening is panning out the way it is. But it's not me, as God is my witness.

Also, God. Hi, it's me. We don't talk often, except when I invoke your name while cursing. But if you could help me out of this particularly sticky situation, I would really appreciate it. And if you do, I promise to be a good, christianly woman in future and give Christmas presents and Easter eggs to poor people and heal the blind and all that kind of stuff... Thanks. It's Maggie by the way. Did I mention that? OK, good.

(MAGGIE steps out of confessional booth and rejoins the others)

MAGGIE
(to GERTIE)

He said he believes me, so I hope you like prison.

HERCULES
Ladies, if you will excuse me. I will now swap notes with the Reverend.

(HERCULES walks over to and enters the confessional booth. Leaving MAGGIE and GERTIE alone).

GERTIE
Don't get any funny ideas, ok? I'm watching you! I know karate.

MAGGIE
You do not.

GERTIE
I know what it is!

MAGGIE
Well, now you do. We both know that until a few weeks ago you thought it was a type of sushi.

GERTIE
I can't believe you would murder all of these good people.

MAGGIE
I didn't. Not that any of them were that good.

GERTIE

I suppose the Colonel deserved it. I can't believe what he did to you. Why didn't you tell me?

MAGGIE

Do you really think that would have helped?

(beat)

Why didn't you tell me about your crush on Ivan? Not that I could have helped, but I could have set you straight there.

GERTIE

(full of remorse)

I've been a terrible friend, Maggie.

MAGGIE

(also remorseful)

So have I.

GERTIE

Can we put it all behind us?

MAGGIE

Of course. Friends?

GERTIE

Friends.

(beat)

Unless you're the murderer.

MAGGIE

(through gritted teeth)

Or you are.

(HERCULES walks out of the confessional box and addresses GERTIE and MAGGIE.)

HERCULES

Ladies, I have made my deliberations and I have something important to announce...

GERTIE

(to MAGGIE)

You're in for it now...

MAGGIE

(to GERTIE)

Please, you already dress like a convict.

HERCULES

But first, the Reverend has something he would like to say…

(One of the confessional booth doors opens, and the REVEREND tumbles out, bloody and dying, a magpie protruding from the palm of each of his hands.)

REVEREND

(groaning, to HERCULES)

You were right! I was next!

(The REVEREND collapses on stage, dead)

GERTIE

Oh my god!

MAGGIE

God was of little help here. Poor Reverend.

HERCULES

Knowing the game was up, the murderer silenced him. And silence is, as we know, golden.

GERTIE

Six for gold!

MAGGIE

But how is that possible?

GERTIE

You killed him!

MAGGIE

Look, I'm not the killer, but if I were, I'd kill you next for being so bloody thick! He was alive when I came out of there!

HERCULES

(solemnly)

And then there were two! Which means the killer is either you, Mrs. Woolworth-Spencer, or you, Miss Lancaster!

(beat)

It is time for the murderer to reveal themselves.

MAGGIE

Gertie, how could you?

GERTIE

(insisting)

I'm not the murderer!

MAGGIE

But it must be you, because it's not me!

GERTIE

I swear it's not! We've known each other for years, how could you think it was me?

MAGGIE

You used to cheat at bridge!

GERTIE

What?

MAGGIE

I saw you do it on several occasions, but I never let on that I knew.

GERTIE

That's a little different to murder, wouldn't you say?

MAGGIE

How?

GERTIE

It doesn't involve harpooning someone with a magpie for starters!

MAGGIE

If you'll cheat at cards who knows what you're capable of?

GERTIE

Well, really!

(pleading to HERCULES)

Mr. Pinot-Noir, it isn't me! It... it has to be her!

MAGGIE

Me? Don't be preposterous!

GERTIE

She could have sent out the invitations! She knew everyone here tonight! She must be the murderer. Her husband died mysteriously. I bet she killed him as well!

HERCULES

You make a good point, madam.

MAGGIE

Poppycock! I'm not a murderer.

HERCULES

(to Gertie)

Madam, you say you are not the murderer and you point the finger at Mrs. Woolworth-Spencer.

(to Maggie)

You deny the charge and instead accuse Miss Lancaster...

THREESOME

BOTH

Yes!

HERCULES

Well, ladies. I am at a dead end. It is, as you say, a draw. A dead heat. Each of you could have performed the evil deeds we have witnessed tonight and the only way we are going to find out which of you actually did it is to give the murderer one last opportunity.

MAGGIE

(aghast)

Are you stark raving mad?

GERTIE

You're crazy. Just arrest her!

(HERCULES walks over to the light switch)

HERCULES

No. I am beaten. The murderer has won! I am now going to turn off the lights. Whomever the murderer is, they clearly want to complete their twisted masterpiece. Well, we shall let them! But know that you will have to savor your triumph in a prison cell, for I, Hercules Pinot-Noir will arrest you as soon as your so-called work-of-art is completed!

MAGGIE

Don't say that! She'll murder you! Oh… actually I'd prefer that to the alternative.

GERTIE

I'll do no such thing! I'm innocent!

HERCULES

But you see, madam, I am safe. I was invited later than everyone else, either to prevent or solve this crime. Alas I have done neither, but if the murderer kills me, then their masterpiece is ruined.

(beat)

But enough talking… on the count of three!!

GERTIE

(frantically running to the front door)

You can't keep me here!! I won't stand for it!

>   HERCULES

All the doors are locked, madam. There is nowhere to run.

>   MAGGIE/GERTIE

Mr. Pinot-Noir, no! / You can't!

>   HERCULES

One!

>   MAGGIE

Gertie, you're like a sister to me!

>   GERTIE

(to HERCULES)

This is a bluff, right? You're bluffing?

>   HERCULES

Two!

>   MAGGIE

Mr. Pinot-Noir this is ridiculous!

>   GERTIE

I'm too young to die!

>   HERCULES

Three!

(Blackout.)

>   MAGGIE

Gertie!

>   GERTIE

Nooooo!

(After a few seconds there is a muffled scream. MAGGIE runs over and turns on the lights. GERTIE is slumped forwards over the bell table, dead with a magpie sticking out of her back.)

MAGGIE

Gertie??!

(confused)

Mr. Pinot-Noir... she's dead!

HERCULES

(wiping his hands)

Yes, madam. The murderer has struck again.

MAGGIE

But she thought *I* was the murderer!

(beat)

I didn't kill her! It wasn't *me*!

HERCULES

Seven for a secret that must never be told. The secret is that you are the murderer. It was such a secret, you didn't even know yourself.

MAGGIE

I'd never kill Gertie! And she's bleeding over a rather rare antique table... I'll never get the stain out.

(sanely)

But wait a minute. I *know* I'm not the murderer...

(beat)

so that must mean...

HERCULES

(innocently)

What, madam?

MAGGIE

It…. It was *you*!

HERCULES
(coolly)

Me, madam?

MAGGIE
Yes, you! *You're* the murderer!!!

HERCULES
I suppose I am.

MAGGIE
Well, of all the nerve!!! You won't get away with this!

HERCULES
There I must disagree with you.

MAGGIE
How did you manage to fool us?

HERCULES
You English aristocrats are so very gullible.

MAGGIE
But why Mr. Pinot-Noir? Why kill these people? What's your motive?

HERCULES
Does there always have to be a reason for everything? Does no one ever think it's odd that I, Hercules Pinot-Noir, just happen to be around when people start dropping like flies?

MAGGIE
Did you even know these people?

HERCULES
I knew none of them.

MAGGIE
Then how did you send them all invitations to get them here tonight?

HERCULES

Your front door, madam; it has no letterbox.

MAGGIE
Doesn't it? Where does the mail get delivered then?

HERCULES
The mail addressed to Magpie Hall is deposited in a mailbox in the guardhouse of your estate.

MAGGIE
Is it?

HERCULES
Yes. And the postman usually comes between eight forty-five and nine am every morning. And you sacked the guardsman many weeks ago.

MAGGIE
You're remarkably well informed about my mail Mr. Pinot-Noir, but what has this got to do with the people you murdered here tonight?

HERCULES
Each of the people here tonight with the exception of your domestic staff, sent you a letter in the past week. From Miss Lancaster: a Thank You card. From the Reverend: a parish newsletter. From Mr. Othello: a love-letter.

MAGGIE
A love-letter?

(laughing)

I wasn't in love with Mr. Othello!

HERCULES
The letter was addressed to your late husband.

MAGGIE
Not him as well? Is there anyone my husband wasn't sleeping with?

HERCULES
Ivan Othello and your husband were lovers. The letter I intercepted proves this. He was unaware that your husband had passed away however, so I invited him, knowing he would not pass up the opportunity of coming to Magpie Hall.

MAGGIE
But he didn't bat an eyelid when he found out my husband was dead.

HERCULES
You are correct. I think this is because a man such as Mr. Othello could only truly love one person.

MAGGIE
And who was that?

HERCULES
Himself.

MAGGIE
Fair point.

HERCULES
Each morning I would watch the postman deliver your mail, knowing that your butler, Jones, would collect it at nine fifteen. That gave me between fifteen and thirty minutes to read your mail and ascertain the names and addresses of all your correspondents. That is how I got their names and addresses and how I knew of their connection to you! That is how they came to be here this evening. *I* invited them all.

(beat)

Like your fat maid, I had heard the story about Magpie Hall and I based tonight's events upon it. There is no actual curse, but the effect was like that of a ghost story: confusion and doubt. Enough time for me to go about my work, secure the keys and lock all the doors.

(beat)

It is a shame that your maid was here this evening, tonight is usually her night off, is it not? Because with my secret told and the death toll already at seven, it all would have tied in nicely with the last line of the rhyme. But no matter… eight is close to seven. I was never particularly good at arithmetic.

(HERCULES takes a step towards MAGGIE)

MAGGIE
No!

THREESOME

(MAGGIE runs to the phone and picks up the receiver.)

HERCULES

The phone is dead, madam. I cut the line myself before I knocked on your front door.

(beat)

There is no escape.

MAGGIE

That can't be true!

HERCULES

It is.

MAGGIE

Where did you hide all the magpies?

HERCULES

Before I was a psychopathic killer, masquerading as an international crime-solving super-sleuth… I was an illusionist. The birds were hidden up the sleeves of my jacket, all evening.

MAGGIE

Ugh. I'd hate to be your dry cleaner!

HERCULES

Yes, my suit now smells a little of bird poo, but it is of no consequence. I will buy myself a thousand suits with some of the Woolworth-Spencer family fortune!

MAGGIE

(laughing)

Family fortune? Is that what this is about? Well you're out of luck Mr. Pinot-Noir. Magpie Hall is bankrupt!

HERCULES

You lie!

MAGGIE

I most certainly do not. I haven't paid the staff for three months.

HERCULES

I do not believe you.

MAGGIE

(incredulous)

This isn't about anything more complicated than money, is it? When it comes down to it, you're just a petty thief!

HERCULES

I am a criminal mastermind, Mrs. Woolworth-Spencer! Do you know how difficult it is to strangle someone with seaweed?

(beat)

I just have a cash flow issue at the moment. It's hard work being an international crime-solving super-sleuth. The police should pay me, but they don't!

MAGGIE

Crimes you solve? You commit the crimes yourself!!!

HERCULES

In English, I believe you call it… "job security."

MAGGIE

You disgust me! But wait! You've already killed seven people. And there were only seven magpies in the coop! You're out of magpies!!!

HERCULES

Am I?

MAGGIE

(counting)

Jones, Ivan Otherllo, Betsy, Lady Swindle, the Colonel, the Reverend, Gertie… that's *seven!*

HERCULES

So, would you like to speculate where *this*…

(HERCULES pulls out a magpie from his sleeve and holds it menacingly)

...came from?

MAGGIE
But that's impossible! Where *did* it come from?

HERCULES
It is, as you say, recycled.

MAGGIE
Ugh, but I've not had my tetanus shot!!

HERCULES
That should be the least of your concerns! And now, madam, the time has come for you to *die*!

MAGGIE
Fine! But before I do, just one question, Mr. Pinot-Noir. Why are you using magpies to kill people? Surely a knife would have been easier? A gun would be too noisy, I understand that, but surely using a magpie as your murder weapon is making life just a tad difficult for yourself?

HERCULES
The reason is simple. Have you ever tried dusting a bird for fingerprints? It is impossible!

(beat)

Also, I poisoned like, half of the people here tonight, and planted the magpies afterwards.

MAGGIE
I knew it!

HERCULES
(menacingly)

Any last requests Mrs. Woolworth-Spencer?

MAGGIE
Not to be viciously murdered?

                          HERCULES
I'm afraid not.

                           MAGGIE
(frantically)

An eighteen-course meal? Clemency? A suit of armor?

                          HERCULES
These will be your last words Mrs. Woolworth-Spencer, choose them well!

(HERCULES walks towards MAGGIE approaching the confessional, ready to strike.)

                           MAGGIE
(wailing)

For God's sake, somebody help me!

(The right door of the confessional opens and there is a loud clunk as HERCULES is hit over the head with a large brass bed pan. He sinks to the floor, out cold. BETSY steps out of the closet, revealing herself as MAGGIE's savior.)

                           BETSY
(proudly)

You called, ma'am?

                           MAGGIE
(relieved, but confused)

Betsy? But how? The last time I saw you, you were lying...

(pointing)

...there dead with a magpie stuffed down your throat.

                           BETSY
Aye, I was, ma'am. But I was in shock, not dead.

                           MAGGIE
But you should have choked to death! How on earth did you survive?

BETSY

Very simple, ma'am. The magpie?

MAGGIE

Yes?

BETSY

I ate it.

MAGGIE

(thrilled)

How marvelously resourceful of you!

BETSY

It was very tasty.

MAGGIE

But how did you get in the confessional?

BETSY

I snuck in when Mr. Pinot-Noir turned the lights off. I knew that the murderer would reveal him or herself, and then I could sneak up on them using the element of surprise!

MAGGIE

And what a lovely surprise it was! You've saved my life! How can I ever repay you?

BETSY

I couldn't say, ma'am.

MAGGIE

(picking up and rummaging through her purse)

Here, have a shilling. Run down to the shops and buy yourself the biggest lump of lard they sell!

BETSY

(gratefully)

Ooh, thank you very much, ma'am.

MAGGIE

And then bring me the change.

(beat)

Oh, and while you're down there put an ad in The Gazette for a new butler, would you?

BETSY

Yes, ma'am.

MAGGIE

(imperiously)

Today has been a very trying day, Betsy, but days like this are sent to test us.

BETSY

Yes ma'am. It's a shame about Miss Lancaster.

MAGGIE

Is it?

(circumspectly)

Yes, I suppose it is… but I never really liked her that much.

BETSY

What about Reverend Whyte?

MAGGIE

I'm a little sad he's dead. He officiated at my husband's funeral you know.

BETSY

It's a shame Mr. Woolworth-Spencer didn't leave you enough money to keep Magpie Hall…

MAGGIE

Well, yes, but…

(she has a brainwave)

Wait a minute!

(excitedly)

I do believe I feature in the wills of at least four of tonight's deceased.

(beat)

I think I'm rich again! Which means I shan't have to sell Magpie Hall after all!

BETSY

Hooray!

MAGGIE

I think we've both earned a holiday, Betsy!

BETSY

Oh yes, ma'am!

MAGGIE

Yours will have to wait. I, on the other hand, am off to the South of France. Dispose of the bodies and have this place shipshape by the time I get back, will you? There are bodies everywhere, you're clearly slacking.

(beat)

Oh, and Betsy?

BETSY

Yes, ma'am?

MAGGIE

Before you scuttle off back downstairs where you belong, be a good sport and give Mr. Pinot-Noir another bash on the head will you? Just to make sure he's dead.

(CURTAIN)

(END OF ACT)

THE GAY DIVORCE

A Play in Two Acts

By

Laurence Watts and Kevin Burnard

Cast of Characters

Brad Cummings — Steve's husband, a realtor in his mid-40s

Steve Smith — Brad's husband, an office man in his mid-40s

Howie Jackson — An African American personal trainer in his mid-20s

Kris Grant — A scrawny retail shop worker in his early 30s

Waiter/Neighbor — A waiter/One of Steve's neighbors

Dr. Fisher — A female therapist (voice only)

Scene:
Various locations across San Francisco's Castro district.

Time:
2020s.

STAGE PLANS

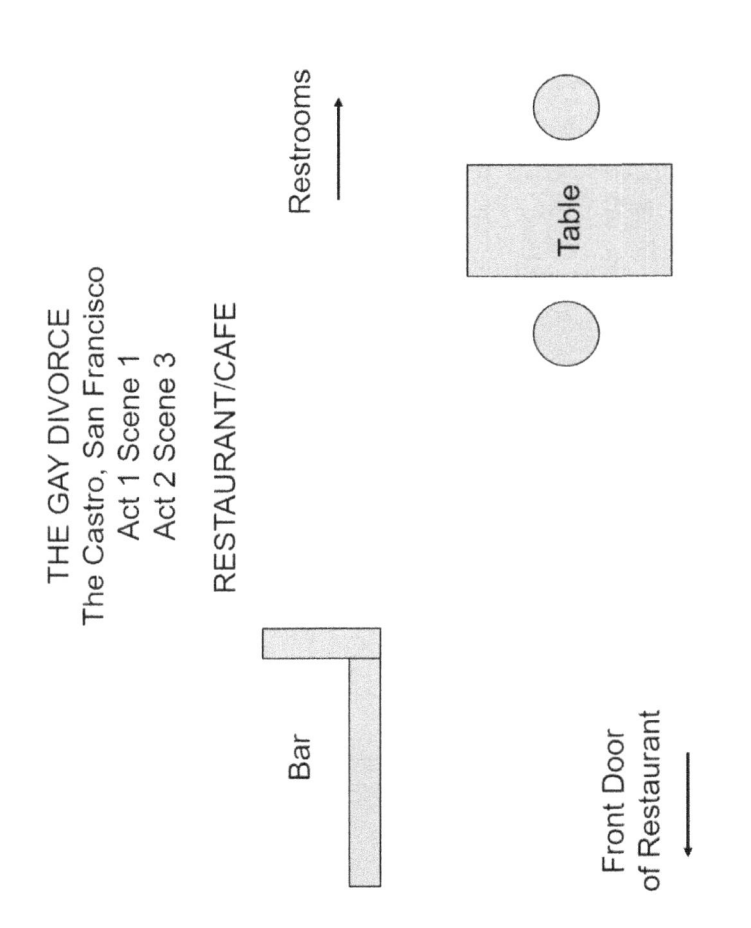

THE GAY DIVORCE
The Castro, San Francisco
Act 1 Scene 1
Act 2 Scene 3

RESTAURANT/CAFE

Restrooms →

Table

Bar

Front Door of Restaurant →

Audience

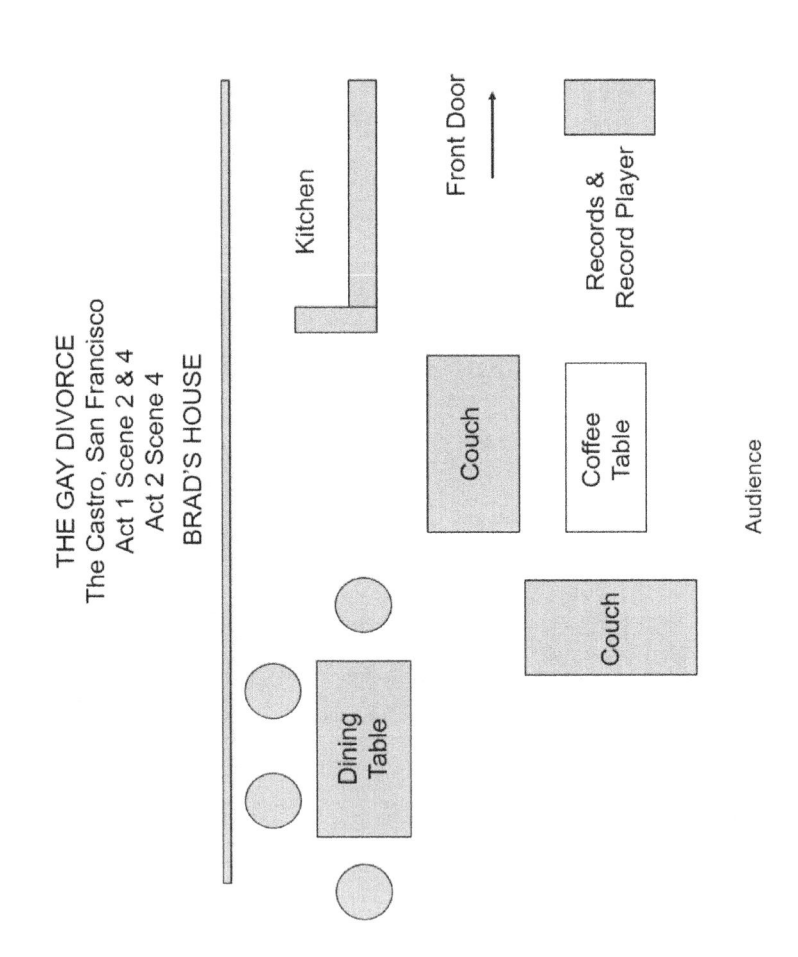

THE GAY DIVORCE
The Castro, San Francisco
Act 1 Scene 2 & 4
Act 2 Scene 4

BRAD'S HOUSE

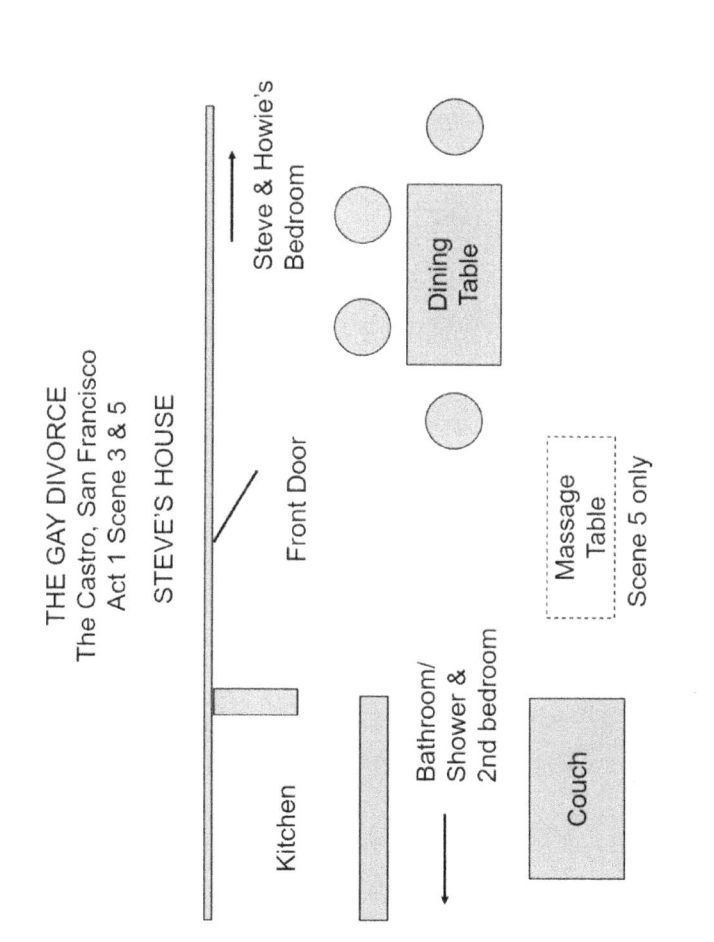

THREESOME

THE GAY DIVORCE
The Castro, San Francisco
Act 1 Scene 3 & 5

STEVE'S HOUSE

Steve & Howie's Bedroom

Front Door

Dining Table

Kitchen

Bathroom/ Shower & 2nd bedroom

Massage Table
Scene 5 only

Couch

Audience

THE GAY DIVORCE
The Castro, San Francisco
Act 1 Scene 6

THE PINNACLE GYM

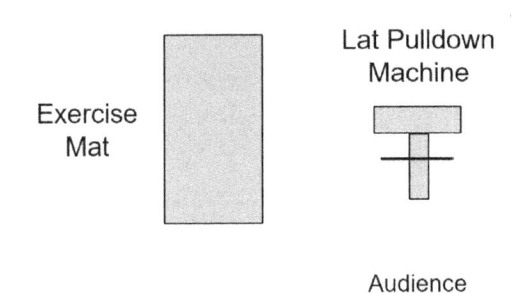

Exercise Mat

Lat Pulldown Machine

Audience

THE GAY DIVORCE
The Castro, San Francisco
Act 2 Scene 1

BRAD'S HOUSE

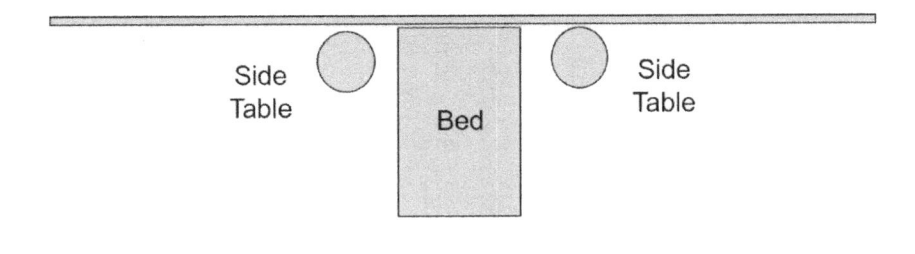

Side Table

Bed

Side Table

Audience

THREESOME

THE GAY DIVORCE
The Castro, San Francisco
Act 2 Scene 2

EXTERIO OF STEVE'S APARTMENT BUILDING

Window

Front Door

Steps

Window

Dumpsters

Audience

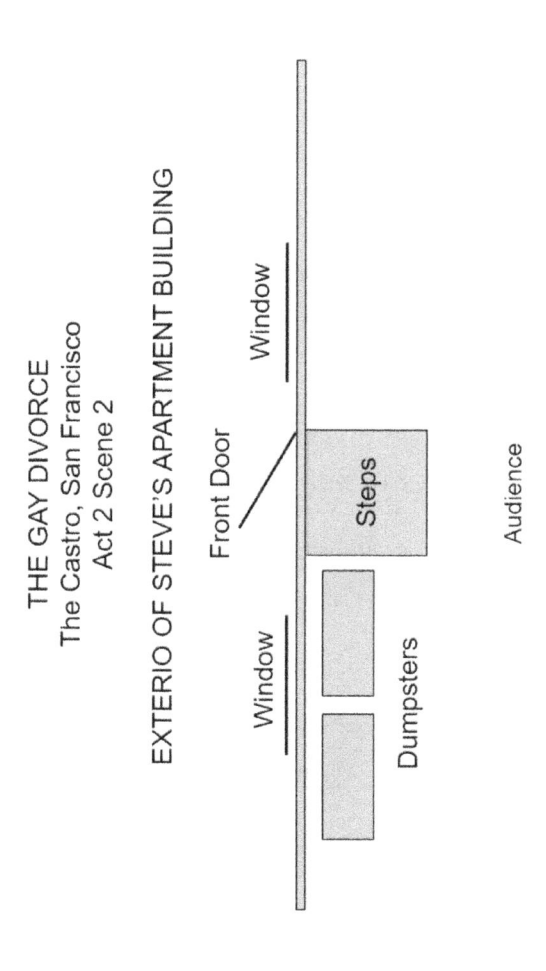

ACT I

Scene 1

SETTING: A restaurant in San Francisco's Castro district.

This is a private table for two, to the side of the rest of the restaurant. Only one table is visible. Lights and sound from other patrons spill in from offstage. There is no menu. A wine bottle stands in the center, as do two glasses, one full, one empty.

AT RISE: BRAD CUMMINGS is seated at the table, looking at his phone.

BRAD
(presses button on phone)

Janet, move tomorrow morning's meeting to ten. Looks like it is going to be a late night.

(puts down phone)

For once in your life, Steve, you had better have a good reason.

(STEVE enters, at a half jog, and slumps into the other seat)

STEVE
(laughing it off)

Sorry, sorry, sorry.

BRAD
And what was it this time?

STEVE
I lost track of—

BRAD
Time.

STEVE
And there was—

BRAD

Traffic, yep.

STEVE
And I had to stop for gas.

BRAD
We have bingo. You know, all these years you've been late for everything, I always thought you were just poorly organized. It now occurs to me you could have just been cruising for dick the whole time.

STEVE
(confused)

While driving?

BRAD
We both know you see driving laws as more of a recommendation than a requirement.

STEVE
Even then...

BRAD
(unsure)

Didn't I give you head once when we were driving through Texas?

STEVE
Ah, the joys of the interstate.

BRAD
Not to mention perfectly straight roads and cruise control.

STEVET
That one evangelical!

BRAD
Her face!

STEVE
And that cow crossing in the road!

                          BRAD
Her car, turning over and over and over...

(BOTH laugh for a moment, remembering what they had)

                          BRAD
(seriously)

Anyone giving you roadhead now?

(STEVE grimaces and reaches for the bottle to fill the empty glass.)

                          BRAD
That one's mine.

                          STEVE
But it's empty!

                          BRAD
You were late.

                          STEVE
Oh.

                          BRAD
Actually, I don't think I want to know.

(beat)

Anyway, this is nice, isn't it? Proof that divorce doesn't have to be acrimonious. We can still be friends.

                          STEVE
Of course.

(STEVE gulps his wine.)

                          BRAD
No reason why we can't be thankful for what we had. Speaking of which, there's something I want to say to you.

                          STEVE

What's that?

BRAD

I love you.

STEVE

(dryly)

What the fuck?

BRAD

(continuing)

We will be happier with other people, but I love you. We got married for a reason, and I still want you to be happy.

(beat)

Just not with me.

STEVE

I think we might have different definitions of the word 'love', but I'll drink to that.

(they clink glasses.)

BRAD

(expectantly)

Now it's your turn.

STEVE

What do you mean 'my turn'?

BRAD

This is where you say it back to me, so we're on the same page.

STEVE

I can't say that.

BRAD

Why not?

STEVE
We're getting divorced, Brad. Don't make this harder.

BRAD
Harder? I was trying to make it easier.

STEVE
Really? Because it's coming across as really weird.

BRAD
What I mean is… we can't undo the past.

STEVE
It was your idea to—

BRAD
(ignoring him)

We had a lot of fun together and I will always cherish the many, many moments we've shared. I wouldn't change it for anything in the world.

STEVE
You wouldn't?

BRAD
No.

STEVE
You wouldn't have wanted to spend this whole time with someone you *could* actually spend the rest of your life with?

BRAD
Well, I mean, *yes*. But I didn't. I spent it with *you*, whenever you were actually there.

STEVE
You cheated on me!

BRAD
I had to do something with the time. I was *bored*.

STEVE
Some-*thing*, yes. Not some-*one*.

THREESOME

BRAD
You made me lonely.

STEVE
How is this my fault. You felt lonely? That's what Instagram is for.

BRAD
To stop feeling lonely?

STEVE
No, to make other people feel just as bad as you do.

BRAD
Well, I didn't have Instagram.

STEVE
Look, let's just put a pin in this, you're always grumpy when you're hungry. Let's order.

(beat)

Where's the menu?

BRAD
I already ordered.

STEVE
Well, I need to order mine.

BRAD
I ordered for you.

STEVE
(dryly)

You did what?

BRAD
You always order beef when we go out.

STEVE
So, you ordered me the beef?

                          BRAD
Of course, not. You're single now. You know what the gays are like, you need to be in shape to have a hope of...

                          STEVE
Did you just call me fat?

                          BRAD
I didn't—

                          STEVE
I can handle my own health, Brad.

                          BRAD
I was just trying to—

                          STEVE
Maybe I don't want beef, or a salad, or whatever you think I want.

(coyly)

What if I've developed a taste for chicken?

                          BRAD
That's what I ordered for you, you moron.

                          STEVE
Oh.

                          BRAD
I did say "I love you", you idiot.

                          STEVE
You also called me fat.

(beat)

And divorced me!

(beat)

Actually, could you do me a favor and stop saying it? Love, I mean, not fat.

I feel like it just makes things harder.

BRAD
I don't see why. But sure…

(beat)

…fatty.

STEVE
(sarcastically)

Thanks.

BRAD
You're welcome. So, look, I wanted to meet because there are a number of things that we need to discuss and I wanted to make sure we're on the same page going into this, before all the lawyers and paperwork take over.

STEVE
OK.

BRAD
We're both professionals, neither of us has depended on the other over the years… I want us to end this marriage as equals, with each of us leaving with exactly what we put in. I don't want anything from you, and I hope you don't want anything from me.

STEVE
That's what I want, too.

(A WAITER arrives with their food, then wordlessly leaves.)

STEVE
(calling out)

Could I get some salt over here?

(The waiter nods)

BRAD
You haven't tasted it yet.

STEVE

I just know I'll want salt. Am I telling you how to eat your food?

(The WAITER returns with salt for the table)

BRAD

No.

STEVE

Right, because that would make me controlling, wouldn't it? And we *both* agree that's a bad quality in a human being, *right?*

(STEVE salts and then passive-aggressively takes a massive bite of the chicken BRAD ordered for him.)

BRAD

Forget I mentioned it. Your salt intake is between you and your cardiologist.

(BRAD nibbles at his own meal. A pause.)

STEVE

Actually, if we're being mature and open, there's something I need to know. When did you decide we were over?

BRAD

(smiling)

What makes you think there was one moment?

STEVE

I'll simplify the question. Was it before or after we tried being 'open'?

BRAD

That was as much your idea as mine. We needed to spice things up.

STEVE

You were already getting spice on the side, I only suggested being open to keep me in the sex loop.

BRAD

Did I think it would help? No.

STEVE
Well, you should have said so at the time. Or did you just want to get some threesomes in on the way out?

BRAD
I wanted to give *us* one last chance. I loved you.

(beat)

Sorry.

STEVE
(faking a businesslike demeanor)

So, you want to talk about assets?

BRAD
I guess not, if we're agreed we both want to be fair. Nobody takes what they didn't bring in.

STEVE
Well, I freed up my whole evening for this. What do you want to talk about, then?

BRAD
How's your mother holding up?

STEVE
She's still dead. Thanks for remembering.

BRAD
(uncertain)

But your father's still alive, right?

STEVE
If you can call it that. How's your sister?

BRAD
Still on welfare.

STEVE
Tell her she can visit if she wants. I'd still be happy to see her.

BRAD
She'd like that. And speaking of 'likes', gotten anyone good online lately?

STEVE
Do you mean, am I seeing anyone?

BRAD
Seeing, sleeping, sucking… interpret the question as you see fit.

STEVE
I am, actually.

BRAD
(choking on his food)

What?

STEVE
Seeing someone.

BRAD
Really?

STEVE
Why so surprised?

BRAD
I'm not, but… is he cute, though?

STEVE
(coyly)

He's alright.

BRAD
And exactly how blind is he?

STEVE
He has 20-20 vision, thank you for asking. Are you seeing someone?

(beat)

Or lots of someones?

BRAD
He's 32. Hung like a beluga whale. Ass you could crack a walnut with.

STEVE
Well, that should be handy at Christmas.

(beat)

Does he have a name, this walnut-cracker?

BRAD
Kris. What's yours called?

STEVE
Howie.

BRAD
Let me guess: fifty years old, combover, tenor in the gay men's chorus?

(STEVE whips out his phone and hands it to BRAD.)

Holy shitballs.

STEVE
(sarcastically)

You called it so well.

BRAD
How much are you paying him?

STEVE
Hourly, he earns more than I do.

BRAD
So, he *is* a hooker?

STEVE
Personal trainer, actually.

BRAD

I don't understand. How did you pull that?

(beat)

What's wrong with him? What's the catch?

STEVE
So far, the only catch is him.

BRAD
Hilarious.

STEVE
But you can judge for yourself, he'll be here in a minute.

BRAD
(alarmed)

He's coming here?

STEVE
Yeah, I hope that's OK?

BRAD
But I didn't order for him.

STEVE
I think he's capable of ordering for himself. In fact…

(Steve stands as HOWIE enters and approaches their table. HOWIE and STEVE kiss. HOWIE takes off his jacket revealing a muscular body under a tank top. BRAD looks on, horrified)

Howie, I'd like you to meet Brad.

BRAD
(stuttering)

Hi…

HOWIE
Oh, you're not at all how I imagined.

THREESOME

BRAD
(recovering)

Better looking, right?

HOWIE

I thought you'd be louder.

(pulls up a chair)

Thanks for freeing up Steve for me.

BRAD
(nervously)

Ha-ha...

HOWIE

So, what are you guys talking about?

STEVE

Just reliving old times.

BRAD

We were just talking about threesomes, actually...

HOWIE

They're never as fun as you'd think, are they?

BRAD

Maybe you've just not had the right company, then.

HOWIE

I've had a pretty good sample size.

STEVE

Let's get you some food, stud.

HOWIE

Actually, I need to use the bathroom. That detox tea was a mistake. Can you order for me?

STEVE

Of course, I can.

(they kiss again)

And stop drinking that shit!

(HOWIE goes off to the bathroom)

BRAD
Tell me he has a small dick.

STEVE
(smugly)

I thought we agreed not to lie to each other.

BRAD
He's weird then?

STEVE
Totally normal and down to earth.

BRAD
Does he make a weird face or sound when he comes?

STEVE
(laughing)

Do you know what *you* sound like?

BRAD
Majestic! Like a breaching whale.

STEVE
More like a damp squib.

BRAD
Then I don't get it. He's hot. He masculine. He's normal. What does he see in *you*?

STEVE
Sincere emotional connection.

THREESOME

BRAD

Bullshit.

(beat)

There isn't even a checkbox for that on Scruff.

STEVE

So, what about yours? What's he see in you?

BRAD

Raw, overwhelming physicality.

STEVE

I give it a month.

BRAD

(cerebrally)

It's like we were made for each other. I'm the yin to his yang, and that circle thing is the shape we make when we're sucking each other's dicks...

STEVE

This is a public restaurant, Brad.

BRAD

We're in the Castro.

(shouted to audience)

Who here likes sucking dick?

(cheers from offstage)

I rest my case.

STEVE

Can I see yours?

BRAD

My dick? I knew you'd miss it.

STEVE

I mean, show me a picture of Kris.

BRAD

I… I don't have one on my phone.

STEVE

Is he on Instagram?

BRAD

No.

(beat)

He's not lonely.

STEVE

Facebook then?

BRAD

He's not allowed to have an account.

STEVE

By his mom?

BRAD

By the CIA. And the FBI.

STEVE

Because he messages kids or something?

BRAD

Because he's a trained killer with top secret security clearance and biceps you could crack walnuts with.

STEVE

I thought you said that about his butt?

BRAD

Pistachios, then.

STEVE

I'm getting very concerned about your nut fetish.

(beat)

Seriously, you guys have never even taken a selfie together.

BRAD

(straining)

He doesn't have a phone.

STEVE

Now I *know* you're lying.

BRAD

Whatever. He's way hotter than your dude.

STEVE

Fiancé.

BRAD

I *beg* your pardon?

STEVE

We're engaged.

BRAD

That's illegal. You can't be engaged to him, you're still married to me.

STEVE

Right. And after you and I get divorced I'll be marrying him.

BRAD

But that's not fair. You can't!

STEVE

You could propose to James Bond if you wanted to.

BRAD

Well, yes, I *could*...

STEVE

Especially if you suddenly come into a lot of nuts you need cracking.

BRAD

Very droll.

STEVE
Why can't you be happy for me? You said you loved me!

BRAD
That doesn't mean I want you to be happy…

(beat)

…without me.

STEVE
You said we were going to be mature about this.

BRAD
You're the one getting married again!

(BRAD's phone buzzes on the table.)

STEVE
Your phone is ringing.

BRAD
I mean, how long have you even known him? He could be a criminal.

STEVE
You said you're dating a trained killer!

(beat)

And your phone is *still* ringing.

BRAD
How long would you have waited if I'd died?

STEVE
It depends. In this hypothetical scenario, was I the one who killed you?

(beat)

Will you please answer your goddamn phone?

STEVE
(answering his phone angrily)

Not now!

(calmer)

Oh, hi, Kris. No, of course I have time to talk to you, I thought you were someone else.

STEVE
So, he does have a phone, then.

BRAD
(into phone)

You're where? No! Stay there. I'll come to you.

STEVE
Is he close? Tell him to come and join us.

BRAD
(into phone)

Security compromised. Abort mission! Abort mission!

(BRAD hangs up the call)

STEVE
For God's sake, tell him to stop by.

BRAD
Impossible. Lives are at stake. We can finish this another day.

STEVE
What are you worried about?

(KRIS enters the restaurant and walks over to BRAD)

KRIS
Hi, guys!

STEVE

(unsure)

Kris?

(BRAD jumps to his feet, puts an arm around KRIS and escorts him to the door.)

BRAD

(angrily)

I told you to "abort mission."

KRIS

And I had no idea what that means

BRAD

It means we're leaving.

KRIS

But I just got here.

BRAD

Exactly.

(BRAD waves excuses and farewell to STEVE and he and KRIS leave. STEVE sits alone at the table until HOWIE returns.)

HOWIE

What did I miss?

STEVE

I think my ex has finally gone insane.

HOWIE

Good thing you've got me, then. Are we staying?

STEVE

I let him spoil fifteen years of my life. I'll be damned if he gets the chance to spoil any more.

HOWIE

Did you order for me?

THREESOME

                    STEVE
Sorry, I was distracted.

                    HOWIE
No worries. What's the beef like?

(STEVE leans forward and kisses HOWIE)

                    STEVE
It's pretty good.

              (BLACKOUT)

            (END OF SCENE)

ACT I

Scene 2

SETTING: Brad's house.

AT RISE: BRAD and KRIS sit on a couch eating microwave dinners in front of the TV.

KRIS
So, are we going to talk about what just happened?

BRAD
It's rude to talk with your mouth full.

(KRIS puts his plastic tray down on the table.)

KRIS
So, why am I eating, or not eating, *this* in front of the TV, instead of a nice dinner out like we planned?

BRAD
(enthusiastically)

Mine's delicious. Besides, restaurants all serve frozen food, anyway.

KRIS
Not the good ones.

BRAD
Steve and I never went to the good ones. That's why life is better with you.

KRIS
Because we eat frozen dinners on the couch at 11 p.m.?

BRAD
Exactly. It's more intimate.

KRIS
I hate that your lame excuses are cute.

BRAD
It's a talent.

(BRAD and KRIS kiss.)

KRIS
So, you're not embarrassed to introduce me to your ex?

BRAD
Yes and no.

KRIS
Not the answer I was looking for.

BRAD
Well, we are exes. It's complicated. Everything we do and everyone we meet ends up being compared to whatever we did during the many dark years we were together.

KRIS
Is that the yes or the no part?

BRAD
That's the yes part.

KRIS
What's the no part?

BRAD
(lying)
I don't think he can take how much better you are than him.

KRIS
Awww…

BRAD
Right? I'm adorable.

KRIS
And a little demonic.

BRAD
That's what makes me adorable.

KRIS

Yes, it is.

(KRIS cuddles up to BRAD.)

So, did I miss any quality drama?

BRAD

His mother's still dead.

KRIS

Oh, that's so sad.

BRAD

Isn't it?

KRIS

When did she die?

BRAD

(indifferently)

Who can say? Steve preferred to talk about feelings rather than the facts of the case.

KRIS

Geez. How did she die?

BRAD

I can't remember exactly, but I think it involved a carelessly placed traffic cone and a steamroller.

KRIS

That's terrible.

BRAD

I'd be guessing, but I imagine it made her very easy to bury.

KRIS

You're such a bullshitter. I love you.

BRAD

What are we watching, by the way? Is this RuPaul's Drug Race?

KRIS
No, but I think you just invented a new genre of entertainment that I wholeheartedly support.

BRAD
So, what is it then?

KRIS
No idea. Some sort of reality TV competition, where someone wins a million dollars and people get voted off one by one.

BRAD
Well, that's original. That guy's pretty hot, though.

KRIS
Didn't think he was your type. Black and muscly? Really?

BRAD
Yeah, you're right, he's not really. Must be the lighting.

(beat)

Not that I'm racist.

KRIS
So, what is your type? I don't look anything like Steve.

BRAD
Not everyone has a type.

KRIS
Does Steve, though? I thought I saw another jacket at dinner. Did he bring some Brad clone along? Is that why you wanted to leave? That'd be so awkward!

BRAD
(laughing)

No.

KRIS
(seriously)

No, he didn't bring someone, or no he didn't look like you?

BRAD

Like he would score this well twice!

KRIS

So, he did bring someone! What was he like?

BRAD

I honestly can't remember.

KRIS

So, not hot then?

BRAD

I mean...

KRIS

(firmly)

Was he hot?

BRAD

Some people might find him hot.

KRIS

Did the man look like a sex machine, Brad?

BRAD

What would you say a sex machine looks like?

KRIS

Was he handsome?

BRAD

Isn't that subjective?

KRIS

Does he look like he works out?

BRAD

I mean, he's probably seen the inside of a gym.

KRIS

Annually or five days a week?

BRAD

Maybe... six?

KRIS

(shocked)

Six times a week?

BRAD

(feebly)

Is it too late to say I meant six times a year?

KRIS

Yes. How big was he?

BRAD

I'm lost now. Are we defining a sex machine or the size of Steve's boyfriend's ripped, muscular body?

KRIS

I knew it!

(KRIS laughs hysterically, then notices BRAD isn't doing the same.)

So, why didn't you want to tell me Steve's got a mid-life crisis boy toy? That's hilarious.

BRAD

(thinking he's off the hook)

It's no big deal.

KRIS

No big…? Wait, you were embarrassed, weren't you?

BRAD

I mean, eating with your ex and his 20-something rebound is pretty embarrassing.

                    KRIS
I mean, you were embarrassed by me. Weren't you?

                    BRAD
Can I just say one thing before we go any further with this conversation?

                    KRIS
Yes?

                    BRAD
I love you.

                    KRIS
Oh my god, you'd *totally* do him, wouldn't you?

                    BRAD
I mean, if I was single… maybe?

                    KRIS
But you're not single.

                    BRAD
Exactly. I'm in a relationship. And it's amazing. Just like this dinner.

(KRIS picks up his tray again, and takes a bite.)

                    KRIS
Yeah. Amazing.

(a moment's silence as they eat.)

So, here's a hypothetical.

                    BRAD
What?

                    KRIS
You're single. You've just left Steve. You're in a club with two strange men, me and this fella….

                    BRAD
Howie.

KRIS
Howie?

BRAD
That's his name.

KRIS
Fine. You're in a club with me and Howie. You don't know anything about either of us. Which of us are you taking home?

BRAD
Well, that's not fair, is it? I don't just love you for your face.

KRIS
So, you're saying he's more handsome?

BRAD
No, I'm saying there's more to you than a pretty face and biceps so big they would force you to buy custom shirts.

KRIS
I don't have to buy custom shirts.

BRAD
Exactly. You're so much more than that.

KRIS
Alright. What part of me do you find hottest?

BRAD
Just *one*?

KRIS
Go on.

BRAD
How do I pick *one*?

KRIS
Do you like my hair?

BRAD

I mean, it's getting a bit long, but…

KRIS

Do you like my body?

BRAD

What about it?

(KRIS leans in close to BRAD, groping his crotch.)

KRIS

Does it turn you on the way Howie's does?

BRAD

You're very different…

(he struggles to free himself of KRIS' grip)

…shapes.

KRIS

It's a yes or no question.

BRAD

(cheerfully)

You have cute ears.

KRIS

Yes or no?

BRAD

Of course, no! He's a fucking personal trainer that works out six times a week, of course he's fucking hotter than you are…

KRIS

I knew it!

BRAD

(recovering)

But you are smarter, kinder, wiser, funnier, and actually clever enough to call me on my bullshit, and not get angry at me just because I find someone else physically attractive. You know *I'm* more than that. And I know *you're* more than that.

KRIS

I get it. We're human. It's unrealistic to expect either one of us to walk around with a pair of blinkers on.

BRAD

Right! It's just annoying that this particular hunk happens to be Steve's new boyfriend.

KRIS

And not yours.

BRAD

Guys like that are cardboard, Kris. They look great, but there's no depth to them. And they probably dissolve in the rain. Fun for a night, but not worth sharing a life with.

KRIS

And I am?

BRAD

Why wouldn't you be? Look, I can lie to you and say that I don't find Howie attractive. I can lie and say I'm happy that Steve has landed himself a total hottie. Or we can admit that gay men are shallow as hell and usually think with the wrong head. You know it's ridiculous. I know it's ridiculous. And yet here we are.

KRIS

Well, he'd better live up to the hype you're giving him. I don't want you getting distracted for anything less than an '8', got it?

BRAD

And that right there is why I love you.

KRIS

Why?

BRAD

Because you get me. You're the full package.

                              KRIS
Ugh. You win for now. I'm off to bed.

(KRIS kisses BRAD and exits.)

                              BRAD
(to himself)

And Steve is going to pay for landing himself a hotter boyfriend than me.

                            (BLACKOUT)

                           (END OF SCENE)

ACT I

Scene 3

SETTING: Steve's apartment

AT RISE: BRAD sits at a table. STEVE carries a tray of snacks over and sets them down, before taking a seat himself.

STEVE
(gesturing to food)

It's nothing fancy.

BRAD
It never was.

(beat)

I'm kidding.

STEVE
So, let's just get down to it. Should be easy enough.

BRAD
Indeed. No arguing, no shouting.

STEVE
We don't have any children to fight over. And we don't even have any pets anymore.

BRAD
Rest in peace, Skippy.

STEVE
You hated that dog.

BRAD
(warmly)

Yes.

(beat)

But as the insurance investigator said, *no one* could have foreseen my brakes failing like that.

STEVE
You are so lucky we agreed not to shout. So, where do we start, the house?

BRAD
Well, we have always earned about the same amount. Always split the mortgage fifty-fifty. So, I'd say the house should be split equally.

STEVE
So, when do you think you'll be moving out?

BRAD
What do you mean?

STEVE
Well, aren't we going to sell it and split the proceeds?

BRAD
Shit, I didn't think about that. Getting a divorce is stressful enough without throwing moving on top. How about I pay the whole mortgage until I do move, and then you'll get your half. Does that seem fair to you?

STEVE
Sure, that sounds reasonable.

BRAD
See? This will be easy.

STEVE
What about the condo in Puerto Vallarta?

BRAD
Sell it.

STEVE
But that's where we spent our first anniversary

BRAD
You *really* want to remember that?

STEVE

Those were good times.

BRAD
It's also where you got arrested for being drunk on the beach at 3 a.m. wearing a sombrero.

STEVE
I wasn't *that* drunk!

BRAD
You were only wearing a sombrero

STEVE
Alright, *mostly* good times. But I love PV!

BRAD
Well, make me an offer for my half. Or you can give me something you have in exchange, like Howie…

(quickly)

…I mean, your car.

STEVE
What do you mean, 'your half'? I paid for most of that condo! I found it, I negotiated it, I found the plumber *and* the interior decorator.

BRAD
He was your ex! And I never liked the tiger print.

STEVE
You said you loved it! That's why I got the thong!

BRAD
We say a lot of things we don't mean when we're in love.

STEVE
And my BMW is worth a lot more than your 'half' share in a vacation home.

BRAD
Have you tried selling a used car before? I'm being generous.

STEVE
I'm not selling Ariana.

BRAD
I refuse to dignify the ridiculous name you gave your car.

STEVE
She's not just a car, she has feelings. Unlike you.

BRAD
Also, I want the TV. It goes with the sound system and I'm not going through another installation again.

STEVE
Fine. Then I get the grill.

BRAD
(serving himself snacks)

But you don't know how to cook!

STEVE
(grabbing BRAD's plate away from him)

No, but I was the only one who ever made the effort to. If you'd had your way we would have lived on takeout for the fifteen years we were together.

BRAD
(BRAD grabs the plate back)

Bar food isn't takeout. It's only takeout if you pick it up and drive it home.

STEVE
So, you want to stay in the house, with the TV and the sound system, and half the condo… and all I get is a grill?

BRAD
And you half of the condo, plus your car, for which I am the registered owner, let me remind you.

STEVE
That's just because that stupid cop gave me a DUI.

(beat)

You were drunker than I was!

BRAD
But you were stupider and decided to drive.

STEVE
Because if I didn't get you out of there, you'd have had an orgy with the host, his husband, and the houseboy.

BRAD
You could have joined in!

STEVE
No, that's not a fair trade. I've made all the payments on that car. If you want to stay in the house, I want the lawnmower and the trailer as well.

BRAD
So, you and Howie can go off to the woods together? I don't think so.

STEVE
You never liked camping.

BRAD
I like you hooking up with some himbo in the woods even less.

STEVE
What has Howie got to do with any of this? You left me!

BRAD
Fine. Have the trailer, but I get the Yoko Ono prints.

STEVE
No. Fucking. Way. Those prints are worth $10,000 a piece!

BRAD
You thought Yoko Ono was a Chinese restaurant!

STEVE
It was an easy mistake.

BRAD

It's a Japanese name! Anyway, I paid for them!

STEVE

With money from our joint account. And I knew who she was, really! It's pretty hard not to Google who someone is when your husband is blowing thousands of dollars on them. Regardless, we should sell them. Unless you want to give me something else. Like your Rolex.

BRAD

(clutching his wristwatch)

This was a gift.

STEVE

Not anymore.

BRAD

You can't take back gifts!

STEVE

But you can take back vows? That makes no sense!

(beat)

I think I still have the receipt somewhere.

BRAD

(threatening)

You take it, I break it! You'll have to cut the damn thing off of my limp, dead wrist.

STEVE

Fine.

BRAD

Fine!

STEVE

I'll need the knife set as well then!

BRAD

Did you just threaten me?

                    STEVE
(laughing)

Of course not.

(STEVE walks back over to the kitchen area and picks up a steak knife and brandishes it)

Because I have a perfectly good knife right here!

(HOWIE enters the apartment in gym attire, having just finished working out. He looks at the knife, and the angry faces before him.)

                    HOWIE
Going about as well as I figured, then.

                    STEVE
(putting the knife down)

Hey, handsome! No, we're just joking.

(STEVE kisses HOWIE)

We agreed not to make a scene.

                    BRAD
Totally amicable.

                    HOWIE
Good, because it looked like you were about to kill each other.

                    STEVE
His face always looks like that.

                    BRAD
And you can't kill something that's been dead inside for years.

                    HOWIE
Amicable? Sure.

                    BRAD
Been working out?

HOWIE

No, I was just working on my doctoral thesis.

(beat)

Just kidding, yeah, blasted these pecs. Alright with you guys if I use the shower? Wouldn't make you uncomfortable or anything?

BRAD

(a little flirtatiously)

No, not uncomfortable at all.

HOWIE

Cool.

(HOWIE takes off his tank top, tossing it over Steve's chair, and exits stage left)

STEVE

Have you finished ogling my boyfriend yet?

BRAD

I can't help it if your boyfriend wants to flirt with me.

STEVE

He was not flirting.

BRAD

He took his shirt off!

STEVE

Howie doesn't like shirts.

BRAD

How awful for you.

STEVE

Anyway, thank you again for reminding me why we didn't work.

BRAD

Seriously though, how the fuck did you land someone like Howie? You don't even like sex! That's why I had to go looking elsewhere.

STEVE
You did *not* just blame me for your infidelity?

BRAD
Ooh, I'm so fancy, I use words like infidelity. It's sex, Steve.

STEVE
The thing is, Brad, I actually like sex. Just not with you.

BRAD
Bullshit.

STEVE
Spit is not enough, Brad.

BRAD
Lies.

STEVE
Foreplay is not optional.

BRAD
Of course, it is. Everyone fast-forwards through those bits anyway, they're just there to make the videos longer.

STEVE
And it is not a race to see who can come first.

BRAD
You're only saying that because I always won.

STEVE
(sigh)

Only you could brag about premature ejaculation.

BRAD
It's not premature, it's exactly when I want it!

STEVE

You know, a considerate lover, like Howie, actually cares about how I feel during sex.

BRAD

Well, he's probably after your money, then.

STEVE

He *loves* me.

BRAD

Oh, you're in love, are you? How long have you been dating, a couple of months? And you're already engaged! What are you, lesbians? Will you be getting matching haircuts too?

STEVE

You are such a cunt.

BRAD

And you are a boring, frigid, dried-up waste of one.

STEVE

Fine, I want the sling we bought and both of the harnesses. They're all packed away in the garage, still in their boxes. Unused.

(At this point, HOWIE walks in in nothing but a towel)

BRAD

If you think I'm going to let you and your little fuck-toy...

HOWIE

(laughing)

Whoa, whoa, whoa... You're arguing over sex toys? I don't want anything the two of you have used.

BRAD

(spitefully, pointing at the solitary towel around HOWIE's waist)

And I want the Martha Stewart towel set!

(BLACKOUT)

(END OF SCENE)

ACT I

Scene 4

SETTING: Brad's house.

AT RISE: KRIS sits on the couch scrolling through his phone. A frenzied BRAD enters.

KRIS
So, how did it go?

BRAD
Well, things are clearer now.

KRIS
You guys sorted it out?

BRAD
No.

(beat)

I'm going to take him down.

KRIS
That doesn't sound like "sorted." I thought we'd all agreed it was going to be amicable.

BRAD
I thought we agreed we weren't going to nag one another.

KRIS
All I'm asking is, did things go the way you wanted them to when you left our house two hours ago.

BRAD
Yes… and no.

KRIS
That is literally impossible. Did you get the BMW?

BRAD

No, he's got a death grip on Ariana. There is no way he's letting me have her.

(beat)

But look, let's not talk about him. I want to do something for us.

KRIS

That sounds nice. What is it?

BRAD

So, I'm going to have to lead into this.

(beat)

You love me, right?

KRIS

That's a scary way to start.

BRAD

What I mean is, there's something I have to say, and I want you to know I love you, and that you trust me, because it's heavy.

KRIS

(squealing)

Oh my God, are you proposing?

BRAD

Don't be stupid, of course I'm not proposing. No, I want to talk about something much more important. There's something that's been eating me up, and it's going to sound terrible, but I need to say it for *us*, because if I don't, it'll ruin our relationship in the end, and I want this to work.

(beat)

Because I love you and all that.

KRIS

And all that?

BRAD

Yes. All that.

KRIS
OK. What is it you want to say?

BRAD
Well, I've had what you might call a revelation.

KRIS
Have you found Jesus?

BRAD
Christ, no. We are not becoming one of *those* couples.

KRIS
Are you turning vegan?

BRAD
No! What am I, a lesbian?

KRIS
Well, maybe the butch kind.

BRAD
Butch, yes, that's good. Now, where to start?

KRIS
You're transitioning?

BRAD
Shut up and let me finish. We both agree that we love each other unconditionally, right? That we both have worth as individuals. We're free to follow our dreams and that we're not going to try and change the other person?

KRIS
Yes.

BRAD
What if there was some incy wincy little thing about you that could be a little better for *us* to work as a couple?

KRIS

Isn't "better" subjective?

BRAD

Not for me.

KRIS

That's the definition of subjective.

BRAD

You see the thing is, Howie, Steve's new boyfriend... he's very... well put together.

(beat)

And you... are

KRIS

Better-educated, better-paid, better-dressed, and better in bed.

BRAD

Do we know that for a fact?

KRIS

I'm your boyfriend, ergo the sex we having is officially the best you've ever had...

(beat)

...or we're breaking up.

BRAD

Yes, but really, how can you judge?

KRIS

Have you ever slept with a guy like Howie?

BRAD

Not yet.

KRIS

I'd prefer "no".

BRAD

OK, "No." Have you?

KRIS

Not with Howie, I've never met the guy. But based on your previous description of "pornstar-tier ebony muscleboy" ... I've had a few.

BRAD

You?

KRIS

No need to sound surprised!

BRAD

Just... I mean... you've never mentioned it before.

KRIS

You've never given me a complete list of who you've boned.

BRAD

Right.

KRIS

Well, if you had a guy like that, you'd know I'm better. Anyone can look like that with enough time and a gym membership, it's just a lazy way to avoid learning to be good in bed.

BRAD

(smiling)

I'm glad you said *anyone* can.

KRIS

Why?

BRAD

(enthusiastically)

I got you a gym membership.

KRIS

You did *what?*

BRAD

We agreed to be honest with each other, right?

KRIS

Yes, but...

BRAD

So, I need to be honest. So, here we go. Howie is way more physically attractive than you are and it's eating me alive that Steve is dating him.

KRIS

What the actual fuck?

BRAD

And it's shallow and base and illogical and all of those things... but it's real, and inescapable and pretending that I feel any other way would be dishonest to us.

KRIS

Did you just say "us"?

BRAD

Yes, because you are my soulmate.

(beat)

Deep down. Beneath...

(beat)

...you.

KRIS

Suddenly, you don't think I'm sexy?

BRAD

It's not that you're not sexy, it's that Howie... is like the physical embodiment of sex.

KRIS

When did you become so fucking shallow?

BRAD

When I got a boner while trying to divorce my ex and his super-hot boyfriend walked in, and it was basically the worst feeling ever.

KRIS
I don't believe this is happening.

BRAD
You can't be mad at me for being honest.

KRIS
Of course, I can. If this is how you feel, maybe you should be dating Howie instead of me.

BRAD
Don't be stupid, I can't do that.

KRIS
Why not?

BRAD
Because Steve's already dating him.

(beat)

And I'm dating you.

KRIS
Oh, and you have to just settle for me, is that it?

BRAD
I'm not settling for you. You are amazing. You are kind, intelligent, you laugh at my jokes, we have similar interests, and you give really good blowjobs.

KRIS
None of those are about my body.

BRAD
But if we could just cut and paste you onto Howie's body, then you'd be better! Objectively! So really, if you think about it, I'm just helping you achieve your full potential. Objectively.

KRIS
How old are you?

BRAD
45.

KRIS
And what do you think you're going to look like in twenty years' time?

BRAD
Still awesome?

KRIS
No. You're already going gray, it's not going to stop. Nor are the stretch marks on your ass, and believe me, they're there. You're going to be haggard and wrinkled, but I don't care because sex and sexual attraction are not the same.

BRAD
You're saying you won't find me attractive in twenty years' time?

KRIS
I don't care how you'll look in twenty years' time. We will still be having amazing sex.

BRAD
I'm not sure I like the picture of the future you're drawing

KRIS
How do you think old couples have sex?

BRAD
Don't be disgusting.

KRIS
Seriously, what did you think they do?

BRAD
Never take their clothes off and slowly decay in retirement homes.

KRIS
There were like fifty old couples on that cruise.

BRAD
Yes, but they weren't screwing each other!

KRIS
They so *were*.

BRAD
Now *I* need to go to the gym.

KRIS
To hold off the inevitable tide of entropy breaking down your shallow little body?

BRAD
No, for the view…

(beat)

… to wash out those images you just dumped into my mind.

KRIS
The point is that physical beauty fades. It's what's inside that counts.

BRAD
And I agree with you one hundred percent.

KRIS
But?

BRAD
But my penis isn't capable of logic. It just likes what it likes. And it likes Howie.

KRIS
Fine. What do I get?

BRAD
(confused)

What do you mean?

KRIS
If it makes you happy, I'll start going to the gym. I'll change my lifestyle to better suit you and what you want. What do I get in return?

BRAD

You get *me*.

KRIS

Nope. I get a better version of you. That's what you're asking of me.

BRAD

How can I be better?

KRIS

I am so glad you asked. There are so many possibilities. Anger management sounds like a good one. You could *join* me in the gym? Couples' classes are more fun.

BRAD

I don't have time for any of that nonsense.

KRIS

Then what I do I get?

BRAD

How about an allowance?

KRIS

No.

BRAD

I could swallow?

KRIS

No!

BRAD

Oh, you always wanted the left-hand side of the bed! It's yours!

KRIS

None of those involve the kind of change you expect of me.

BRAD

I offered to swallow!

KRIS

You need to see a therapist.

BRAD
I take it back, I'll join you at the gym.

KRIS
Nope. You need to sit down with someone, on a regular basis, and talk about your feelings and how they relate to me and the rest of your life.

BRAD
But that is so much work!

KRIS
So is bodybuilding, babe.

BRAD
But…

KRIS
No buts. I will start going to the gym. You will start seeing a therapist. Are we agreed?

BRAD
(suspiciously)

And you'll look more like Howie?

KRIS
If that's what you want, then yes. And you'll learn to stop obsessing over other people's relationships and unhealthily comparing them to your own.

BRAD
You think that's what therapy will be like?

KRIS
I can only hope.

BRAD
Deal! I bought you dumbbells on Amazon too, they're arriving tomorrow.

KRIS
You are a piece of work. OK, I need to return some books to the library.

BRAD

Is that still a thing?

KRIS

For those of us that actually read, yes.

(beat)

But I'm glad we got to have this heart to heart. It proves that we discuss these kind of issues like adults.

BRAD

In a calm, mature and measured way.

KRIS

Exactly.

(KRIS leaves. BRAD immediately dials a number on his phone)

BRAD

(into phone)

Hi, is that Bradshaw, Burns and Wallace?

(beat)

You're divorce lawyers, right?

(beat)

So, how much to rip the entrails of a man out through his throat, but, like, legally?

(beat)

Sold!

(BLACKOUT)

(END OF SCENE)

ACT I

Scene 5

SETTING: Steve's apartment. There is a massage table center stage.

AT RISE: STEVE enters in a bathrobe and turns down the lights. He ignites some scented candles and puts on an overly romantic instrumental version of ABBA's 'Fernando'.

HOWIE enters from stage left. They kiss passionately. HOWIE gestures to the table, which STEVE approaches. And then...

STEVE
(bashfully)

Could you... humor me and turn around?

HOWIE
Why?

STEVE
(gripping bathrobe)

It's just...

HOWIE
You're kidding.

STEVE
No, I'm serious.

HOWIE
There isn't a part of your body I don't already know intimately.

STEVE
Yeah, but that's when we're, like, in bed. This is different.

HOWIE
How?

STEVE
It just is.

HOWIE

(giving in)

Fine!

(STEVE tastefully disrobes and climbs on to the massage table underneath a white sheet)

HOWIE

(oiling STEVE's back)

You're ridiculous.

STEVE

Just shut up and rub me.

HOWIE

Wow, you're really tense.

STEVE

Why do you think?

HOWIE

Brad?

STEVE

I had a call from my ooooooowwwwwww!

HOWIE

Well, you need to relax.

STEVE

(shouting)

I am relaxing. This is me relaxed… and going through a divorce.

HOWIE

Where do you feel it?

STEVE

In my wallet, mainly.

THREESOME

HOWIE

I meant the tension.

STEVE

So, did I. A little high…. Mmm.

HOWIE

Right there?

STEVE

Mmmmfblegbleblmmmf.

HOWIE

Who was the phone call from?

STEVE

From mmmmmy lawyer, which is doubly stressful. Firstly, because I know Brad has thought up some new ridiculous demand, and secondly because it's knowing costing me $500 just for my lawyer to tell me what it is.

HOWIE

Why can't the two of you just work it out together?

STEVE

(laughs maniacally)

You'd think two grown-ups could, right? But it turns out that divorce turns you into children, and you need to pay other grown-ups to divide the toys between you. Can you get a little lower?

HOWIE

(running hands down Steve's spine)

What did you ever see in that guy?

STEVE

He's confident. Energetic. Fun. Or at least, he was at the beginning. Always seemed to know what he wanted, even if it was never consistent. Life with him was the proverbial roller coaster.

HOWIE

So, what happened?

STEVE

I got motion sickness.

(beat)

That and all of a sudden, I wasn't enough for him.

HOWIE

If you were, would you two still…

STEVE

I hope not. Because now I know he wasn't enough for me, either. We were both so young when we got together. Gay life was different back then. These days I think young guys should play the field before they settle down. That way they can better understand what it is they want.

HOWIE

How young was young?

STEVE

We were in our twenties. But twenty was younger back then.

HOWIE

I'm twenty-five. You saying I don't know what I want?

STEVE

(HOWIE pushes too hard)

Ow!

HOWIE

Sorry, lost focus. You were saying I don't know what I want.

STEVE

Do you?

HOWIE

I mean, this feels right, the two of us together. It feels like what I need. I love you.

(silence.)

Did you just tense up? Because I said the L word?

STEVE
Right now, the L word for me is "lawyer."

HOWIE
Do you think I can't love you because it's only been six months?

STEVE
You know, there was one-time Brad and I didn't talk for six months. I'm not even kidding. We were remodeling the lounge and...

HOWIE
...didn't agree on the paint color?

STEVE
No, we agreed on the color, just not on the name for it. You know, paint stores always give colors ridiculous names? Well, they had this one in Home Depot we both loved. Purple Midnight. But the name pissed Brad off, because he'd keep saying that midnight isn't purple, it's black. And because he kept blowing up about it, I kept using the name, in and out of context, just to annoy him.

I remember hearing someone once refer to "that special person you want to annoy for the rest of your life." And that's one of the great things about spending so much time with someone. You get to learn where all of their buttons are, and you get to push them one by one. Sometimes you change up the order to see if it makes a different tune. And sometimes you press all of them at once, just like a kid in an elevator.

Anyway, it got to the point where we couldn't sit in the room without arguing. And then we couldn't think about the room without arguing. And then we couldn't talk without arguing, so we just didn't.

For six months.

And then one day, we were just sitting in the lounge, not talking, and he said, "Let's paint it beige."

And I said, "Fine."

Six months, over like that.

HOWIE

Well, six months is a long time to me. And I love you, even if you don't love me.

STEVE
Of course, I love you, Howie. I mean, what isn't there to love? You're perfect. I think love just takes on a different meaning when you've previously seen it turn to ash.

HOWIE
You remember we're engaged right?

STEVE
Of course, I do, but we agreed to a long engagement and I explained to you why that needed to be the case.

(he sighs)

You see, marriage is all about love and passion and romance. Whereas divorce is about deadlines, depositions and disclosure. And who in their wisdom decided that, in the State of California, two people can get married in just twenty-four hours, but can't get divorced in less than nine months?

HOWIE
Do you think we have any issues?

STEVE
Every couple has issues. You show me a couple that doesn't have issues and I'll show you a burial plot for two.

HOWIE
What issues do we have?

STEVE
Seriously?

HOWIE
Yeah. How can I get better if I don't know my faults are?

STEVE
Well, for one thing, you're arguing with me when you're supposed to be giving me a massage. If you weren't doing it for free, I'd ask for a refund.

HOWIE

Turn over for me.

(STEVE turns over onto his back, looking up at HOWIE)

STEVE
But seriously there's nothing I'd change about you. Maybe that's a fault in and of itself.

HOWIE
Are you going to ask me?

STEVE
Ask you what?

HOWIE
What your faults are.

STEVE
I thought you said I was perfect just the way I am.

HOWIE
You are. Or you would be if you lost 20 pounds.

STEVE
(outraged)

20 pounds? Are you calling me fat as well?

HOWIE
(calmly)

I'm saying you're older than me, and I want you to live as long as possible. We don't have as long as I would have if I dated someone my own age.

STEVE
I'm not dying! It's called 'middle age' because you still have half of your life ahead of you.

HOWIE
Not the way you eat.

STEVE
Is this about that Keto thing again?

HOWIE

It doesn't have to be Keto. But come on, maybe try some vegetables that aren't fried. Eat less Oreos? It's not rocket science.

STEVE

Fine. Only if you cook them.

HOWIE

You always complain when I cook.

STEVE

That's because you use vegetables.

HOWIE

OK, fine.

STEVE

I want something else as well.

HOWIE

What?

STEVE

A vacation.

HOWIE

We've talked about this. It's fine for you, you get paid time off. I'm self-employed. And if I go away, my clients don't get to work out.

STEVE

I know, which is why I'll pay for the trip. I just want some time away from our everyday lives somewhere with sunshine, margaritas and a beach. And if you want me to start eating kale and wheatgrass, then you have to give me this.

HOWIE

I could get Julio to train my clients while we're gone.

STEVE

See, that wasn't so hard was it?

HOWIE

OK, let's work the rest of those knots out. Then we're good.

STEVE
I love it when you're assertive.

HOWIE
Ha. You're usually the one bossing me around.

STEVE
Am I?

HOWIE
Yes.

STEVE
Well then, ditch those clothes and join me on the table.

HOWIE
Can it even hold us both?

STEVE
Who knows? Only one way to find out.

(HOWIE takes his shirt off and joins STEVE on the table.)

(BLACKOUT)

(END OF SCENE)

ACT I

Scene 6

SETTING: Pinnacle Gym, the Castro

AT RISE: KRIS is sitting, working out on the lat pull-down machine. His form is wrong. HOWIE enters.

HOWIE
Whoa, stop!

(KRIS lets go suddenly. We hear the weights drop.)

KRIS
What?

HOWIE
Don't drop the weights!

KRIS
Then don't startle me!

HOWIE
I was trying to stop you from throwing your back out! You were leaning back way too much. Bad form can really get you hurt.

KRIS
Wait, you mean trying to get healthy can be super dangerous?

HOWIE
Yeah. Couldn't you feel the strain in your back?

KRIS
I assumed the strain was the muscles growing.

HOWIE
You really need to learn what you're doing. Weight training is a skillset like anything else. You should sign up for some personal training sessions.

KRIS
Is that what you did?

HOWIE
No, all this is natural.

KRIS
Really?

HOWIE
Of course not. I was a sportsman all through college, I've got a degree in kinesiology, and I work out almost every day.

KRIS
You can get a degree in lifting things?

HOWIE
It's more than just lifting. Nutrition, muscle movement, physiology. But you don't have to know all that, because you've got me.

KRIS
I do?

HOWIE
If you want. I know my shit.

KRIS
You definitely look like it.

HOWIE
I'm a trainer here. Sign up for some private sessions with me!

KRIS
I can do that?

HOWIE
For sixty-five dollars an hour. It's cheaper if you buy a package. And you get to make a commitment to yourself at the same time. It keeps you coming back.

KRIS
But it's on top of the cost of my gym membership?

HOWIE
Think of it like college. You can pay tuition, but you've still got to get textbooks. And believe me, they're expensive as hell.

KRIS
And you've got to put in the hours, right?

HOWIE
Damn straight.

KRIS
How often do you work out?

HOWIE
Well, I try to work out twice a day, but it's normally only six times a week.

KRIS
Only? That's a commitment.

HOWIE
What can I say? You get out of it what you put in.

KRIS
Sounds like a relationship.

HOWIE
What are your fitness goals? Why are you here?

KRIS
Goals?

HOWIE
Are you trying to lift a certain weight? Lose fat? Gain muscle? Give boys whiplash looking at that caboose?

KRIS
I don't know? I want to look 'fit', I guess?

HOWIE
There are a lot of kinds of 'fit'.

KRIS
There are?

HOWIE
Those long-distance runners from Ethiopia are fit. You want to look like

them?

KRIS
They look like they could use a sandwich.

HOWIE
So, what kind of body do you want? Bodybuilder, jock, twink, twunk? What do you think looks hot on a guy?

KRIS
What makes you think I'm gay?

HOWIE
You were staring the way they all do.

KRIS
Wait, you're not--?

HOWIE
Of course, I am, bitch: gay and fabulous.

KRIS
I was actually admiring your... shorts. Where did you get them?

HOWIE
A follower of mine on Instagram sent them. He wanted to see me in them. Bit weird, but they're my size, I like them, and they were free, so, like, score.

KRIS
Does that happen a lot?

HOWIE
Usually with things a lot less socially acceptable than gym shorts.

KRIS
So... and this is not a come-on... do you have a boyfriend? Is he okay with that?

HOWIE
Sure do. And not really, but he likes them on me, too, so we're good.

KRIS
And he likes the way you look?

HOWIE
What's not to like? Your guy digs you, right?

KRIS
Let's just say he bought me the gym membership as a 'gift'?

HOWIE
Damn, that's cold.

(beat)

But look, it's paining me to see you use this stuff wrong, and my usual 1:30's moved to P-town, so I'm free for a bit. Why don't I give you a free session so you don't look totally clueless, maybe help you have a little fun with lifting.

KRIS
And you're not going to charge me?

HOWIE
That's what free means where I come from.

KRIS
That would be awesome.

HOWIE
Well, since you're on the pulldown machine, we might as well do back day. So, let's start with the right posture.

(HOWIE helps KRIS adjust his seated position on the pulldown machine.)

Back straight. Head up. Don't lean forward. Arms like this.

(HOWIE adjusts KRIS' elbows)

And let's take the weight down to something you can actually lift properly!

KRIS
I tried 60! It was too easy!

HOWIE
That's because you were doing it wrong. Start small, do more reps.

(KRIS starts the pulldown)

KRIS
This is the right form?

HOWIE
Sure is.

KRIS
But it feels harder.

HOWIE
It does when you're doing it properly. It means you're isolating the muscle.

(beat)

So, why are you with this guy if he doesn't like the way you look?

KRIS
Of course, he likes the way I look. Otherwise, he would be mentally torturing someone else right now. He wants me, but, like… more…

HOWIE
Well, if you're gonna get bigger or whatever. Do it for yourself, not for him. Anyway, you've already got that hot nerd vibe going for you.

KRIS
Is that even a thing?

HOWIE
You don't think that guy that plays Spider-Man is hot?

KRIS
As long as you're not referring to Tobey Maguire.

HOWIE
Then it's a thing. Peter Parker: ultimate hot nerd. That's enough reps, by the way, take a breather.

(beat)

So, is your fella into working out?

KRIS

I don't think he's ever seen the inside of a gym outside of porn.

HOWIE

But he expects you to be?

KRIS

Honestly, it might just be a phase. He gets like this about dumb things sometimes. But I guess this is one of the better ones? It's healthy to be muscly, right?

HOWIE

It can be.

KRIS

What does your boyfriend look like? Do you guys work out together?

HOWIE

No, I do this for me, I don't think it should be a requirement. My guy's different. A bit older, actually.

KRIS

Mine too. Older guys are hot.

HOWIE

Right? All that experience and confidence. It's comfy.

KRIS

Comfy? Are you dating a sofa?

HOWIE

You know what I mean.

KRIS

Sounds like someone has some daddy issues.

HOWIE

Maybe. I can still appreciate younger guys. I just like a guy with a bit of substance and culture. Millennials are just so... flakey.

KRIS

Nah, I know what it is.

HOWIE
What?

KRIS
You just want someone who gets adulting better than you do.

HOWIE
Okay, you got me. How are those muscles feeling?

KRIS
Kinda tight?

HOWIE
You didn't stretch, did you?

KRIS
I have to stretch?

HOWIE
Come on.

(HOWIE pulls KRIS over to an exercise mat, lays him down, and helps him stretch. As they talk, they work through various stretches, getting more intimate with contact.)

KRIS
I feel like old people have life so easy.

HOWIE
I mean, boomers, right? They have no clue. "Just ask them for a job," I mean, are you kidding me? Nobody hires that way anymore!

KRIS
And do they know how much student debt I have? I can't just take any job.

HOWIE
And how many jobs is that degree getting you?

KRIS
None.

HOWIE

Preach. And they blame avocado toast for us not having savings.

KRIS

I've never even bought avocado toast!

HOWIE

Me either! Who does that?

KRIS

And Heaven forbid we even think about owning a house one day. Like, no one earns that kind of money!

HOWIE

Sometimes I wonder if I'm dating an older guy just so I can just inherit his stuff when he dies.

KRIS

Modern financial planning for the young, hot and gay.

HOWIE

It works!

KRIS

Mine keeps talking about savings, investments and...

(shudders)

...pensions.

HOWIE

What even is a pension?

KRIS

Right? But you know what the really scary thing is?

HOWIE

What?

KRIS

We're probably going to need to know what it is one day.

HOWIE

God, I hope not.

KRIS
Hopefully the seas will rise and society will collapse first.

HOWIE
You're really smart, you know that?

KRIS
Not smart enough to stretch beforehand.

HOWIE
None of the people here are.

KRIS
You mean you don't stretch all of them out on an exercise mat?

HOWIE
Only the cute ones.

KRIS
You think I'm cute?

HOWIE
You don't?

(KRIS moves in and kisses HOWIE)

HOWIE
Wow.

KRIS
Sorry.

HOWIE
Don't be.

(HOWIE pulls KRIS into a longer kiss.)

(CURTAIN)

(END OF ACT)

ACT 2

Scene 1

SETTING: Brad's house.

There is a bed center stage with TWO BODIES under the covers.

AT RISE: They are asleep.

(STEVE sits up in bed. Smiles to himself, looking around the room. Sees the lump of a body next to him. Double-take. STEVE jumps out of bed.)

                              STEVE

Oh, my fucking God!

(STEVE runs to his phone to check the time and for text messages. His phone has died)

Shit.

(STEVE hesitates to wake the other man, but has no other option. He shakes him.)

Hey. You awake?

(STEVE shakes him again.)

Oh, come on, we both know you sleep with one eye open.

(STEVE shoves the OTHER MAN out of the bed and onto the floor)

WAKE UP!

                              BRAD
(picking himself up off of the floor and getting back into bed)

What the fuck is your problem?

                              STEVE

My problem? We just… never mind what we just did or didn't do, where you do you keep your phone charger?

BRAD
(rolling to his feet and standing)

In the drawer, on this side.

STEVE
(retrieving the charger and charging his phone)

Why don't you have it plugged into the wall like any normal human being?

BRAD
It wastes power.

STEVE
When the fuck did you ever care about the environment?

BRAD
I care about the bill.

STEVE
(looking at his phone)

Why do these things take so long to turn on?

BRAD
What's the emergency?

STEVE
We just fucked and my boyfriend will want to know where I am.

BRAD
So, we did fuck? A second ago you didn't seem certain.

STEVE
I *was* certain, I just didn't want to be.

BRAD
Well, that's OK then. I mean, no one wants their love-making to be unmemorable.

STEVE
That was *not* love.

BRAD
Calm down, it's just a figure of speech.

STEVE
Finally! God, Howie, I'm so sorry... oh.

BRAD
He is panicking, then?

STEVE
(calmly)

No voicemail. Zero texts.

BRAD
Oh. Maybe he forgot that has a fiancé?

STEVE
Don't be such a vindictive bitch.

BRAD
(enthusiastically)

Or maybe he's in the hospital? And they took his phone away? Maybe you should start calling around.

STEVE
Nice try, but you just missed the obvious explanation.

BRAD
Which is?

STEVE
Maybe he just trusts me enough to stay out for the night and come home in the morning...

(beat)

... and I completely abused that trust by fucking you behind his back!

BRAD
Yeah, you did. How does it feel to be the awful one of us for a change?

STEVE
Oh, fuck off, you're still worse.

BRAD
(smugly)

I know.

STEVE
(brainwave)

I'll text him!

BRAD
And say what?

STEVE
I'll say I was drunk--

BRAD
You were.

STEVE
I was drunk and passed out on a co-worker's couch.

BRAD
But which one?

STEVE
Shit. Lucy, maybe? Howie doesn't like her, he'd never check.

BRAD
If he doesn't like her, how is you spending the night at hers going to make him feel?

STEVE
Good point. Damn it.

BRAD
Why don't you just tell him the truth. You got drunk, you fell into some old habits, and you spent the night being pounded by your soon-to-be-ex-husband?

STEVE
(aghast)

That is NOT what happened.

BRAD

It's what I remember. Geez, Steve, get your story straight. If you can't convince me, you won't convince him.

STEVE

I was drunk, granted, but you came on to me.

(beat)

And then you gave me tequila.

BRAD

And head.

STEVE

For God's sake, Brad, you know what tequila does to me!

BRAD
(bullshitting)

How could I possibly know that?

STEVE
(ignoring him)

Especially after a bottle of red wine.

BRAD

Two.

STEVE

You shit, you did this on purpose!

BRAD

Yet intent is so hard to prove, isn't it?

STEVE

You are the worst.

(to himself)

What can I text Howie?

BRAD
Tell Mr. Muscles I said 'hi'.

STEVE
Fuck off.

BRAD
Whatever you do, don't say that.

STEVE
(reading out loud)

"Hey, Mr. Muscles..."

BRAD
You're welcome.

STEVE
(continuing)

"Drank too much last night and ended up crashing on Lucy's couch. Be home soon." Sent.

BRAD
Shakespeare could not have done better!

STEVE
Can you even name five of Shakespeare's plays?

BRAD
Romeo and Juliet, Macbeth... The Great Gatsby?

STEVE
No.

BRAD
Death of a Salesman?

STEVE
You're not even trying, are you?

BRAD
Harry Potter and the Cursed Child?

STEVE
I'm leaving. But before I do, I have to ask you an important question.

BRAD
I'm all ears, and other assorted appendages.

STEVE
Did we use protection?

BRAD
We? I mean, did *you*?

STEVE
Don't fuck with me.

BRAD
That's literally what we did.

STEVE
Did you use a condom?

BRAD
I don't remember.

STEVE
How can you not remember?

BRAD
Well, you don't remember.

STEVE
I was off my face, which is the only reason last night happened.

BRAD
I know a way to check.

STEVE
How?

BRAD
There's a box of condoms in the top draw on your side. Count how many are in there.

(STEVE retrieves the box and counts them.)

STEVE
Five.

BRAD
(pretending to count on his fingers)

Then no, we didn't.

(STEVE sits down on the bed with his head in his hands.)

STEVE
Shit. When was the last time you were tested?

BRAD
For?

STEVE
Syphilis? Gonorrhea? Chlamydia? Herpes?

BRAD
Dude, I'm on PReP.

STEVE
That is not how PReP works, you dumb fuck. Jesus, no wonder STIs are on the rise.

BRAD
I'm sure we're both fine. I saw my doctor Tuesday, and I haven't slept with anyone other than Kris in… Three weeks.

STEVE
You guys are open?

BRAD

Well, I am.

STEVE
He doesn't know, does he? Did you learn nothing from us?

BRAD
No, but I don't forget to text when I'm not coming home.

STEVE
If I end up giving Howie chlamydia, I'm going to kill you.

BRAD
And if you don't and he still wants it, give him my number.

STEVE
You are a piece of human garbage. Where is Kris anyway?

BRAD
He's at Coachella.

STEVE
Why aren't you with him?

BRAD
Shockingly, stoned orgies with the great unwashed aren't my thing.

STEVE
Since when did you develop standards?

BRAD
After we split up.

(beat)

By the way, I'm selling the car.

STEVE
What car?

BRAD
The BMW.

STEVE

We talked about this. You are not selling Ariana. I'm the one who made all the payments on her.

BRAD

But my name is on the paperwork.

(beat)

And I would think given your sensitivity to what happened last night, that you might now be more amenable to the idea…

STEVE

Are you blackmailing me?

BRAD

I don't know, am I?

STEVE

But Kris would find out, too.

BRAD

I can get another Kris. Can you get another Howie?

STEVE
(about to argue, but able to control himself)

Fine. Sell the BMW, you conniving prick. I need a new car, anyway. But you'd better not breathe a word about last night to anyone.

BRAD

Or what?

STEVE
(struggling to find the words)

Ugh. One of these days, Brad.

(STEVE exits)

BRAD
(to himself)

Phase One complete, now for Phase Two.

(BRAD falls back on the bed, fake-laughing like a supervillain.)

(BLACKOUT)

(END OF SCENE)

ACT 2

Scene 2

SETTING: Outside Steve's apartment. A front door, center. Two dumpsters stand outside.

AT RISE: BRAD is loitering, looking shifty.

(A NEIGHBOR approaches the front door.)

BRAD
Hey, so, weird question, but could you tell me which dumpster is yours?

(The NEIGHBOR walks into the building without answering)

BRAD
Rude!

(beat)

OK. Shouldn't be too hard to figure out.

(BRAD approaches the two dumpsters and lifts the lid on the first one.)

BRAD
And what do we have here? Jesus, when did the garbage truck last swing by.

(BRAD starts rummaging through, looking occasionally at items, but then returning them to the dumpster)

(sheepishly, to audience as if they are passers-by)

Don't worry! Just lost my keys. Not some weirdo. Keep walking!

(BRAD looks at the small pile of trash he's dug out, then into the dumpster. A pause. He climbs in)

Oh, God!

(BRAD throws used diapers out of the dumpster)
Wrong one! Wrong one!

(BRAD's head peeks over the edge of the bin as he tries to climb out. He slips and falls back in.)

Ew! What the—whose garbage contains used condoms and diapers, what kind of sick heterosexuals live here?

(BRAD finally climbs out, falls to the floor. Looks to the audience and shudders. His clothes are now stained)

I'm fine. Everything is normal.

(calmly walks to the other dumpster)

So, you must be the one, then!

(BRAD lifts the lid with determination. He reaches in, straining.)

Protein shakes. Yes!

(BRAD pulls his arm out, looks down at his stained clothes.)

Fuck it.

(BRAD climbs into the second dumpster.)

Wow, Steve, you really haven't got the hang of recycling, have you? Anyone could see your receipts…

(Brad surfaces with some receipts in his hand, which he scrutinizes. Then his phone rings. He answers it)

Hello?

DR. FISHER
(voice only for entire scene)

Brad Cummings?

BRAD
Yes. Who is this?

DR. FISHER

My name is Dr. Zara Fisher. I'm meant to be your therapist.

BRAD

My therapist? Oh, that's right! Yes, how are you?

DR. FISHER

I'm more interested in how you are, Brad. So far you've missed every one of our appointments. I count five, in total.

(BRAD removes a banana peel from his shoulder)

BRAD

Yes, I've been a bit busy.

DR. FISHER

On five separate occasions?

BRAD

(flinging the banana peel into street)

That's what busy means.

DR. FISHER

Too busy to call me and rearrange? Or to tell me you're not coming?

BRAD

What are you complaining about? You get paid either way!

DR. FISHER

I do, Mr. Cummings, but oddly, I didn't enter this profession just to get paid. I did it to help people.

BRAD

(under his breath)

Ugh, you're one of those.

DR. FISHER

I'm sorry?

BRAD

You can help me by taking my money and never contacting me again.

DR. FISHER
That's not how therapy works.

BRAD
Let me be honest, I only made the appointments with you to appease my boyfriend. He thinks I need to talk through my feelings and talk about my problems, but I'm perfectly sane, perfectly happy.

DR. FISHER
What are you doing now?

BRAD
What do you mean?

DR. FISHER
Well, we're supposed to have an appointment now, and you're obviously not busy because you're free to answer my call. So, what are you doing?

BRAD
(looking again at the receipts he has)

I'm sorting through some old paperwork.

DR. FISHER
Well, why don't you stop doing that and come by my office.

BRAD
I told you, I'm totally fine.

DR. FISHER
Then why does your boyfriend think you need to see a therapist?

(BRAD clambers out, and sits on the side of the dumpster)

BRAD
He and I made a deal. You're my toll.

DR. FISHER
I don't think you're taking this seriously.

BRAD
Really? Whatever gave you that idea?

DR. FISHER
Your sarcasm may be hiding a very insecure ego.

BRAD
(laughing)

Is that what your fancy psychology degree taught you?

DR. FISHER
No, it's what my ex-girlfriend taught me. You get the professional stuff when you come into my office.

BRAD
You and I both know I won't do that.

DR. FISHER
How old are you, Mr. Cummings?

BRAD
(smiling)

A gentleman never reveals his age.

DR. FISHER
Do you think you're going through a midlife crisis?

BRAD
I wouldn't call it a crisis…

DR. FISHER
Is your boyfriend considerably younger than you, Mr. Cummings?

BRAD
A bit. But you wouldn't know looking at the two of us.

DR. FISHER
Have you recently exhibited any atypical or unusual behavior?

BRAD
Does talking to a therapist count?

DR. FISHER
No.

BRAD
(looking around him at the dumpsters)

Then I can't think of anything.

DR. FISHER
Look, I can't make you tell me anything you don't want to, but I am here to help, so if there's anything on your mind that you do want to talk about, I'm all ears.

BRAD
(pause)

And anything I tell you is confidential, right?

DR. FISHER
Absolutely.

BRAD
Settle something for me, then. Hypothetically, if someone went through his ex's dumpster, searching for dirt to hold against him as part of an increasingly acrimonious divorce… how would that sit with you?

DR. FISHER
Is this something he did to you?

BRAD
That's *exactly* what he did.

(beat)

Is he insane?

DR. FISHER
I mean, it speaks of desperation.

BRAD
What if he was driven to do it?

DR. FISHER
By what?

                              BRAD
(guessing)

Work pressure? An unhappy childhood? Being replaced by a significantly hotter boyfriend.

                           DR. FISHER
We're still talking about your ex, right?

                              BRAD
That's what I said. Unless you mean the hotter boyfriend, because…

(thinking)

…that would be mine. Obviously.

                           DR. FISHER
Tell me, Mr. Cummings, are you in the dumpster right now?

(BRAD drops the phone into the dumpster in shock. He curses and jumps back in to retrieve it)

Mr. Cummings?

                              BRAD
Sorry, just dropped my phone! My boyfriend is always saying I'm so clumsy!

                           DR. FISHER
And this would be--?

(BRAD starts to climb out, but sees HOWIE approaching, drinking from a can)

                              BRAD
Howie.

(beat)

Kris, I mean Kris. Sorry, I misheard your question. Shit!

(BRAD ducks back into the dumpster.)

HOWIE
(to dumpster)

Thought I closed you.

(HOWIE tosses the can in and closes the lid. He goes inside.)

BRAD
(horrified)

Oh my God.

(ecstatic)

Oh my God!

(The dumpster lid flies open and BRAD clambers out, triumphant, holding his phone in one hand and a new receipt in the other)

BRAD

YES!!!!!!

DR. FISHER

Mr. Cummings?

BRAD

I've found it!

DR. FISHER

Found what?

BRAD

Proof that Howie is cheating on Steve!

DR. FISHER

Mr. Cummings. I have no idea what you're doing or whether your boyfriend is called Kris, Howie or Steve, but whatever his name is, we need to talk. I think you may have some serious issues.

BRAD

So will Howie and Steve when they find out about this!

DR. FISHER

I have reason to believe you may need to practice healthy coping mechanisms. Mr. Cummings? Can you hear me?

BRAD

Oh, I'm sorry, you're breaking up!

(he ends the call and studies the receipt again)

And so are my ex and his boy toy! Ha!

(BLACKOUT)

(END OF SCENE)

LAURENCE WATTS & KEVIN BURNARD

ACT 2

Scene 3

SETTING: Cafe in The Castro

AT RISE: KRIS is seated at a table waiting for BRAD, who is late. BRAD arrives.

KRIS

You took your time.

BRAD

It was worth it, I promise.

KRIS

You know there are other men out there who know how to tell the time and arrive promptly?

BRAD

No, I'm not just saying I'm worth it, I'm saying I found something that's worth--

KRIS

This was meant to be our time. Just us. No distractions, no plots.

BRAD

(pulling phone out)

Yes, but look--

KRIS

Actually, could you turn your phone off? So, we're not interrupted.

BRAD

What do you mean off? How will someone call to talk to me?

KRIS

They won't.

BRAD

(putting phone on table)

No one's going to call me. I'll just put it here, face-down. See? You've got my full attention.

KRIS

Fine. How was therapy?

BRAD

Therapy?

(beat)

Oh, it was great! We made some major progress

KRIS

You guys are digging deep?

BRAD

Something like that.

KRIS

And what did you find?

BRAD

A lot of Steve's shit.

KRIS

(upbeat)

I think that sounds constructive.

BRAD

Trust me, it's going to prove very useful. How are your gym sessions going?

KRIS

I guess I'm getting some results.

BRAD

Yeah? You getting some muscle on you?

KRIS

More than you would think.

(beat)

So, look, I just wanted to--

(BRAD's phone rings. He reaches out--)

KRIS

Don't you dare.

BRAD

It could be important.

(BRAD answers the phone)

KRIS

I'm important.

BRAD

(talking into the phone)

Brad Cummings.

KRIS

You're unbelievable.

BRAD

(into phone)

No! What kind of weirdo would do that? How did you even get this number?

KRIS

Who is it?

BRAD

(into phone)

Fine, you caught me. I'm the weirdo. But I had a very good reason to be going through your dumpster!

KRIS

You did *what?*

BRAD
(into phone)

No, it's a very messy divorce, you'll understand one day--

(KRIS forcefully grabs the phone from BRAD. BRAD speaks into it as long as possible)

No need for language like that! You don't even recycle!

KRIS
(into phone)

He'll call you back.

(to BRAD)

Please tell me that wasn't Steve's neighbor complaining about you going through his trash.

BRAD

It's worse than that.

KRIS

What could be worse than that?

BRAD

Well, yes, it was Steve's neighbor complaining about me going through his trash, but on top of that I also…

(a thousand words a minute:)

…left my wallet at the scene of the crime which means you have to pay for lunch.

KRIS

Un-fucking-believable.

BRAD

But it was all worth it. I found evidence that Howie is cheating on Steve!

KRIS
(suddenly nervous)

Howie?

BRAD
Steve's boyfriend? It's funny, I thought you guys had met, I guess you haven't.

KRIS
(defensively)

No, we've never met. Why would you think that?

BRAD
Anyway, the point is we can use what I found to win the divorce.

(BRAD'S phone rings. He reaches out, hesitates.)

BRAD
I'll leave it.

KRIS
(conciliatory)

No, by all means.

BRAD
But I thought you didn't want me taking calls during lunch?

KRIS
(picking up and answering BRAD'S phone)

Brad Cummings?

(to BRAD)

It's for you.

BRAD
Well, of course it is, it's my fucking phone!

KRIS
It's your lawyer.

                              BRAD
It is? Give me that.

(snatches phone from KRIS)

Hello?

(beat)

Well, blackmail is a very strong word.

(beat)

No, I don't know the legal definition.

(whispering to KRIS)

He's defining blackmail for me.

(into the phone again)

What do you mean, is it true? Define true! Well, you were able to define blackmail.

(beat)

Of course it's not black and white! I thought you were a lawyer!

(beat)

I am not giving him the car.

(to KRIS)

He wants the car.

                              KRIS
Your lawyer wants the car?

                              BRAD
No, Steve! Pay attention!

(into phone)

No, not you. Who would he tell? The police?

(beat)

And what would they do?

(beat)

And how long would I get?

(beat)

It's almost worth it. But wait, how can he be blackmailing me into going to the police saying that I blackmailed him?

KRIS

It's called client-attorney privilege.

BRAD

(snarkily to KRIS)

This is a private phone call, thank you very much.

(into phone)

Look, how do we get out of this? Of course, it's fucking true, but that's beside the point.

(beat)

But we've spent months trying to come to an agreement, how would talking to him yet again, help us?

KRIS

How would digging through his fucking trash for blackmail material?

BRAD

(to KRIS)

Be quiet! He doesn't know about that yet.

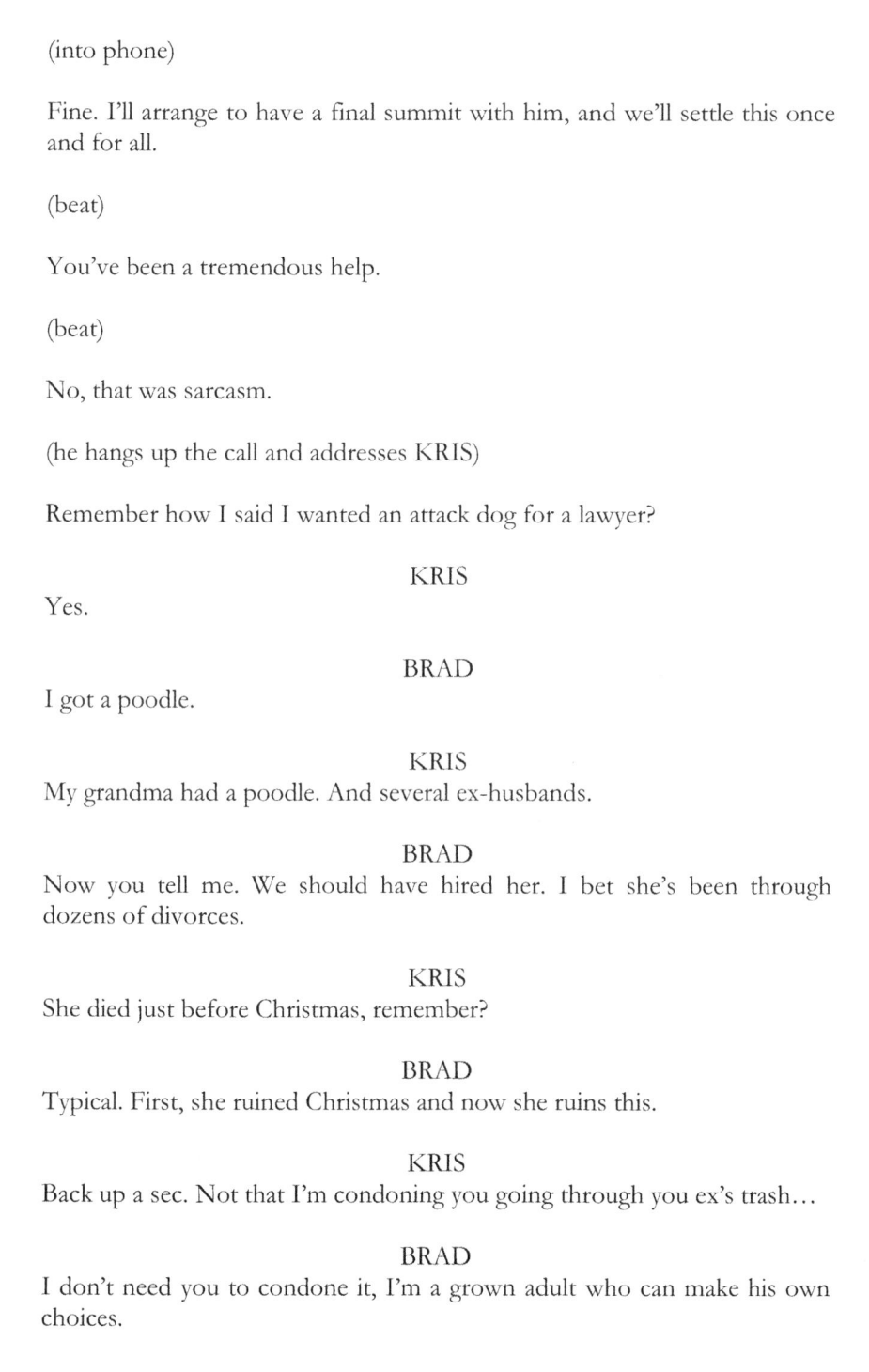

(into phone)

Fine. I'll arrange to have a final summit with him, and we'll settle this once and for all.

(beat)

You've been a tremendous help.

(beat)

No, that was sarcasm.

(he hangs up the call and addresses KRIS)

Remember how I said I wanted an attack dog for a lawyer?

KRIS
Yes.

BRAD
I got a poodle.

KRIS
My grandma had a poodle. And several ex-husbands.

BRAD
Now you tell me. We should have hired her. I bet she's been through dozens of divorces.

KRIS
She died just before Christmas, remember?

BRAD
Typical. First, she ruined Christmas and now she ruins this.

KRIS
Back up a sec. Not that I'm condoning you going through you ex's trash…

BRAD
I don't need you to condone it, I'm a grown adult who can make his own choices.

KRIS

…but how do you know that Howie is cheating on Steve?

BRAD

I'm glad you asked. See this? It's a motel receipt for a weekend when Steve was away on business. Who books a motel in their hometown if it's not to screw?

KRIS

If Steve was away, and Howie was cheating on him, why didn't he just take whoever it was home?

BRAD

Are you an amateur? Rule number one of cheating is, don't leave any evidence behind. Rule number two is, if you bring them back to yours you will always leave evidence. You won't even know you did it, but there will be a stain or a splash, or a used coffee cup…

KRIS

You've thought a lot about this.

BRAD

It's just what I've heard.

(beat)

From friends. But there's more! Because I found this, as well!

KRIS

And that would be…?

BRAD

Another receipt! Dinner for two. At Catch, that place you like. If Steve's out of town, who's diner number two?

KRIS

(defensively)

I don't like that place.

BRAD

Yes, you do. You wanted to go there for your birthday.

KRIS
You actually remembered?

BRAD
Yes, stupid, I actually like you.

KRIS
Though not enough to actually take me.

BRAD
It's the thought that counts. Anyway, back to the point; how can we leverage this to finally beat Steve in the divorce?

KRIS
(confused)

Wait, if the lawyer didn't know about your dumpster-diving, what were you using to blackmail Steve…

(BRAD's phone rings)

BRAD
Hold whatever excellent thought it is you're having…

(answering phone)

Brad Cummings. This is he. You're calling from where? Yes, I'm sure I have it somewhere.

(to KRIS)

It's my doctor with my blood results. I don't know why they screen for STDs when I'm on PReP.

(BRAD finds a piece of paper in his pocket and reads from it into the phone)

It's 857-492.

(to KRIS, smiling)

HIV, negative. Syphilis, negative. Hepatitis alphabet soup…

(beat)

...negative. Gonorrhea...

(beat)

I'm sorry, could you repeat that?

(beat)

Right, and exactly how contagious would that be?

(KRIS faceplants on the table in exasperation)

I see. Thank you. Yes, I will. Goodbye.

(to KRIS)

So... good news and bad news...

(brightly)

I don't have syphilis!

KRIS
So, in all likelihood that means I also...

BRAD
...do not have syphilis.

(beat)

We should meet with Steve as soon as possible...

(beat)

... to talk about the divorce.

KRIS
Yeah. We definitely should.

BRAD
I must have picked it up from a toilet seat or something

(WAITER approaches the table)

WAITER
Who wanted crabs?

KRIS
Nobody, but here we are.

(BLACKOUT)

(END OF SCENE)

ACT 2

Scene 4

SETTING: Brad's house.

AT RISE: BRAD and KRIS are in the kitchen cooking dinner.

BRAD
(while straining vegetables)

Now remember, let me do all the talking.

KRIS
Of course, I'm just here to be pretty and silent.

BRAD
Don't be snarky. The last thing we need is for Steve and his lump of meat to see us fighting.

KRIS
(composing himself)

You know what? You're right.

BRAD
This is why I love you.

(BRAD and KRIS kiss awkwardly. The doorbell rings.)

Get that!

KRIS
What did your last slave die of?

BRAD
(reprising, brightly)

Not syphilis!

(KRIS opens the front door. HOWIE is standing there.)

HOWIE

(awkwardly)

Hi, you must be Kris. I'm Howie.

KRIS

Pleased to meet you

(beat)

Oh yeah, I'm Kris.

HOWIE

Steve's gonna be a moment, he was having trouble carrying the dish he made. He sent me on ahead.

BRAD

(shouted from kitchen, where he's still busy)

I said don't bring anything!

KRIS

Brad's just finishing up in the kitchen. Guess we have a moment.

(HOWIE and KRIS check that the coast is clear and kiss and hug.)

HOWIE

The last few weeks have been…

KRIS

Amazing, yeah

(Their embrace is interrupted by STEVE, who appears behind them.)

STEVE

Good to see you two are getting along. You've not met before, have you?

HOWIE

First time.

KRIS

Please, do come in.

BRAD

(looking up)

I told you not to bring anything.

(STEVE kisses BRAD and hands him the dish.)

BRAD
What the fuck is this?

STEVE
Ceviche with passion fruit jalapeno vinaigrette.

BRAD
What's in it?

STEVE
Maize, octopus, scallops, shrimp, corvina, and mussels--

KRIS
Glad you brought muscles.

(HOWIE and KRIS exchange a glance)

STEVE
… all in a passion fruit-jalapeno vinaigrette.

BRAD
(suspiciously to STEVE)

Did you make it or buy it?

STEVE
Of course, I fucking made it! What did you make?

BRAD
Steaks, I think. Kris did most of the work. I mainly supervised.

STEVE
Good to see you haven't changed.

BRAD
Interesting to see that you have.

(to KRIS)

Kris, why don't you show Howie your vinyl collection while us grown-ups have a summit before dinner?

(KRIS groans and walks HOWIE over to the couch, where he shows him some vinyl records. On the other side of the stage, BRAD and STEVE talk in the kitchen.)

(to STEVE)

We need to talk.

STEVE
We are talking. Why are you so serious?

BRAD
You gave me gonorrhea!

STEVE
(loudly)

Gonorrhea????

BRAD
Shhhhhhhhh.

(HOWIE and KRIS look over. BRAD and STEVE are all smiles, pretending nothing untoward is happening.)

(in the living room)

HOWIE
(holding a vinyl record)

They're the size of dinner plates!

KRIS
They're not all mine. That one's Brad's - *Clap Your Hands* by The Black-Eyed Peas. It's his favorite. He only just got it.

(beat)

The clap.

HOWIE
Never heard of it.

KRIS
No, he's got the clap. I'm being subtle.

HOWIE
Right.

KRIS
You get me?

HOWIE
What's the clap?

(back in the kitchen)

STEVE
(to BRAD)

How the hell would I give you gonorrhea?

BRAD
Well, you had it and we had sex, do you need a diagram? PowerPoint slides? A mime?

(BRAD mimes anal sex with his hands)

STEVE
Why do you think I had it?

BRAD
Because I have it now.

STEVE
What, so it's my fault? Who did I get it from then?

BRAD
Your skank-ass boyfriend, probably.

STEVE

(scoffing)

Howie doesn't sleep around.

(in the living room)

                KRIS

(to HOWIE)

It's a sexually transmitted disease. And Brad has it. Which means…

                HOWIE

(the penny drops)

…that you might have it.

                KRIS

Which in turn means…

                HOWIE

(too loud)

Shit!

                BRAD

(from the kitchen)

Everything OK over there?

                HOWIE

The Black-Eyed Peas! They were shit after… that one dude left.

                KRIS

(to BRAD and STEVE)

He means Fergie

(to HOWIE)

Fergie's a woman.

(back in the kitchen)

STEVE
(quietly to BRAD)

Are they talking about a rock band?

BRAD
(quietly to STEVE)

I have no idea. I get one vinyl record a week for myself to keep the boy happy. Never listen to them. Means we have something in common though.

STEVE

Whereas your true hobby is actually "not listening to people."

BRAD
(smiling)

I only ignore the ones I love.

STEVE
(realizing)

Wait, but that means I could have given it to Howie!

BRAD

What are you talking about? The little muscle-slut probably gave to you. He's probably sleeping with half of San Francisco.

(in the living room)

HOWIE
(to KRIS)

It figures. I've seen your boyfriend's Grindr, bet he's slept with half of San Francisco.

KRIS

Grindr? He said he only uses that to keep in touch with friends.

HOWIE

Nobody uses it to keep in touch with friends. Friends with benefits, maybe. Anyway, I didn't wanna say, but he messaged me a while ago.

THREESOME

(beat)

And he sent me this.

(HOWIE shows KRIS a photo on his phone.)

KRIS
That's *friendly*. How long's "a while"?

HOWIE
Every other night for the past two weeks. I saved the pictures to my phone to show you, but I deleted the messages.

KRIS
Wait, what are *you* doing on Grindr?

HOWIE
You wouldn't believe how many clients I get through that app. People pay top-dollar for an hour with a personal trainer they want to fuck.

KRIS
And do you?

HOWIE
(winking)

They wouldn't keep coming back if I did.

KRIS
I would.

(back in the kitchen)

STEVE
So, what do I do? I'll have to tell him the truth.

BRAD
Why? I bet he lies to you all the time.

(beat)

I hear he's permanently on Grindr… flirting outrageously.

STEVE

He uses it for work

BRAD

And how would you know?

STEVE

He's had me message a few clients for him.

BRAD

(uneasily)

You have access to his profile? To his messages?

STEVE

Yeah, it's how I know I can trust him

BRAD

You help him get clients through Grindr? You're basically his pimp! No wonder you're both diseased.

KRIS

(from the living room)

So, are we actually going to eat or are we meant to stare at vinyl for a few more hours?

BRAD

You're the cook. You tell us!

KRIS

Fine! Let's move to the dining table, then.

STEVE

I'll help you.

(KRIS and STEVE go into the kitchen and serve the food, while BRAD and HOWIE sit down at the table.)

BRAD

(to HOWIE)

Got any interesting messages on any apps recently?

HOWIE
Oh, don't worry, Steve's seen nothing. I delete all the messages from horny old men who can't take no for an answer.

BRAD
I'll have you know I am two months younger than your current boyfriend.

HOWIE
I suppose it's the wrinkles that make you look older, then.

BRAD
It's just this body has seen a lot of use.

HOWIE
Should I clap?

BRAD
What did you say?

(STEVE and KRIS reach the table with dinner.)

HOWIE
(to BRAD)

So, this is the house where you and Steve spent all those happy years?

BRAD
Happy years, plural? I think I can remember one. One and a quarter, maybe?

STEVE
Was I there?

BRAD
I think so. In the background maybe.

(beat)

This fish is cold.

STEVE
It's meant to be, it's raw.

KRIS
Raw? Can't you catch stuff from raw meat?

BRAD
Not if you pull out in time.

STEVE
(slamming his hands down on the table)

We need to tell you something.

BRAD
Which "we" are you referring to?

STEVE
Fine, Brad needs to tell you something.

BRAD
No, I don't.

STEVE
Either you tell them, or I will.

BRAD
Good, because you gave it to me.

KRIS
Did you just say what I think you said?

BRAD
No?

KRIS
You two didn't--!

BRAD
Sometimes you can get these things from toilet seats.

STEVE
(unable to hold it in any longer)

Brad and I slept together. I'm so sorry, Howie. And you, Kris.

THREESOME

BRAD
(hurriedly)

Of course we slept together. We were married.

STEVE
Last week.

BRAD
And now I have gonorrhea.

STEVE
We don't know that you got it from me!

HOWIE
You hooked up? You guys barely slept together when you were married!

BRAD
He seduced me.

(beat)

I was powerless to resist

KRIS
Cock existing is enough to seduce you.

BRAD
(smiling)

What can I say? I enjoy life's many pleasures.

(beat)

Anyway, Steve gave me gonorrhea, which means, Kris, you probably have it, and you, Howie, probably gave it to Steve.

HOWIE
Dude, I studied health. I get tested regularly, and I don't sleep around. If I have it, it's your fault!

BRAD

(reaching into his pocket and a pulling out two receipts)

Then how do you explain these?

HOWIE
What are those?

BRAD
Receipts showing that you stayed in a motel when Steve was away on business and had dinner for two beforehand.

STEVE
Enough with the bullshitting, Brad!

BRAD
No, here's the amazing thing: for the first time ever I don't have to lie. It's fun, isn't it? I should do this more often. His name's on it and everything. Care to explain, Howie?

HOWIE
(laughing)

It was a birthday present for a friend.

BRAD
You fucked someone as a birthday present?

(beat)

My birthday's coming up.

HOWIE
You can kiss my ass. How did you get this?

BRAD
I... found it.

KRIS
He went through your dumpster.

STEVE
What?

BRAD

I was looking for Kompromat!

HOWIE

What?

BRAD

It's what the Russians had on Donald Trump.

(beat)

Dirt, you idiots, I was looking for dirt!

STEVE

In a dumpster? Genius. Did you find any?

KRIS

He was covered in it.

HOWIE

More like full of it.

BRAD

Oh, you're one to talk, muscleboy. Are you going to tell us who you were sleeping with? A friend? A "client?" Do you even know the difference anymore?

HOWIE

It's none of your goddam business.

STEVE

(concerned)

You're being very defensive, all of a sudden.

HOWIE

You cheated on me with this guy. Even if I had a hookup, you can't judge!

STEVE

I don't want to judge. I just want us all to be honest. I want to talk.

HOWIE

(getting up to leave)

Well, I don't want to talk right now.

STEVE
Howie, please, don't go.

HOWIE
I'm not mad at you. Him, yeah, but not you. But I can't be here right now, not without punching him in his smug little face.

(he puts his jacket on)

I'm going to go work this off at the gym.

STEVE
I love you, Howie.

HOWIE
I know you do. I'll see you at home later.

(HOWIE leaves, exchanging a glance with KRIS as he does so. STEVE is dumbstruck)

BRAD
I knew he'd leave you.

STEVE
He hasn't left me. The miracle here is why anyone would choose to be with you, no offense, Kris.

KRIS
You did.

STEVE
Well, that makes us both idiots then, doesn't it?

KRIS
Speak for yourself.

STEVE
What makes you think he's going to be any different with you? You know he's not faithful. You know he's a colossal dick. Why make my mistakes?

BRAD
(raising his hand)

I'm sitting *right here*.

STEVE

Good. You need to hear it, too.

BRAD

I need to hear it, do I? Because I'm always the problem, never Steve. God forbid anyone see anything in me. Oh, wait, you both did! Case closed. You know what really gets on my tits, Steve? We spent years talking about how we were sexually incompatible, but we stayed together because we loved one another. Because we were more than just sex.

STEVE

More like Stockholm syndrome.

BRAD

But you wouldn't bottom for me, Steve. Plain and simple. And that cut through our marriage like a hot knife through fisting cream.

STEVE

You wouldn't bottom for me either!

BRAD

And yet, what do we find on Howie's Grindr profile?

(takes out his phone)

"26-year-old African American jock."

(beat)

"Top only."

(beat)

So, what the fuck makes him more special than me?

STEVE

It's just different with him.

BRAD

So, he's more special than the guy you pledged your life to. I loved you, Steve. Sure, you can pretend I'm this callous curmudgeon, but I fucking loved you. And you wouldn't give me anything back! What does he have that I didn't?

STEVE

It just works!

BRAD

(mimicking)

"It just works!"

STEVE

With him life doesn't' feel like it's a competition… or one long argument.

BRAD

Jesus Christ, nag, nag, nag, it's like we're married all over again.

STEVE

Fine, let me tell you about Howie.

(as STEVE gives his speech, KRIS watches closely)

He may be half our age, but he is more mature than you will ever be. He knows who he is. He's not trying to fuck everything that moves just to get validation. He isn't trying to beat everyone he meets, like life is some kind of game. He's just living his truth, while you bury yourself in lies like a dung beetle buries itself in shit.

(beat)

Howie is good, and smart, and kind, and thoughtful, and romantic. And he loves me.

(KRIS' phone buzzes. He checks it.)

BRAD

I can't help it that I have a bit of life in me! A bit of zest. That I have a brain. And I like to have fun. I'm sorry I never bought you cheap flowers from a gas station on Valentine's Day or a stuffed toy holding a balloon that says, "I love you".

(beat)

And anyway, where is this knight in shining Under Armour? Gone! Like an emotionally stunted… Armadillo. But where is Kris? Right here, next to me, like the mature adult we both need in our lives. And he is loyal, organized, patient, clean, capable of compromise, and a much better cook than you.

KRIS

I didn't know you felt that way about me.

BRAD

Of course I do.

KRIS

Well, this is awkward.

STEVE

You're telling me.

KRIS

I just got a text from Howie, he's outside. Says he left a bag.

STEVE

Oh, right, excuse me, then.

KRIS

(getting up)

He says he's not ready to see you yet.

(beat)

I'll take it to him.

(KRIS picks up HOWIE's bag, pauses, and turns to BRAD and STEVE)

You two: figure this shit out. If I've learned one thing tonight, it's that you two actually managed to love each other once. Try remembering that, and figure out your whole stupid divorce once and for all. Stop dragging the two of us into it.

(KRIS exits)

STEVE
You know what? That makes sense.

BRAD
Told you he was a catch.

(beat)

So, how do we do this?

STEVE
You know what? I don't care anymore. Take what you want, and try to be fair.

BRAD
As long as you have Howie?

STEVE
That's all I need. You win.

BRAD
I always do.

(beat)

But maybe this time, you do too.

STEVE
Did you really go through my dumpster?

BRAD
Yes.

(beat)

Whatever it takes.

STEVE
Well, you get 10/10 for effort.

BRAD

Never less than 100% Remember that Black Friday sale the year we got married?

STEVE
That poor cashier's face!

BRAD
But I got you that watch, didn't I?

STEVE
Ten stitches for a cut-price watch.

(beat)

Remember when watches were a thing? We've gotten old.

BRAD
We had some good times, though, didn't we?

(a phone vibrates.)

BRAD
What was that?

STEVE
It's not mine.

BRAD
Kris must have left his phone here.

STEVE
(picking up a phone from the table)

No, it's yours. You have a text.

BRAD
Don't be ridiculous, no one texts me.

STEVE
It's from Kris.

(showing him the phone)

Look, it says so.

BRAD
Kris would never text me.

STEVE
Why not?

BRAD
Because the writing's too fucking small, that's why.

STEVE
Well, it is from him. And just bite the bullet and wear your glasses, for goodness sake.

BRAD
You read it. I don't think I can take the eye strain.

(STEVE takes the phone and reads. He goes cold.)

Well, what's it say?

STEVE
You weren't kidding about the strain.

BRAD
I've heard you can make the font bigger, if you know how to do that kind of thing.

STEVE
Not that kind of strain.

BRAD
Just read it to me!

STEVE
"I'm not coming back."

BRAD
What?

STEVE
There's more: "You probably think it's impossible that anyone would leave

you. Maybe it's because your ego is that big, or maybe it's just because Steve let it get that big. Either way, I know now it's something I can't live with, that I deserve better.

BRAD
Better? What the fuck does that mean?

STEVE
He means better than you.

BRAD
I know what he means! I mean, why is he leaving? Has he found someone else? Is he coming back for his things?

STEVE
"I'm not coming back" doesn't really leave a lot of wiggle room.

BRAD
Fine, at least I get the dickhead's TV, then. And his vinyl record collection. Wait a minute, where is the TV? It's gone. The little prick was planning this!

STEVE
Wow. I should have done the same. He put more thought into this than I ever did.

BRAD
Oh, of course you take his side!

STEVE
No, Brad, I take my side. I'm focusing on me from now on. I have my life with Howie to treasure now, and I'm not going to fuck this up the way you did.

(BRAD's phone vibrates.)

BRAD
What now?

(STEVE reads the text and breaks down in tears)

Steve!

(STEVE keeps wailing and gestures with his hands)

Can you try using words to explain what is happening?

(hitting STEVE with a chair cushion)

Oh, for fuck's sake, snap out of it!

STEVE
(STEVE grabs the cushion and hits BRAD with it)

You heartless bitch!

BRAD
Oh, so you *can* speak!

STEVE
(in a high-pitched wail)

Howie and Kris have run off *together!* He just broke up with me over text!

BRAD
Ouch. But wait, I thought you were talking to Kris?

STEVE
I was.

BRAD
(gleeful)

Oh, that's *much* worse. Your text didn't even come from your boyfriend. It came from his lover.

(beat)

And was sent to your ex-lover's phone.

STEVE
Do you want another pillow to the face?

BRAD
But none of this makes any sense. They only met each other for the first time tonight. Kris only leaves the house to go to the record store and the gym.

STEVE
You made that scrawny boy go to the gym?

BRAD
Yep. I even paid for him to have personal training sessions.

STEVE
(suspiciously)

What was the name of the gym you sent him to?

BRAD
The Pinnacle.

STEVE
(the penny drops)

That's where Howie works! That's where they must have met!

(beat)

So, this is all your fault. Your jealousy caused all of this!

BRAD
Envy, actually, not jealousy. Jealousy is fear of something you have being taken away. Envy is desiring what someone else has.

STEVE
Why am I even still here?

BRAD
Because we're friends!

STEVE
You just screwed me over in the divorce. You took seven of the best years of my life. You cheated on me AND you gave me gonorrhea...

BRAD
That has yet to be determined!

(he has a brainwave)

Kris and Howie could have given us gonorrhea!

STEVE

Why would they... actually, you know what, it kind of helps to think of it as their fault.

BRAD

I do what I do for a reason.

(beat)

Do the texts say anything else? Like where they are going? Or how long the affair has been going on?

STEVE

(reading and sighing)

They're going to LA.

BRAD

Like the trash taking itself to the dumpster.

STEVE

Neither of them will like LA.

BRAD

Nobody likes LA. The people who live there just pretend to like it for Instagram.

STEVE

Well, they'll fit in perfectly, then. They pretended to love us for at least a couple months. And... Kris says they've been seeing each other for seven weeks. "We didn't expect to fall for each other. Nobody wanted to cheat. But we just fit better."

BRAD

There's that "better" word again. Whatever happened to making do with what you have? Honestly the kids these days want everything.

STEVE

(throwing his hands up)

So, what now?

BRAD
What now, indeed? I mean, who's going to clean up and do the dishes? And we didn't even have desert!

STEVE
What is it?

BRAD
Lemon meringue pie. That's what it says on the box anyway.

STEVE
You bought it from a store?

BRAD
Well, I wasn't going to make it from scratch, was I? Who has time for that?

STEVE
Do you even know where the forks are kept?

BRAD
I think so.

(BRAD retrieves a pie and forks from the kitchen. They begin eating.)

STEVE
Hmm. Bitter and sweet.

BRAD
Quite appropriate really. Did my cunt of an ex say anything else?

STEVE
(giggling)

Nothing important yet.

BRAD
You're laughing.

STEVE
I'm not reading it word for word, but the general gist is that you're having a midlife crisis.

BRAD
Ridiculous. That home DNA test I took said I'll live until at least 95, so I'm *years* away from midlife.

STEVE
Your capacity for denial never ceases to amaze me.

BRAD
Are we having a midlife crisis?

STEVE
We were both dating guys a decade younger than us and competing over whose boyfriend was hotter. It's possible.

BRAD
Well, you were normally wrong about these kinds of things…

STEVE
I knew you'd say something like that.

BRAD
Well, take it from someone who's driven two perfectly nice guys away by being a dick, you didn't do that. Howie didn't leave you because you're a bad person, or because you're boring, or because you're not hot enough and rocking a sick bod. I mean, he wouldn't have picked Kris if he was doing that.

Sometimes two people just aren't meant to be together. Sometimes, the grass seems greener on the other side and people can't just make the most of the lawn they have and just throw a barbecue like normal people. Sometimes, a relationship is a box that someone just doesn't fit into, and you just have to let them go.

STEVE
When did you get so wise?

BRAD
It was a gift at birth.

STEVE
(glancing at his phone)

God, it's late. I can't even imagine driving home right now.

BRAD
Well, you can stay the night here if you want?

STEVE
Shouldn't we both see a doctor first?

BRAD
What?

STEVE
Well, if you want me to stay the night?

BRAD
On the couch, dumbass.

STEVE
Oh.

BRAD
(fetching STEVE a pillow and blanket from offstage)

I may be turning into a softie, but I know not to make the same mistake twice. We can talk more about your sad and pathetic existence in the morning.

STEVE
Only if I get to judge yours, too.

BRAD
That's what friends are for.

(STEVE makes his bed on the couch while BRAD leaves. The lights dim, just a lamp next to the couch remaining.)

STEVE
Goodnight!

BRAD
(offstage)

Goodnight!

(beat.)

STEVE

I love you.

BRAD

Fuck off and go to sleep, you loser.

(STEVE laughs quietly and switches off the lamp.)

(CURTAIN)

(END OF ACT)

ABOUT THE AUTHORS

Laurence Watts is a British-born, American writer and editor.

He co-edited the final installment of Quentin Crisp's autobiography *The Last Word*, published in 2017, and its companion *And One More Thing*, published in 2018.

In 2018, he published *Life After Phillip Morris*, which he co-wrote with four-time prison-escapee and conman Steven Jay Russell.

The following year, he edited transgender flag creator and activist Monica Helms' autobiography *More Than Just A Flag*, published in March 2019.

In 2020, he published *Threesome*, a collection of three plays written with Kevin Burnard.

He has written for CNN, the BBC, The Guardian, The Huffington Post and Pink News. He studied at Queens' College, Cambridge University. He lives in San Diego, California.

Kevin Burnard is an American writer and filmmaker.

He wrote the short film *Schrodinger's Box* for the Santa Barbara International Film Festival 10-10-10 program in 2018.

In October that year, his short story *The Shot Seen Round The World* was published in the science fiction anthology 10,000 Dawns, Poor Man's Iliad.

He has written several scripts for film and audio drama, including the third episode of 2019's podcast drama Verity Weaver, titled *Goodnight, Starlight*, for AudioHour productions.

He has also served in various production roles in documentary film and television, including a producer credit on *Under Her Wing* a short documentary featured at the 2018 Santa Barbara International Film Festival and NatureTrack film festival.

In 2020, he published *Threesome*, a collection of three plays, written with Laurence Watts.

He studied at the University of California, Santa Barbara, graduating in Film and Media with honors. He lives in San Diego, California.

Made in the USA
Monee, IL
15 January 2021